ASCENDANCE
OF THE
FORGOTTEN PRINCE

ELIJAH HER

Cover Design: Elijah Her
Interior Art: Canva
Cover Art: kidana_artis
Title Page Art: artmaniac.lili

ISBN: 979-8-9927299-6-2 (paperback)
ISBN: 979-8-9927299-8-6 (hardback)
ISBN: 979-8-9927299-7-9 (ebook)

F90 PRESS

www.f90press.com

To those who fight to reclaim their name and forge their own destiny—May you find strength in vulnerability, power in love, and courage in the face of betrayal. May you ascend.

CONTENT NOTES

Ascendance of the Forgotten Prince includes themes some may be sensitive to or find triggering:

Graphic depictions of gore, violence, and brutality, including descriptions of death and body horror. Power abuse, hegemonic imperialism, slavery, and exploitation. Graphic depiction of explicit sexual scenes. Themes of sexual harassment and dubious-consent.

PRONUNCIATION GUIDE

Akhsarun (*Ahk-sah-roon*)

Amalthea (*Ah-mal-thay-ah*)

Aqaynah (*Ah-kai-nah*)

Ashti-Yasu (*Ash-tee Yah-soo*)

Ayame (*Ah-yah-meh*)

Azariel (*Ah-zah-ree-el*)

Darius (*Dah-ree-us*)

Durathar (*Der-rah-thar*)

Eien (*Eh-ehn*)

Emiko (*Eh-mee-koh*)

Gamal (*Gah-mahl*)

Hiro (*Hee-roh*)

Ilay (*Ee-lay*)

Jiro Asahi (*Jee-roh Ah-sah-hee*)

Kaito (*Kai-toh*)

Kamishen (*Kah-mee-shen*)

Kyo (*K'yoh*)

Lunrae (*Loon-ray*)

Nayila (*Nah-yee-lah*)

Nisshen (*Nees-shen*)

Pahlavan (*Pah-lah-vahn*)

Renjiro (*Ren-jee-roh*)

Rohan (*Ro-hahn*)

Rustam (*Roos-tahm*)

Seiryu (*Sair-yoo*)

Shahmizan (*Shah-mee-zahn*)

Soraya (*Soh-rah-yah*)

Sulqadir (*Sool-kah-deer*)

Tairasa (*Tear-rah-sah*)

Tenishen (*Teh-nee-shen*)

Vorynthia (*Voh-rin-thee-ah*)

Yuehama (*Yoo-eh-hah-mah*)

Yuka (*Yoo-kah*)

Zurathi (*Zir-rah-thee*)

CHAPTER ONE

My hands trembled as I raced through the palace halls, the thick scent of blood heavy in the air, clinging to every breath I took. Until now, death had been a distant thing—an abstract concept that others carried on their shoulders, not me. I had never seen the light drain from a man's eyes, never witnessed the delicate unraveling of life from flesh. That was the burden of the imperial guard. But in the span of mere minutes, I had watched two lives extinguish before me.

Ayame, my father—the Emperor of Yuehama—had fallen. I had been too slow. Too late. The memory was as sharp as the blade that claimed him. I had seen its edge glinting in the moonlight the instant I entered the chamber, yet I could not reach him in time. The blade cut deep, severing not only his body but the very heartbeat of our empire. The last of his warmth still lingered in the air, a fleeting reminder of all that had been.

My gaze drifted to the tranquil pond recessed in the floor. Smooth stones bordered the water's edge, lush with green fronds; koi glided beneath the surface, their scales flashing like coins. Lilies and lotuses floated in languid circles. It was meant as a touch of beauty in the palace, a symbol of harmony. But under my will, it would become something far darker.

My fingers stopped trembling as fury steadied my hands, my gaze locking onto the man who had stolen my father from us—Darius, Emperor and General of Durathar. His sword, still slick with my father's blood, glinted as he prepared to strike me down next.

Drawing a deep breath, I brought my hands forward, summoning the waters around me, feeling them pulse with my will. I was like the moon and the ponds the tide. It responded to my call, the tranquil surface breaking, churning as they surged past me in a fierce wave. With a single twist of my fingers, the water obeyed, forming sinuous ropes that lashed around Darius' limbs and throat. One swift pull, and a red mist painted the palace walls, staining the stones, the columns, and the depths of my own soul.

With grim purpose, I picked up Darius' sword and cast a final glance toward my father, warmth stinging my eyes. But there was no time for grief. I had to secure the throne. I had to find the royal council. Each step echoed in the silence as I approached the towering doors of the imperial hall, pressing my hand against their cold, unforgiving surface. Beyond them lay the throne, my birthright, the seat from which I would proclaim my vengeance. I had slain their emperor, and by that act, I should have been the victor. Yet as I pushed the doors open, a dark foreboding swept over me, heavy and ominous.

My footsteps slowed, my heart pounding in my ears. The hall was bathed in the golden glow of the braziers, casting long, distorted shadows that seemed to twist and writhe along the wooden floor. And there, at the center, my gaze fell upon a scene that froze the blood in my veins. My uncle stood with a blade pressed to his throat. The sword glinted in the low light, its curve deadly, its edge resting precariously against his skin by a Bazifir, a Duratharian soldier.

Instinct drove my hand to the hilt of Darius' sword, fingers twitching in readiness. But before I could act, Renjiro's voice pierced the silence, calm and deliberate.

"Ashti-Yasu," he declared—the ancient rite of rest, an invocation of temporary peace. Even the savage Durathar would honor that truce.

The blade lowered with a slow, metallic hiss, and the Duratharian Bazifir holding it spoke, his voice harsh and unyielding. "Where is your prince?" His words cracked like a whip, more command than question.

"Dead," Renjiro replied, his voice calm, his eyes never once shifting towards me. He did not acknowledge me, did not even dare a glance in my direction.

I tried to speak, to argue that I still lived, that I had slain their Emperor, but my throat tightened, my voice bound. Something dark coiled around my words, silencing me. I opened my mouth, but nothing came. *I am the prince. I have taken your Emperor's life.* Yet, the truth remained locked in the hollow of my chest, suffocating.

"The Emperor and his heir no longer live," Renjiro said, his tone steady as he knelt before the Duratharian. "I am all that remains of royal blood. Durathar has won this battle."

Coward. Betrayer. What was he doing? I had crushed their line with my blade, leaving them with nothing but Rohan's bastard, a man unfit to claim the Durathar throne. His blood was impure, sullied by the womb of a slave. The strength of Yuehama was not broken; I lived. I was the rightful Emperor of the Kamishen people, of my people.

I took a step forward, but my body faltered. My gaze darted toward Renjiro, and in that moment, I saw it—the subtle bend of his fingers, the delicate tension in his hand. He held me, bound by a spell I could not break. He knew I was here, that I was witnessing.

"One hundred Kamishen slaves," Renjiro said, his voice as unyielding as stone, bartering our people's lives with a deadly calm. "Two thousand pounds of gold."

Ashti-Yasu was always sealed with a price—blood, pride, and gold.

The Bazifir sheathed his sword with a soft metallic click, his eyes narrowing as he regarded my uncle. "You have one month to fulfill your promise, *Emperor Renjiro.*" His voice dripped with disdain, though his posture betrayed none of it. As he turned, his gaze flickered toward me, his eyes passing over me as though I were no more than a servant of the court.

The sound of his retreating footsteps echoed long after he had vanished from the hall, swallowed by the vastness of the palace. Renjiro approached me, his presence cold and calculating, the echo of his boots ringing like the toll of a bell, announcing the death of something far more precious than an empire.

"One day, you will understand," he murmured, his voice tender in a way that made my skin crawl. He reached out, his fingers brushing my forehead, as though he believed this treachery was an act of mercy. "This is for the good of Yuehama."

His thumb traced a line across my brow, and with a single whispered word—"Sleep"—my vision darkened. The world slipped away, falling into shadow. I tried to fight, but his power washed over me like a tide, inescapable. My limbs grew heavy, my thoughts fragmented, sinking deeper into the abyss.

And then, there was nothing.

✦·🕱·🐚·🌾

The air was thick and stifling, the scent of sweat and heat filling the cramped space around me. Sunlight streamed in thin beams through the wooden cracks of the caravan, casting sharp lines of light into the murky darkness. My body ached, muscles sore and stiff, as though I had been bound by more than just sleep. Because I was, my wrists and ankles were shackled, the rough metal biting into my skin. I was no longer dressed in the royal garbs of Yuehama, but in coarse, plain robes—the clothing of a commoner.

I blinked, the haze of sleep clinging to me like fog, refusing to lift entirely. The world around me was dim, suffocating, the air too thick to breathe, too hot to bear. Nothing like the cool, earthy breeze of Yuehama. The stench of sweat and fear mingled in the close quarters, where men and women with pointed ears huddled, their Kamishen features unmistakable. They were my people, mostly commoners and servants to the crown. Their faces were gaunt, hollowed by exhaustion, their eyes vacant, yet filled with an unspoken dread. The quiet murmur of despair hummed through the cramped space like a low chant, fragile and resigned.

I shifted, a sharp sting searing my neck to my chest, a familiar burn that made my breath catch. My hand instinctively rose, fingers tracing the sensitive flesh. The last time I felt this, it was beneath the sacred sigils of the celestials, inked into my skin to strengthen my magic. But this was different—brutal, foreign—not my own doing.

The chime of metal echoed as my hand raised higher, until they tangled in the uneven strands of my hair. My breath wavered, and my throat tightened as I swallowed hard against the ache threatening to spill free. This hair, my hair, once a flowing emblem of my status, of my lineage, of *me*. Now it lay in jagged, brutal ends, a cruel testament to what had been stripped away. I clenched my hand into a fist, pulling it away as if burned. *What had happened to me?* My thoughts stirred sluggishly, fragmented memories clawing their way to the surface.

Durathar... they had infiltrated our capital. The palace had fallen, crumbling beneath their siege. And then—my father. Pain knotted itself tightly in my chest, squeezing, choking. I could still see him, the glint of the blade, the blood staining the floor. My breath stilled. The imperial hall, the coldness in Renjiro's eyes. The Ashti-Yasu—he had invoked it. For what? Temporary peace? My uncle had not even fought. He was our Vizier, our Grand Shiryū. He had simply handed over our people, cowardly surrendering us to our fate.

I glanced at the Kamishen around me, their silent suffering mirrored my own. Renjiro had betrayed us. Peace was a lie. The Durathar would not stop. They had already devoured Akhsarun, and our kingdom was next. After that, only Lunrae stood in their way. Half the continent of Tairasa belonged to Durathar. We were all that remained—the two kingdoms of the Kamishen people.

"You are awake?" A voice, soft but steady, broke through the silence. I turned to see a woman beside me, her face shadowed by the dim light, though she seemed close to my age—twenty-two summers or perhaps younger.

"We thought you were dead," she continued, her voice laced with faint relief. "You've been unconscious for days now."

"Days?" I rasped, my throat dry, the words scraping against my vocal cords.

She nodded. "Yes. They loaded you on like that, and you stayed that way. A few tried to rouse you, but you wouldn't stir."

I swallowed, her words sinking in. *Days?* How long had it been since that night, since my world had unraveled? Time felt like an abstract thing now, slipping between my fingers like water.

"I am Yuka," she offered quietly, her gaze lingering on me. "What's your name?"

The question struck me like a blow. *My name.* She didn't know who I was? The thought seemed absurd, but then again, perhaps my face was not as familiar to the Kamishen as I had assumed. I was the prince, the only heir of Emperor Ayame and the late Empress Emiko. Everyone in Yuehama should have known me.

"I am—" I tried to speak, but the words caught in my throat, turning to ash on my tongue. I swallowed, attempted again, but it was as if some unseen force had bound my voice.

"I am—" But nothing came. My throat constricted, my own name refusing to leave my lips.

Yuka's brow furrowed in concern. "Do you not remember?" she asked gently. "Perhaps that's why you were out for so long—a concussion, maybe? Or fever?" Her hands rose, the chains attached to her shackles clinking softly as she touched my forehead with surprising tenderness. "You don't feel sick. Are you alright?"

"Yes, I just..." The words faltered as the caravan jolted to a sudden halt, silencing the murmur of voices. Every eye turned toward the wooden door at the back, anticipation thick in the air.

The wood groaned as it was wrenched apart, the brightness beyond it spilling in like molten gold. My eyes, now unaccustomed to such unforgiving light, narrowed into a squint as the harsh sun bore down, its heat already crawling across my skin. The shadows of towering bazifir filled the entrance, their frames vast and imposing, their words a cadence of low growls and clipped consonants, unmistakably Duratharian.

"We must be in Durathar now," Yuka said softly, her voice barely more than a breath. Her gaze lingered on the men, the unease threading through her words like a fine, invisible cord.

"Out," one of the bazifirs commanded, his accent thick, the weight of his tongue wrapping around the word. When no one moved, he reached forward, seizing a Kamishen by the arm and yanking them into the light. The others followed, too afraid of being dragged out by force.

When my boots met the sand, it scorched even through the leather, the heat rising in thick, palpable waves. Durathar's landscape unfurled before me—an endless stretch of ochre and gold. This was Durathar, the homeland of the Zurathi people, the children of the Wilds.

The horizon rippled with heat, blurring the outlines of jagged stone structures and the distant, looming walls of the capital. The air was dry, relentless, carrying the scent of hot stone and smoke. It clung to me, foreign, oppressive. It was a far cry from the cool, mist-covered mountains of Yuehama, where jade and sakura trees dotted the landscape, and rivers ran clear beneath our feet. Here, the land was scorched, barren, as though life itself had been burned out of the soil.

We were herded like cattle, the caravan split before my eyes—Kamishen lives parceled out like chattel, each body measured, each fate sealed. Some were selected for labor or household servitude, their shoulders already bowed beneath the phantom weight of more chains yet to bind them. Others were claimed for fates darker still. The submissive and beautiful would be offered to the twisted desires of the privileged, stripped of the dignity to refuse. The strong and unyielding were cast into the arena, doomed to face beasts or men, to bleed for the savage pleasure of the crowd.

It was my turn. A bazifir with a scarred face and eyes the color of iron gripped my chin roughly, tilting my head up to meet his gaze. His thumb pressed painfully into my skin, forcing me to hold still beneath his inspection. "Pretty," he muttered, the word dripping with disdain, as if beauty in a man was a weakness. I jerked back instinctively, a low growl rising in my throat. But his grip was unyielding, his strength a cage around my defiance.

I reached for my magic then, a desperate, instinctual pull, but it was as if I were grasping at smoke. Nothing. A pulse of heat flared at the base of my neck, a reminder of the sigils that I had yet to inspect—the ones that had stolen not only my name, but seemed to have taken the very power that defined me as well.

He squeezed my bicep next, testing the firmness of my muscle, then his hand moved to my waist, his fingers digging into the flesh as though assessing me for some unseen worth. "Sturdy," he remarked in his thick accent, his voice slurring with the cadence of a Duratharian, the vowels drawn out. His lip curled into a sneer. "Arena."

He released me with a shove, and I stumbled forward, rage licking at my insides, but powerless to act. As I steadied myself, I spat into the sand by his feet, watching the wet stain sink and disappear in the heat. The Zurathi only laughed, as if my defiance was nothing more than an amusement, a trivial display from a mere slave.

I joined the group destined for the arena, my heart pounding with a helpless fury. As I stood among them, my thoughts turned to Yuka. She had been a stranger, yes, but there was a kindness in her, a beauty that had softened the brutality of our captivity. I searched the crowd, straining to catch a glimpse of her, but she was lost among the sea of bodies. Fear curled in my chest—what fate had been chosen for her? I did not know, but I feared it would be far worse than mine.

We were led through the gates of Durathar's arena, the vast structure looming above us like a temple to violence, its grandeur undeniable even in its cruelty. The walls, towering and intricate, were etched with the delicate artistry—sharp geometric patterns weaving through smooth stone. As we were pushed forward, I glimpsed the arena through a break in the columns—a circular expanse of sand, stained with the memory of countless battles, surrounded by rows upon rows of stone seats, where the people of Durathar would sit, waiting for the spectacle of death to unfold beneath their gaze.

It was a strange and terrible beauty. The arches overhead were carved with symbols I couldn't understand, the high domes soaring above like the heavens mocked us in their splendor. Every inch of the structure had been designed for the delight of the crowd, the architecture not just functional, but meant to evoke awe, even reverence.

I had heard whispers of the arenas here—spoken not as places of battle, but as crucibles where lives were extinguished for sport, where men were stripped of name and dignity, reduced to mere pawns in a game of power and spectacle.

I glanced up at the seats, imagining the faces that would fill them—Zurathi nobles with their glittering eyes, hungry for violence, their voices rising like a storm over the screams of those forced to fight below. I could almost hear the roar of the crowd, taste the metallic tang of blood in the air, feel the suffocating weight of all those eyes upon us.

We were ushered beneath the arches, down a narrow passage that wound its way into the belly of the arena. The air grew thick, damp with the smell of stone, the sunlight above was swallowed by the shadows. The underground chambers stretched out before us, a labyrinth of cells. Each one was a hollow, cold space—bare, unforgiving. Yet, somehow, this place had been designed with the same careful attention to detail as the arena above, the stone walls inlaid with delicate carvings, as though beauty could soften the brutality of our fate.

The cells were cramped, but some rooms had been hollowed out into larger, barrack-like spaces, filled with thin straw mattresses that offered little more than the illusion of rest. Slaves moved silently in and out of the shadows, their faces hollowed with exhaustion, some of them too far gone to even glance our way. A few lifted their eyes as we passed, their gazes empty, resigned to the inevitability of this place. They were ghosts, wandering the space between life and death, forgotten by the outside world. Realization settled over me like a shroud—this place would break us if we let it. This was a place where names were forgotten, where souls were swallowed by the darkness, where hope was bled dry in the sand above.

The shackles fell from my wrists with a clink, and I was handed a new set of clothes. As they led me to my assigned cell, I glanced at the others, all alike, stripped of their former lives, clothed in rags that were of Durathar. Some were Zurathi, with their proud, once-defiant gazes now dulled by defeat. Others were human, and seldomly I caught glimpses of other races from other kingdoms and continents I never had the pleasure of stepping foot in. No matter who, their faces were all the same, hollow, already resigned to whatever fate awaited them. There was no fight left in them, no spark of rebellion. Perhaps that was why we were freed from our shackles—where could we run? What was the point of defiance when there was nowhere to flee, nothing to gain but a quicker death?

"You'll stay on that side. I'll stay on mine. Understand?" The voice belonged to the human I was to share my cell with, rough and edged with disdain. He sat on a worn mattress, his frame muscular but lean, built for speed and endurance rather than brute strength. His brown locks fell naturally over his angular strong features, framing dark hazel eyes. I was certain that if one looked beyond the rough exterior—the scars, the wear of time, and the unruly beard—they would find that he held a rugged handsomeness to him.

I said nothing, stepping toward the corner where my own thin mat lay. Untying the belt at my waist, I shrugged off the rest of the garment. The clothing I was given—if they could even be called that, was designed less for modesty and more for enduring the sweltering heat of Durathar. A strip of fabric, thin and worn, that draped loosely across my chest and shoulders, leaving much of my upper body bare to the elements. The trousers were made of a similar material, loose but slung low on my hips, exposing more skin than they covered.

I could feel his gaze on me, appraising, judgmental. He didn't bother to hide his assessment of me, his eyes lingering on the exposed skin of my chest, my arms, searching for weaknesses. "Not a single scar. Do all Shen live such soft, privileged lives?" His voice even-toned. "Mage blood doesn't serve any good here. There's no celestial magic to save you."

His words bit deep, though I didn't let it show. The Celestial Bodies—the sun, the moon, the stars—were the Shen's source of power. Kamishen specifically were children of the moon, blessed with abilities that could manipulate our surroundings and command the tides.

My fingers brushed over the sigil etched into the back of my neck, its form so familiar I didn't need to see it to understand. A binding spell. Severing us from the moon itself. Our own people must have been the ones to ink it into our skin, their hands heavy with reluctance, but bound by Renjiro's command before sending us off to Durathar.

I met his gaze, my expression hard. "I suppose you'll just have to wait and see how many of us Kamishen know how to wield a sword. For your sake, hope they're skilled enough to end you quickly."

His head tilted, just slightly. Brows knitting in a flicker of surprise, though amusement soon softened the edges. There was something almost leisurely in the way he regarded me, as if I were a curiosity rather than a threat or liability. Perhaps he had expected silence—tears, even, or trembling. Something soft, broken and scared.

"One can only hope," he murmured, the words drawn out as a lazy smile ghosted across his lips. "Name's Gamal."

I hesitated before giving him a name, one that wasn't truly mine. "Kaito," I said, my voice steady, though the sound of it felt wrong.

CHAPTER TWO

Gamal and I stood by the iron bars, our gazes locked on the spectacle unfolding in the arena. The muffled roar of the crowd echoed around us, distant and detached, as though we watched from another world entirely. Through the thin slits of the barred window, I could see him—a beast of a man, larger than any Zurathi I had ever seen, even for their kind. The children of the Wilds, they were naturally vast, their bodies honed by strength that seemed to pulse from the ground beneath them. But this one was different. There was something unnatural in his movements, in the sheer force he wielded, as though he were an extension of the Wilds themselves.

"Rustam," Gamal murmured beside me, his voice low. "He invokes the great bear spirit, Dubkhers, before every fight."

I tore my eyes from the scene for a moment. "They allow that?" The Zurathi wielded a power that was raw and untamed, bound to the spirits of nature. Unlike the Celestials, whose gifts flowed innately through our blood, the Zurathi forged bonds with these ancient spirits, calling upon them in exchange for fleeting but formidable blessings. Their power wasn't inherited—it was bargained for, an agreement between mortals and the Wilds.

A human opponent, smaller and utterly dwarfed by Rustam's hulking figure, was lifted like a doll and slammed into the dirt, the sound of bones cracking sharp even through the distance. The man's breath left him in a wheezing gasp, his body limp, but not yet dead. The inevitability of his fate was written in the curve of his spine, in the surrender etched into the lines of his face. A part of me mourned for him already as I saw the quiet acceptance in his eyes as death loomed ever closer.

"Gifts from the Spirits may not be allowed for most," Gamal said, his gaze steady and unwavering. "The Zurathi have their own ways of severing their people from magic. Did you notice?" He inclined his head. "Rustam doesn't wear one of those black metal collars like the rest of them. He has the Emperor's favor."

I frowned. "What do you mean by favor?"

"The nobles don't just watch us fight," he explained, his voice tinged with bitterness. "They choose their favorites, make champions of those they think have potential. To them, we're little more than sport, their playthings. They bet on us, flaunt us, parade us like prized beasts. Champions... they're treated differently. They don't sleep in the cells below. They eat better, live better. Exceptions are made for them."

I closed my eyes briefly, the brutality of the scene pressing in from all sides. Another sickening thud, the final blow, and the crowd's uproar told me the fight was over. I didn't need to look to know that the man had met his end. Instead, I turned my gaze to Gamal. "And they're not afraid? That by giving us that much power, we might turn on them?"

He shook his head, a humorless smile playing at his lips. "Why would they be? Most champions become drunk on the glory. They stop thinking of escape, of rebellion. All they want is more of the crowd's cheers, more of the nobles' praise." He nodded toward the arena, where Rustam raised his bloodied fist high in triumph, the corpse of his opponent dangling from his other hand like a trophy. The crowd roared in approval, their bloodlust sated for the moment.

I watched with a quiet, seething disgust, the taste of bile rising in my throat. Everything about this place repulsed me. The glorification of death, the worship of strength above all else—it was barbaric, monstrous. These people didn't care for honor, or life. Only power, only blood. My lip curled involuntarily, and Gamal caught the expression before I could hide it.

"If you're ever put against Rustam," he said, his voice soft but edged with warning, "it means someone wants to see you dead."

I didn't doubt that.

If Durathar ever discovered who I truly was—what I had done to Darius—there would be no mercy. My end would be as brutal as it was inevitable, and death would not come swiftly. Death by a brute like Gamal seemed fitting for me.

"He's putting on quite the show for the Emperor," Gamal remarked, his tone as flat as his expression.

I stepped closer to the iron bars, my gaze climbing to the dais where the crown sat. The new emperor, perched high above us all, watched his champion with an impassive stare. From this distance, I couldn't discern whether it was pride or something darker that colored his gaze. Was he not pleased with his beast?

"With the Zurathi having strength like Rustam's, I'm surprised no one has risen to challenge Rohan's bastard for the throne," I muttered, my voice low but weighted with the thought.

The politics of this land were something my father had spoken of with measured disdain. Bloodlines mattered here, but not in the way they did elsewhere. In Durathar, it wasn't merely ancestry that held power but the glory attached to a family's name, the strength of its legacy. The Zurathi prized strength above all—brutal, unrelenting power. The Pahlavans had always been a family steeped in glory, their lineage etched into Durathar's history with the blood of warriors. They had earned the fear and respect of their people with each generation.

And yet, for all their renown, Darius had fallen to me, a Kamishen. A quiet scoff escaped me at the memory. *So much for formidable offspring.*

Still, it puzzled me why no one had yet sought to unseat the half-breed emperor. My gaze lingered on him, his figure commanding attention even from this distance. He was large, yes, especially when measured against humans or Kamishen, but compared to a pure Zurathi like Rustam, he seemed diminished. His mother's blood had softened his edges, made him something other. But less formidable? I couldn't decide.

"What do you know of Azariel?" Gamal's voice drew my attention back, both of us now fixed on the Emperor.

"That his mother wasn't Zurathi. That he was the forgotten prince, a shadow in a house of giants. He has a temper, or so I've heard, but with Zurathi blood, that hardly surprises me." I crossed my arms, leaning against the cold stone as I spoke.

"You can only challenge the crown here if you deem yourself stronger than the Emperor," Gamal continued, his voice softening with something like intrigue. "Azariel is part Tenishen... So he possesses something the Zurathi do not."

"Celestial magic," I breathed, the realization stealing the air from my lungs. My voice was barely above a whisper as I stared, disbelief threading through my thoughts. I had believed the children of the stars, the Tenishen, had perished long ago—their race extinguished in the ancient wars, lost to time. My gaze returned to the emperor, lingering now with a deeper sense of unease. The Tenishen were said to be angelic, winged beings that bridged the heavens and land, the closest children of the celestial bodies. But there were no wings on Azariel, no ethereal softness about him. He looked to be all sharp edges and cold indifference, a storm contained in human form.

"The rumors of his temper are true. Volatile. Impulsive." Gamal's fingers slipped through the dark coils of his hair, his voice low, almost reverent. "And when he wants something, there's no stopping him. He'll have it—exactly as he desires."

There was a tension in his words that lingered, something unspoken. I watched him closely, trying to decipher if it was admiration or warning that edged his tone. But before I could decide, the Zurathi overseer approached. His presence, as always, carried the weight of ice. Without a glance in my direction, his gaze settled on Gamal, sharp and indifferent.

"To the gate. You're next." He said before he turned on his heel, disappearing into the shadowed corridors of the arena.

Gamal gave a short, humorless laugh, patting my shoulder with a firmness that felt more like a goodbye. "If I don't make it back, there's a bottle of spirit tucked beneath my mattress. Drink it, and think of me when you do."

His hand lingered a beat longer, his grip grounding me in the present, before he strode off after the overseer, his steps steady, resigned. I watched him leave, the sound of his boots fading into the distance, swallowed by the ominous quiet that always settled before the bloodshed began.

I stepped back over to the bars, my hands curling around the cold iron as I watched Gamal stride into the arena, his form small against the expanse of blood-soaked dirt. A pang of discomfort twisted in my chest, knowing that soon, his opponent—my kin—would fall. It should have stirred some sense of loyalty in me, a desire to root for my own kind. But in the arena, survival knew no allegiance, no ties of blood.

Gamal stood there, poised and calm, facing the Kamishen slave across from him, and I could see it—the control in his stance, the fluid grace in every step, every breath. This wasn't a fight to him. It was a dance, a practiced ritual of evasion and precision. He waited, always waited, for the moment when his opponent left the smallest crack in their defenses. And then he struck, swift and unerring.

The Kamishen lunged, but Gamal was already moving, slipping out of reach with a grace that seemed almost unnatural. His strikes were like whispers—silent, deadly, and impossible to predict. Watching him fight, I couldn't help but wonder if he had once been a warrior before this life. His movements spoke of years of training, honed in battlefields far beyond this wretched pit.

It had been a week since I arrived in Durathar, and this was the third time I'd watched him fight. Each time, the outcome had been the same—swift victory. Yet, despite his skill, he remained not a champion. It puzzled me, for surely the nobles had seen what I had. Perhaps he was too controlled, too detached. They preferred savagery, bloodlust, fighters who stirred the crowd with brutality, not with the art of survival.

The roar of the spectators broke through my thoughts, signaling the inevitable. Another Kamishen lay dead, his blood seeping into the land like so many before him. This land, drenched in the life of my people, a land they should never have set foot on. Yet, here we all were, trapped in a cycle of death and survival.

Gamal raised his eyes to the crowd, his expression unreadable. Victory was his once more, but the triumph in their eyes never seemed to touch him.

♯·⚖·ㄅ·朿

Another Kamishen, Hiro, helped me haul one of the bodies into the creaking wooden cart. The weight of it was dead, not just in mass but in spirit, a heavy reminder of what this place demanded. Already, the body had begun to stiffen, the pungent smell of death clinging to the air like a second skin. It filled the arena, mingling with sweat, blood, and despair. A stench of a life reduced to nothing.

The only time we fighters were allowed to breathe freely, to speak more than grunts of pain or labored breaths, was when they let us out to eat, or to clean and train in the arena. Outside the confines of our cells, we could stretch our legs, if not our minds. But even here, in this fleeting respite, we carried the weight of bodies—both the ones we fought and the ones we became.

"I don't understand why the Grand Shiryū didn't fight," Hiro said, panting as we hoisted another limp body onto the cart. The wood groaned under the strain, a protest against the dead weight we piled onto it. "Emperor Ayame and Prince Kyo fought to the very end. Kyo even felled Darius. I'm sure if

Renjiro had taken them we would have pushed them out of Gahara—the capital. Maybe even out of Yuehama..."

His words hung in the air. What could I say to him? That Renjiro was a coward? That he craved power at any cost, even at the sacrifice of his brother and nephew? I said nothing. The truth was bitter, and there was no comfort in voicing it.

"Prince Kyo would've made a good Emperor," Hiro continued, his voice softening as though speaking of someone he knew intimately. "He was kind. Pragmatic. He looked out for his people." My chest tightened, but I forced my expression to remain neutral.

I was never so entangled in courtly games that I didn't know how my people saw me, but hearing it struck another cord. I had tried, always, to walk in my father's shadow with grace, though its breadth often dwarfed me. He was the kind of ruler legends cradled gently in their telling: just, unyielding, and empathetic.

He didn't rule for dominion, but for change. For the common folk whose names would never echo in the palace halls. Even beyond Yuehama, his concern stretched. His heart tethered to Tairasa as a whole, as though no border could dull his sense of duty. *Without your people, a kingdom is nothing*, he would say. And I believed him. I still do.

"Have you ever met the royal family, Kaito?"

"I have not," I said, my voice steady.

"I have. My father and I met them once. We went to petition for more guards to patrol the borders of our village. The

Prince himself vouched for us, gave us coin for what we lost to the bandits." There was warmth in his voice now.

"You met the Prince?" My heart stilled for a moment as memories stirred within me. Qingehe Village... I remembered it now—a quiet place, peaceful until the bandits came. They had taken the villagers' crops, their livestock, even their women. His father and he had come to the palace to plead for aid.

"What else do you remember of the Prince? Do you remember what he looked like?" I asked, my voice softer now.

Hiro frowned, his brow furrowing in thought. "I... I should. But I can't seem to recall. It's strange, isn't it? Now that I think of it, I don't even remember his hair color."

He scratched his head, as if the memories might come loose if he tried hard enough. But they wouldn't. I had learned that my people could not remember me. It was a double-edged sword, offering me safety from being exposed to my enemies, yet it cut deep in another way. I was nameless. Faceless. Forgotten.

"I'm sure it'll come back to you soon," I said, my voice quiet, almost gentle. "Let us move on. I'm famished."

The sun was beginning its descent and though the day's heat still clung to the air, I could already feel the night's chill creeping in. The cold here was ruthless, biting at your bones the moment the sun vanished. If the arena didn't kill you, the climate might. The heat scorched you by day, the cold froze you by night. There was no respite.

We walked through the inner walls of the arena, descending into the dining hall they used for us. It was a vast, bleak space. The stone walls were bare, save for the flickering torches. No windows. No art. Just rows of worn wooden tables and benches, stained by time and suffering.

"Kaito," Gamal said, sitting beside me, his voice low. "This room reeks of death and sweat. In honesty, I'd rather eat in my cell."

He unwrapped a piece of flatbread, tearing off a bite. The taste of something, anything, to ward off the gnawing hunger that lived inside us all.

"I miss bathing," I groaned, staring down at the bowl of rice and lentils in front of me, my appetite absent. I stirred the spoon idly, not out of hunger but habit. The food was tasteless, just sustenance to keep us fighting, nothing more. I miss the food of my country, the baths, the softness of my bed... *I miss freedom.*

I had lived a life of privilege, a life I had taken for granted. I never imagined I would end up here, in a cage, my identity erased. Most of my days had been steeped in ceremony and scholarship. I had been trained to inherit not just a throne, but a legacy.

I was made to hone my celestial gifts with reverence and determination. To study the rise and fall of empires, memorize the treaties of Tairasa as I shadowed my father through counsel halls and villages alike. I had ideas, visions of change and my father would listen. He'd nod, perhaps smile and tell me I was wise beyond my years, but it was always tempered with the notion: I needed to first learn to listen more than I spoke. At the time, I secretly resented the waiting. I mistook the cocoon for a cage.

But now I would return to it in a breath. Not for the silks, the comfort. But for the people. I missed them more than the luxuries of my past life. My companions. My father. I wondered if Renjiro had laid my father to rest properly. Had he honored his wish to be buried beside my mother?

"Become a champion, and you'll earn a bath. Or wait until the overseer tires of us and lets us bathe with a cloth and bucket," Gamal said with a low chuckle, his tone light despite the weight of the world we lived in.

I had yet to step into the arena. There weren't fights every day, and not every slave was called to fight each time. Still, I knew my time would come. I was trained to wield a blade, to pierce a target with arrows, to fight even without a weapon. Yet those skills were always tested against wood and straw, or the palace guards, never in the life-and-death stakes of this place—except for that fateful day with Darius. However, my true talents lay in my magic, the sigils etched into my memory and flesh, in my cunning, my reflexes. But here, none of that mattered. Here, physical prowess was the only currency.

A loud thud shattered my thoughts. Gamal and I turned in unison toward the source. A Zurathi slave lay partially on the ground, his legs still draped over the wooden bench, his hands clutched to his throat. Blood seeped through his fingers, staining the stone floor beneath him as he choked on his own blood. The wet, ragged sound filled the hall, a macabre symphony of desperation.

On the opposite side of the table stood a human slave, his eyes wide, a knife trembling in his hand. The color had drained from his face, as though he hadn't quite processed what he'd done. The knife gleamed, slick with blood, a forbidden weapon that should never have been in his grasp.

"How did he get a knife?" I whispered, my voice barely audible over the dying gasps of the Zurathi.

In the arena, we were not permitted weapons beyond what the overseers gave us. For meals, we used wooden utensils, crude and harmless. Yet here, in this slave's hand, was a blade sharp enough to kill. How had it come to him?

Before we could think further, bazifirs stormed into the hall. Their hulking figures moved with swift purpose, seizing the human with rough, unyielding hands. His eyes were empty, devoid of comprehension, as if his mind had slipped away the moment the blade struck. "I didn't mean to... He just-... I'm sorry..." His words were barely a whisper, a fading plea drowned by the chaos of his own actions.

As they dragged him out, his voice disappeared into the dim corridors, leaving only the body behind. The lifeless Zurathi, now a motionless heap on the ground. A hollow feeling gnawed at my chest. I had thought my death would find me in the arena, under the weight of a sword or the force of a blow. Now, I realized, it could just as easily come from the hands of another slave, a fellow prisoner driven mad by fear, by hunger, by the suffocating weight of survival.

My gaze drifted back to the scene—drawn like a moth to the flicker of danger. My body moved of its own accord, rising from the bench, but a firm grip caught my forearm before I could fully stand

"Don't," Gamal said. His voice was low, quiet, yet there was steel beneath it. His gaze locked with mine—steadfast, unwavering.

"What? I'm not doing anything, I just..." The words stumbled from my tongue, trailing into the dry air. I needed to know. How had the knife gotten past the bazifirs? Fighters were permitted advantages by the hands of the nobles, sure, but there were no champions here—at least, none declared. But perhaps...

"I am not daft. My brother wears that same look when curiosity gnaws at him," Gamal murmured, releasing my arm. "You would be wise to keep your head down, Kaito. Survival means winning your matches and being unnoticed."

His hand withdrew, and I let my arm fall to my lap, heavy with restraint. Perhaps he was right. Whatever secrets brewed beneath the sands of this place, it was not yet my time to uncover them.

The last thing I needed was to be seen digging too deep—especially in a place where the price of interest could be my identity.

CHAPTER THREE

The day had come at last, the day I had dreaded and yet could not escape. My heart thundered in my chest as I approached the portcullis, each step heavier than the last. The air was thick with dust and sweat, the scent of blood ever-present in this place. I had seen this gate open countless times, watched men—some I knew, some I did not—disappear through its iron maw and return as lifeless bodies, or worse, more broken than before.

But today, it was my turn.

Normally, the gates would creak open on either side simultaneously, the grinding of metal on stone like the herald of death itself. But today, it was different. Only one side opened, slowly, with an ominous hesitation, as if even the gate itself pitied what lay ahead. My gaze flickered to the small, barred windows carved into the walls of the arena, knowing that somewhere behind them, Gamal was watching. I could almost hear him muttering a prayer, hoping that if death came for me, it would be swift.

The gate yawned wider as I stepped toward the center of the arena. My heart pounded so violently I thought it might leap from my chest. The sky above seemed endless, a cruel expanse that offered no escape, no mercy. I sent a silent prayer to the Spirits, not for victory, but for mercy. Let my opponent be someone unknown to me—perhaps even someone I disliked. Anything to make the burden of taking a life more bearable.

But then I saw it, and my breath caught in my throat.

Was that... a karkadann?

My mind stuttered, disbelief seizing me. That was a karkadann.

Spirits damn me.

The great beast, impossibly large, pawed at the sand, snorting in agitation. Its thick, stone-like hide gleamed beneath the harsh light of the sun, its single horn sharp as death itself. The ground trembled beneath its weight as it charged toward me, each thunderous step kicking up clouds of dust.

Panic surged through my veins. My eyes darted around the arena, searching for anything—*anything*—that could serve as shelter, a shield, a weapon. But there was nothing. No crates, no pillars, no weapons, not even the crude spear I had half-expected. The overseer, in his cruelty, had sent me in with nothing.

I had heard whispers among the fighters, matches of men being pitted against beasts rather than one another, but to face such an enormous creature without so much as a blade? It was madness.

My body moved before my mind could catch up. The instinct to survive overpowered everything else. My feet kicked into motion, and I ran—ran as fast as my legs could carry me, the sand slipping beneath my heels. I could hear the beast behind me, its breath hot, its snorts filled with fury. There was no time to think, no time to strategize. Only the raw, primal urge to live another moment, to evade the crushing weight of the karkadann's charge.

There was no honor here, no grand battle of skill or strength. Just the sheer, desperate race to outrun death.

I fled back to the edge of the arena, heart racing, lungs burning. The portcullis loomed ahead—closed, immovable. It would not open until one of us was declared victor, but I needed space. I needed to think. I would not die here, not on foreign land, and certainly not beneath the crushing weight of a wild beast.

May the fury of the Wilds take Renjiro, I thought bitterly, *and the horn of a karkadann finds its way up his ass.*

I turned sharply, veering away from the gate as the karkadann thundered toward me, its monstrous body too slow to avoid the collision. The sound of flesh and muscle meeting iron echoed behind me as it crashed into the gate, shaking the very ground beneath my feet.

Glancing up, I saw the bazifirs stationed above, their spears glinting in the harsh light as they leaned over the edge to watch the spectacle unfold. If only I could grasp one, if only my magic were not bound. I stretched my fingers out toward the nearest spear, desperation filling my veins, trying to seize it through sheer force of will. Nothing. The sigil at the base of my neck flared, a searing reminder of the barrier between me and my celestial gifts.

"Please," I whispered to myself, voice hoarse.

I tried again, the strain building behind my eyes, the burn at the nape of my neck intensifying until it felt as though fire had been etched into my flesh. Renjiro's words echoed in my mind, like a cruel taunt.

"*Destroy the sigil,*" he had said, voice dripping with condescension. "*Remember, Kyo—sigils are locks. The one who creates them holds the key, but the truly powerful can destroy them outright.*"

The ground trembled beneath me as the karkadann resumed its charge. I ran, legs burning, lungs screaming for air. My hand found the raised scars of the sigil, tracing the lines with trembling fingers. I would not wait for a key. I was the key.

I dug my nails into my skin, tearing into the flesh, carving a new sigil atop the old one. Pain shot through me, sharp and biting, as blood trickled down my neck and between my shoulder blades. I winced, but there was no time for weakness. This sigil was not my uncle's work—no, it was crafted by a lesser shiryū, and I could unravel it, even if only for a moment.

Blood dripped down my spine, warm and wet. My gaze darted to the bazifirs once more, hand outstretched, focusing on the spear I so desperately needed. My concentration slipped, and in that brief moment, I felt the world shift.

A shadow fell over me.

Then, something massive struck my back. All the breath was driven from my lungs as I was lifted off the ground, weightless for a heartbeat before I slammed back into the earth. Sand and dirt exploded around me as I lay sprawled on my stomach, every bone and muscle screaming in protest.

Get up, I willed myself. *You have to get up. You cannot die here.*

The ground trembled again, each step of the karkadann growing nearer. With agonizing effort, I rolled onto my side, my vision blurring as I saw the crimson trail staining the sand beneath me. Its horn had pierced my back. Blood poured from the wound, warm and constant.

Blood.

Blood is water. And I am a child of the Moon Spirit.

My fingers trembled as they dipped into the pool of blood collecting beneath me. I could feel the pull of the tides in my veins, the ancient power that had always answered my call. The old sigil burned, resisting—but not enough to stop me now.

I closed my eyes briefly, focusing, feeling the blood respond, shaping it into a lance, sharp and shimmering with my essence. It hovered in the air before me, suspended by my will alone. My vision darkened further, black spots dancing at the edges as exhaustion threatened to take me under.

The karkadann charged again, its heavy breaths shaking the air, each step closer, closer still. I waited, watching, timing my strike as my world narrowed to this one, final moment.

I released the lance with all that I had left in me.

Darkness closed in, pulling me down, but in those final seconds, I heard the thunderous fall of the beast as it crashed to the earth. The ground trembled one last time, and then, silence.

.⚶·⚸⚶⚶

The first thing I noticed was the air, heavy with the scent of honey and dried herbs, rich and cloying, lingering just on the edge of sweetness. My body felt weightless, cushioned beneath what I realized was an impossibly soft mattress, its comfort foreign to the rough bedding I had grown used to. I dared not open my eyes, afraid the feeling was some cruel illusion—that at any moment, I would be pulled back into the biting ache of the arena floor, and the merciless grit of sand against my skin.

But I wasn't there. No, there was softness beneath me, silk sheets that felt like water against my bare skin, their texture too smooth, too cool. My body ached, a dull throb in every limb, yet I could feel the weight of clean cloth binding my torso and neck, wrapping me in what must have been meticulous care. I had been tended to, my skin washed free of the blood and dust I remembered. I felt almost... whole.

I cracked my eyes open, blinking against the gentle light filtering through a canopy above, rich in deep, dark hues embroidered with silver that looked like threads of moonlight. I could see a few cushions stacked beside me, their embroidery catching the light, almost blinding in its beauty.

With an ache in my chest that spread through every muscle, I shifted, pushing myself just slightly to get a better look—only to feel a sharp, burning pain course through me, forcing a wince from my lips.

"Don't move." Her voice was a whisper, firm yet soft, washing over me like the balm on my wounds. "You'll injure yourself further."

I turned my gaze to the sound, my heart beating just a bit faster. Yuka stood at the bedside.

"What are you doing here?" I asked, taking her in, piece by delicate piece. Her long ashy blonde hair gathered in a careful knot, each strand obedient and refined. Her robes—a mix of ivory, soft earth-browns, and whispers of tan—hung around her in graceful folds, lending her a quiet dignity. Relief flooded me as I realized this kind stranger, this soul from my homeland, had not met some perverse fate in the emperor's courts. She looked well, the bright glint in her pale lavender eyes seemed to be untarnished by the cruelty of this place, and a weight I had not realized I bore melted away.

"I told him I knew you," she said, her voice soft. "I thought it might be easier for you to wake to a familiar face in such an unfamiliar place."

"Told who?"

"Emperor Azariel," she murmured, the name slipping through her lips like a dark secret. "I think he means to make you a champion. They only permit sages to tend to champions."

So, this was her new role—a herbalist, a healer. It was likely the best outcome one could hope for, especially for a woman from Yuehama.

"I was nearly killed by a wild animal, and he wishes to make me his champion?" I asked, the skepticism laced through my tone, unwilling to conceal the absurdity of it all.

"*Nearly killed, you survived.*"

The low voice seemed to seep into the room, drawing shadows into sharper focus. Yuka's head bowed immediately, her eyes casting downward as though in respect or fear.

"Your Majesty," she whispered.

"You are dismissed." The words carried a quiet command, and Yuka rose without a word, leaving the air heavy with an unspoken tension.

And then, at last, he stepped into view—Azariel, the emperor. I had only seen him from a distance, his figure draped upon the raised dais overlooking the arena like a cold, untouchable divine being. I had mistaken him then, thinking him devoid of the ethereal quality that his Tenishen blood should have imbued. Up close, he was a sight to behold, a vision of celestial beauty woven with something darker, something almost predatory.

His form towered, each broad shoulder and the chiseled line of his chest cutting a powerful figure, yet there was elegance in the way his frame tapered to a lean waist. Snowy hair, a contrast against the deep umber of his skin, fell like a curtain around a face that balanced angular edges with a certain cruel grace. His eyes were a marvel, stormy and dark, they glimmered with a subtle, molten gold at their centers, an inner light that flickered like the stars themself. And upon his skin were not tattoos or painted markings, as I had once thought from afar, but living veins of gold that coursed just above the surface, cleaves, pulsing with a life of their own—a manifestation of celestial power straining against the Zurathi vessel that held it.

He was beautiful, but his beauty held an edge, a cold intimidation that pressed upon the air. His smile, when it came, never touched his eyes. Instead, those dark, hungry eyes stared with a malice that was as chilling as it was concealed, the kind of smile that promised kindness but carried the shadow of cruelty.

"How did you do it?" Azariel's voice curled through the silence, cool and curious.

"Pardon?"

"How did you break the sigil?" He lowered himself to the edge of the bed, his weight sinking into the softness beside me, the press of his hand grazing the silken coverlet. His gaze held me, dark and unyielding, watching every breath, every flicker of movement. I felt dwarfed beneath him, as though the very air grew thinner, caution weaving through me like a taut string pulled tight. My instincts screamed danger, whispering that if I valued my life, I should run. My heart thudded in my chest, each beat loud enough, I was certain, for him to hear.

"I-" I forced myself to swallow, to steady my voice. "In Yuehama, I served under the palace's Grand Shiryū. Sigils are nothing new to me."

He held my gaze in silence, his expression unreadable, his eyes assessing, dissecting. But my words were no fabrication, my uncle had been my teacher.

A thought crept into my mind, bold as a flame: *I could kill him here and now.* It would be so simple, wouldn't it? Just a twist of the sheets around his throat, a brief struggle as the emperor's breath left him, and with it, his rule. In Durathar, such things were not met with the same disdain as they would be in Yuehama—here, one took the crown by any means, blood and blade or no. The light would die in his eyes, and his kingdom would fall into my hands.

"Such hatred in your eyes," Azariel murmured, a dark chuckle slipping past his lips, eerie and unsettling.

"Can you blame me?" I hissed, my voice low, edged with a bitter fire. "Your people seized mine, forcing them to either amuse you or die in their attempts. And now, what? You've come to make me your latest pawn? Your champion? To have me slaughter my own kin for the glory of your name?" My fists tightened around the sheets, the cloth twisting under my grip, the pulse of my own heartbeat pounding against my skin.

"You were fortunate this time," he said, his voice smooth, my disdain gliding off him like water over stone. "But tell me, do you think the Spirits will favor you again, should I withdraw my hand? What if your next match were against a champion?" His smile was sly, dark amusement dancing at the edges.

Gamal's warning came unbidden, a ghostly whisper in my mind. *"If you're ever put against Rustam, it means someone wants you dead."* The weight of it lingered, a chill settling over me. What if my defiance sealed my fate, making my next match my last? Would he tolerate insolence and refusal from someone like me?

"Do I even have a choice?" I asked, feeling the shadows of his unspoken threat stretch between us.

"There are always choices." His gaze was unwavering, cold and absolute. "You may choose to accept my offer, become one of my champions. Gain a foothold in these games and survive. Or... persist in your defiance, testing the limits of your capabilities until it shatters your body." His hand pressed against my chest, and instinctively, I recoiled, my spine biting into the bedding as pain flared sharp and unyielding.

"What's your choice, Kamishen?" His hand pressed further into me. His touch was unnaturally warm, a twisted soothing feel even as it heightened my agony.

"Survival," I breathed, each syllable catching in my throat, my voice betraying the shame that clawed within me.

"Good." His voice was soft, almost tender, smug satisfaction glinting in his eyes as he drew his hand back and rose to stand. "Rest, heal. This is your new cell now, a gift befitting one of my own."

My jaw clenched, bitterness flooding my mouth. I had sold myself, a proud man reduced to a pawn in his games, bound by the whims of an enemy. The truth burned beneath my ribs—I was nothing but a horse for his bets, a slave to survival, a coward.

As the heavy door thudded shut behind him, I forced myself upright, defying the sharp, pulsing ache that swept through me. I could not lie idle in this bed, soft as it was, as though yielding to his whims. No, I needed to see, to understand, to prepare. I refused to play the docile slave for him.

The room unfolded before me, spacious and refined—a chamber crafted for a guest, someone of court from foreign lands perhaps. The bed was its heart, a magnificent expanse draped in silks, smaller than the one I knew in my homeland but leagues above the straw mat of my cell. To one side rested a divan, its delicate curves beckoning like a distant comfort, a low table in the center of the room surrounded by broad, plush cushions in muted jewel tones.

My gaze traced upward, to the towering ceilings and the high-set windows that allowed beams of sunlight and fresh air to spill in through the chamber. They were well beyond reach, though the arched double doors with intricate latticework of mashrabiya panels and stained glass, seemed within the realm of possibility for escape. A terrace. A strange kindness, almost... careless.

Yet, as I looked upon it all, unease settled within me like a shadow. The comfort, the finery—it felt like something I should not possess, not while my people bore the weight of servitude and discomfort elsewhere. There was an urge to escape, to twist this token into my own defiance.

CHAPTER FOUR

Azariel had not appeared since that night, his absence hanging over me like a specter. Three days had passed in a languid haze, and I could almost picture Gamal shaking his head, assuming I had perished in the ring or had been taken and left to fade without care in a cell. Perhaps he would even believe they had let me die in their presence—if not through indifference, then through a deliberate silence, a choice made to be a sick source of entertainment.

I had learned the truth of the terrace though—that faint whisper of escape was, in fact, a cruel jest. The doors did not open to freedom but led only to another threshold, another wall. The terrace stretched forward, open to the winds and sky, yet iron bars clung to the railings, fastening me to the palace's edge. A delicate ruse, meant to taste of freedom while delivering yet another bitter sip of confinement, reminding me that I had merely traded one cell for another.

"Raise your arms, Kaito," Ilay murmured, a hint of reluctance threading through his voice. I obliged, though not without a roll of my eyes as he brought the damp cloth across my skin, its coolness meeting the warmth of my body and the scent of rose water unfurling in the air around us, delicate yet excessive.

"I'm capable of washing myself," I said, tone sharp. The indignant words barely masked my discomfort beneath his careful hands.

"Of that, I have no doubt," he replied, a faint sigh underscoring the formality. "But we both know I am bound to the Emperor's orders."

Ilay served as Azariel's Bearer, a position demanding absolute loyalty and deference—a title not easily won or given. It surprised me, still, to see him in this role, for something in his bearing hinted at mixed blood that had perhaps been diluted over generations. His Zurathi lineage felt softened somehow, his frame slight and graceful, more fitting for a noble in the northern courts of Tairasa than for a servant of Durathar.

"The nobles of the court are presenting their champions at a feast tonight," he continued, guiding my arms down as he drew the cloth over the sigil marked upon my skin, a series of them I had painstakingly etched myself years ago. "You and Rustam are expected to attend, to show yourselves—to stoke the court's appetite for wagers." His stormy blue eyes lingered on the sigils, perhaps in quiet awe or quiet fear. "It was requested you wear something that reveals these. They say it adds... a certain allure."

His tone softened, then, as he stepped back, setting the cloth aside before arranging my attire on the bed: a tunic that barely veiled my chest and left my arms entirely bare, a sash meant to drape across my hips with studied elegance, tailored trousers, and a band of gleaming gold intended to clasp around my bicep, each piece chosen to expose my markings like a tapestry while dress me up like a doll.

"I will leave you to dress," he said, bowing slightly, his raven-black locks falling to obscure his view. "When you are ready, I will escort you to the Hall of Starlight." With that, he slipped from the room, leaving only the echo of rose water and his words lingering behind.

As I crossed the threshold into the Hall of Starlight, I felt the weight of it settle over me—the hushed splendor, the quiet, unassuming power that pressed down like a lover's hand, cold and insistent. The last rays of the setting sun cast a golden glow across the vast expanse of mirrored walls and mosaics. The large terrace doors were wide open, allowing a cool, fragrant breeze to drift through the hall, carrying with it the soft sounds of distant desert life. The light filtered in through the doors and windows, catching on the small mirrored tiles that lined the walls and archways, casting flecks of amber and gold that danced along the floors and ceiling, as if the room itself were shimmering in response to the sun's retreat.

Nobles of Durathar lounged throughout the hall, draped across plush, colorful cushions arranged in small, intimate clusters. Some reclined, fingers lazily dipping into plates of jeweled fruits, sweet honey-drenched pastries, and succulent meats. They sipped dark wine from goblets carved with intricate designs, their laughter mingling with the gentle murmur of conversation. Silken pipes sat by their sides, their exotic tobacco smoke curling upward, creating clouds of scented haze that hung in the cooling air. The nobles' gaze flitted toward the center of the room, where nearly unclothed performers wielding shimmering blades moved with practiced grace, their bodies twisting and turning in hypnotic, dangerous beauty.

Others stood at the periphery, sipping their wine as they conversed, their attention shifting between one another and the men and women stationed at their sides. These individuals, unmistakable as champions of the arena, were draped in finery designed to accentuate the muscle and scars won in battle. They were like prized beasts on display. They thrived on the scraps of power tossed their way, basking in the fleeting glories that came with their proximity to influence. Their docility was an act—a performance of submission woven from ambition and desperation, a calculated strategy to ensure survival.

But there were other companions here—pleasure slaves. They possessed a different kind of quiet surrender. There was no feigned bravado in their submission, only a yearning so palpable it lingered in the air around them. They leaned into caresses, melted under whispered promises, and sought the gaze of anyone who might find them desirable. Their docility was born of a hollow hunger, a craving to be more than an ornament, to be claimed as something permanent.

Perhaps they dreamed of catching the favor of a noble, of being elevated to the rank of courtesan.

Champion, slave, servant. Here, in this place, it didn't matter. To the nobles, they were all possessions and prizes, nothing more. Their worth wasn't in their humanity but in their ability to adorn, to amuse, to serve. And as I watched them—their glances soft as silk, their bodies draped in finery that disguised the chains binding their spirits—I wondered which was worse: to crave power in captivity or to hunger for love in a world that would never offer it.

At the heart of it all sat Azariel, upon an elevated stone dais of layered cushions and fur, an idle hand resting upon the bare bronzed back of a woman who draped herself across his lap. She was nearly naked, save for a silver collar and a gossamer cloth at her hips that seemed a mockery of modesty, something meant to tempt more than conceal. Her fingers traced circles upon his knee, her movements languid and artful, like the rest of them—those raised to beauty, to artifice, to submission. She wore his wealth and power as plainly as if it were a brand upon her skin.

Azariel's eyes caught mine, dark and all-knowing, and a ghost of a smile passed across his lips. I felt it as a weight, a silent acknowledgment of what I was brought here to be—a vessel, a means, an amusement to him and those around him. I felt their eyes upon me, countless and unrelenting, appraising me as one might a horse bred for speed or a blade crafted to kill. I was no more than a curiosity in that moment, a thing to be studied and then forgotten.

A voice, low and feminine, stirred me from my wary observation of the Emperor. "I caught your match against the karkadann," she said, her words soft but carrying a sharpened edge that left me raw under her gaze. "It was... bold, the way you used your own body like that."

She looked at me as if she were peeling back layers, unraveling secrets with her amber eyes. I felt the weight of her scrutiny settle over me, prickling my skin. It was strange, this rare feeling of exposure under someone's gaze, and I couldn't tell if it was her curiosity or her judgment that I found more unsettling.

"Thank you," I replied simply, keeping my voice measured, while my gaze fell briefly to the jewels draped over her neck and wrists—gold and blood-red rubies that gleamed in the dim light, a perfect match for her wine-colored dress. This was wealth: the kind wrested from other kingdoms, plundered from foreign hands. I forced my mouth into stillness, quelling the contempt that nearly rose to betray me.

With a practiced ease, she reached out, her fingers cool and audacious as they groped the muscle of my arm, tracing the edge of the golden band resting against my bicep. Normally, she was exactly the type of woman I'd crave—smooth ivory skin, auburn locks, and soft curves that tempted the hand. But there was a darkness in her, a shadowed edge that kept me on guard. "Nayila Sulqadir," she murmured, her voice like silk veiling steel. "And you are?"

"Kaito," I said, tempering my tone with just a hint of softness. Her name echoed in my mind; I knew it well enough.

Daughter of the Duratharian Vizier, a figure who wielded influence with his words as well as his prowess. Her gaze was one of conquest, studying me with the hunger of a predator circling wounded prey. But I knew this game, and how to play it. Perhaps she could be useful. I allowed my gaze to drift downward, lingering on the delicate curve of her breast. Giving the illusion that I was captivated by the gentle rise and fall of her soft, measured breaths that caused them to swell against the crimson fabric.

"You are far too handsome to be a fighter," she purred, her fingers trailing boldly to my chest, pressing her hand over my heart as if it beat for her command. For a moment, I imagined my fingers closing around her wrist, bones breaking beneath my grip. But instead, I met her gaze, a naive smile curving my lips.

"And if not a fighter," I asked, tilting my head, "what would I be?"

"*My* concubine," she replied, her voice as brazen as her words were offensive. Her fingers moved to trace the sigils etched over my skin, as if she thought them a decoration to be admired, not symbols of power and confinement. My jaw tightened, but I kept the smile frozen on my face, unyielding.

"Oh, really?" I said, my hand closing over her wrist, my fingers digging in as her eyes flickered to mine, a dark gleam in them that was both thrilling and deadly. Her composure slipped as my grip tightened, a subtle tremor betraying her.

"Nayila, has no one told you not to toy with things that do not belong to you?" A voice intervened, low and unmistakably amused. I released her wrist, and she withdrew, nursing her wounded flesh along with her pride as she bowed her head toward the figure beside me.

"Azariel," she said, her voice slipping into deference, though a flicker of defiance lingered in her eyes. "Forgive me, majesty. The wine dulls one's sense of decorum."

Azariel's gaze lingered on her, heavy and unrelenting, his silence stretching long enough to unsettle even her. I could feel his warmth beside me, an oppressive presence, his celestial essence radiating from his skin and burning through the cool linen of his robe.

"Perhaps your father is looking for you," he said at last, dismissing her with an elegance that only deepened her shame. She shot me a final glance, the lust in her eyes now edged with disdain and challenge.

"A viper," he murmured, his lips curving near my ear. "Be cautious in the den." His voice, quiet as it was, sent a shiver through me.

"I had it handled," I replied, stepping back, shaking free of his warmth.

A hum escaped him, noncommittal, before he glanced over his shoulder. "Time for you to meet the other champions." He walked ahead, his gait indifferent, leaving me to follow or be left behind.

And so, I followed. Face after face blurred before me, each a pawn of courtly games, champions paraded like prized horses, nobles wrapped in silks richer than the land. Their names and titles slipped away, replaced by an unsettling realization. No one asked about the sigils—the markings that breached the wall between flesh and spirit. They asked nothing of the magic I wielded, power I shouldn't have been able to touch at all. They didn't care. They were too absorbed in their spectacle of blood and sport to see what lie hidden in their slaves. Only those who conjured this monstrous game could understand. Those were the ones who held the power here, who twisted fate like strings, drawing us ever deeper into this theater of cruelty. The ones who had champions.

"Why was I set against a beast and not a man?" I asked as we moved away from the press of voices.

Azariel gave me a sidelong glance, ignoring my question entirely. "I notice you've yet to touch your drink," he remarked, his gaze slipping to the untouched wine in my hand. "Information here, like favors, is not given freely. Finish it, and I'll answer you."

I bit down lightly on the inside of my cheek, looking to the crimson wine. It's dark surface shimmered beneath the mirrored lights, and for a moment, it seemed I held a cup of starlight. I had avoided drinking intentionally, unwilling to let anything cloud my senses.

"Are all Kamishen so unyielding, or is it simply you who lacks the art of enjoyment?" His tone was relaxed, almost mocking. "Or is it that you expect us to poison you? A wasteful choice, really. We are not as conniving as you may think."

I hadn't feared poison; no, it was never that simple with the Zurathi. Death for them was a display, a test of strength, and I felt no safer in their courts than I did in their pits. "Not poison," I said, my voice calm, eyes fixed on his. "Only that my senses remain sharp. As you said, we stand in a den of vipers. Shouldn't I be wary... Your Highness?" I let the title fall with a trace of disdain.

He only arched a brow, an amused twist at the corner of his mouth. "No great design led you to face the karkadann," he said finally. "It was chosen only because it would entertain. A test, to see if a man would even rise, weaponless, against it."

Entertainment. So I was nothing more than a whim, a name thrown at random into the jaws of a beast. Rage coiled beneath my skin, but I said nothing. My grip on the glass tightened, the surface slick under the tension of my fingers.

"Does that answer not satisfy, Kamishen?"

"My name is not Kamishen. It's Kaito."

"Kaito." He echoed it, each syllable slipping slowly from his lips, amusement glinting in his eyes. A restless ache gnawed at me. I would be neither his companion nor his pet any longer for this spectacle. Without another word, I stepped away, letting the distance grow between us.

I had no destination in mind, only a need to be anywhere else, to regain the fragments of composure I felt slipping through my hands in his presence. But a name caught my ear, softly spoken—Gamal's name, hushed between a Zurathi and his master.

Keeping my stance casual, I raised the glass to my lips, feigning interest in the taste while I lingered within earshot, my mind racing.

"You'll invoke Jānga when you fight him tomorrow," she said, her tone casual, as though they spoke of dinner. "Make it slow, draw it out, and give them a good show. Think you can manage that?"

A soft chuckle interrupted and drowned out the rest of their words, and I turned to find Azariel behind me. "Not the most subtle in your schemes, are you?" His words were smooth, laced with a playful scorn. "Eavesdropping hardly befits a champion."

I kept my voice steady, resisting the urge to glare at him. "Surely there are softer entertainments to occupy you tonight than following me. Like a set of breasts," I said, casting my gaze back toward the pair, but they'd moved on, their murmurs faded beyond reach.

His smirk widened. "Far more interesting to watch you blunder through this place."

My expression soured, amusement failing me entirely. "What is Jānga?" I asked, the unfamiliar Durathian word twisting awkwardly in my mouth.

Azariel's eyes dropped to my untouched glass, a brow arched with an expectancy.

Suppressing a sigh, I raised the cup to my lips, draining the liquid in a single pull, willing my displeasure not to show as I shoved the empty glass toward him. The bitter taste lingered on my tongue, warm and bracing.

"Jānga," he began as he took the glass from my hand, "is a serpent spirit of the desert... Does the Wilds intrigue you?" His voice took on a mock curiosity.

"I was curious, nothing more," I lied, turning and stepping away from him before he could savor the shift in my mood. The heat of his gaze prickled against my back, but I ignored it, my eyes scanning the chamber for Ilay's form.

"You forget yourself, Kaito." His fingers reached out and tightened around my forearm, arresting my retreat. "Perhaps I've indulged you too freely tonight."

The offense in his gaze was palpable, a flare of something cold and indignant at my repeated retreats. "Does it wound your pride, Emperor? Are you so easily perturbed that a Kamishenian slave has no interest in your company?"

He laughed, a sound low and smooth, laced with a dark amusement. "You imagine I follow you for company?" The mocking in his tone stung like an open flame. "Your vanity's unbecoming."

My jaw clenched. "Then why is it you keep following?" I held his gaze, letting the words land with all the disdain I could muster. "I humored you, didn't I? Allowed myself to be paraded, now, I'll retire as I see fit."

He leaned close, voice dropping to a taunt. "You still don't grasp the politics of a champion's place here, do you?" His words dripped with condescension. "You're nothing more than a tool—an extension of me. I *parade* you to build anticipation, to make them hunger for your performance. If you have no use to entertain them, the only thing they'll desire is your death."

I held his gaze, something cold settling within me. They might see only a pawn, a showpiece for their sport. But I am a prince—*no*, an emperor, even if they remain ignorant of it. I have no interest in these barbaric games.

My arm tore free from his grip, the act too sharp to ignore. Eyes turned toward us, curious mutters rising around the hall. I felt the weight of every gaze, knew I'd invited consequences by challenging him openly. But pride had kept me standing firm, refusing to bow beneath the scrutiny.

But then I felt a gentle hand on my shoulder. "Kaito," Ilay's voice was collected, "the drinks must have made you bold. Come, I'll see you back to your quarters."

One last glance to Azariel showed a glint of something venomous in his eyes, a smoldering darkness that churned just beneath his cool exterior. It sent a chill through me. But in an instant, he composed himself, his gaze shifting to a woman who slid her hand around his waist, stealing his attention as I followed Ilay into the dim corridors beyond.

CHAPTER FIVE

The next day, I was finally granted leave to train with the other fighters. The palace's luxuries had offered some comfort, yet they felt wrong, undeserved, a cloak that did not quite fit. I found my spirit more at ease here, standing among my own people, bearing witness to their struggles, feeling the grit of the sand beneath my boots.

"I never thought you dead," Gamal remarked, his breath even despite the hours we'd spent sparring. "You're too stubborn to fall that easily." His eyes were sharp as he continued, "But when I heard the palace sages were summoned to tend to you, I knew they'd chosen you as a champion. I just... I didn't expect the Emperor himself would claim you."

I raised a hand, signaling a break, bending over to catch my breath. "He's... intrigued by the sigil," I replied, rising to face him again. "Intrigued that I managed to break it, if only for a moment."

Gamal's brow furrowed. "From what I've heard, you're the first to even try tampering with the binding in that way."

"Usually, it's futile. For commoners, breaking a sigil as complex as a binding spell is near impossible," I admitted, the memory of my attempt fresh in my mind, seared with the pain it had cost. "I wasn't even certain I could do it."

"They'll expect you to try again. You know that, don't you?" There was a trace of worry in his gaze. "Do you think you'll succeed?"

"I believe I will," I replied, though quietly, almost as if speaking the thought too loudly would break the fragile hope. I'd already started piecing the sigil together in my mind, though without a mirror, without a way to see its full form, it was a struggle. But I would find a way to force that lock open, to keep it open. Once I could free myself, I would unlock the same for my people. Then, perhaps, we could find a way out of this place entirely.

"They only want to see how much you'll hurt yourself in the name of survival," he murmured. "They revel in it, the thrill of watching you surprise them, defy them. Be cautious, Kaito."

I nodded, a quiet promise escaping my lips as we joined the others at the gate. Though we both bore the scars of Durathar's cruelty, his wounds had been carved more openly, more deeply. Gamal was Akhsarian—one of the conquered. He had not known Akhsarun in her days of sovereign splendor, when her banners flew untamed across its lands, when her tongue and traditions shaped the rhythm of daily life. But his father had. And his father before that.

He had lived through the conquest—the aftermath that came not with swords, but with decrees. The slow unraveling of identity. The young taught to praise Durathar's "unity," while the old whispered in corners what had been taken. They called it strength. Integration. Prosperity. For Tairasa, they claim, can only stand strong under Durathar's rule. A lie repeated often enough that even those who suffer it began to believe it were true.

"Gamal, there's something I need to tell you."

His gaze sharpened with curiosity. "Hm?"

"There was a feast for the champions," I began, lowering my voice. "I overheard one speaking with his master. I'm certain you'll face a champion tonight."

He arched a brow. "Do you know who?"

Azariel had introduced us briefly, but the name had slipped through my memory. "I can't recall his name, but I heard his master telling him to invoke the spirit Jānga, to 'put on a good show' as he kills you."

"Jānga," he echoed, a shadow passing over his face. "I know the champion you speak of. He draws on Jānga's power to paralyze his foes, then kills them slowly—prolonging their agony." Gamal's gaze grew distant, calculating. "I'm fast, but he'll be faster, faster than I could counter. It seems someone has painted a target on my back tonight."

I felt a tightening in my chest. "How does Jānga's power work exactly?"

The cloth pressed hard against my neck, pressure to stop the bleeding. The ache was a dull companion as I gripped the iron bars, gaze fixed on the arena. Gamal had just entered, his form steady as he adjusted the crude bandage around his forearm, waiting for his opponent. Across from him, the Zurathi fighter strode in, arrogant in his bearing. They were both given shamshirs for this fight—a choice designed not for strategy, but for brutality.

The Zurathi relished in their so-called superiority, casting "mage blood" as lesser, unworthy. They wielded powers born from the Wilds, powers to dominate and destroy. Shen, the celestial gifts, they mocked as simple manipulations of the elements. But they would learn—today, they would learn—that survival forges strength they could never hope to contain.

The battle began. The Zurathi fighter moved with inhuman speed, his strikes snakelike, his limbs an unyielding blur—the very essence of Jãnga's spirit. Gamal's pace was ordinary in comparison, and he was forced onto the defense, struggling to keep up. My chest tightened as I watched, caught between anticipation and dread. And then it happened—the Zurathi's blade swept low, catching Gamal's ankle, sending him crashing to the dust. His face pressed into the dirt, the weight of the Zurathi pressing him down as his opponent kneeled on his back.

With a sickening grin, the Zurathi leaned in, sinking his teeth into the flesh of Gamal's shoulder. He released him just as quickly, the venom left to seep into Gamal's blood, the real spectacle about to begin.

The Zurathi circled, wiping blood from his mouth, watching Gamal struggle to his feet, waiting for his venom to do its work, to paralyze Gamal's body and leave him helpless for the crowd's amusement. But Gamal pushed to his feet with a swiftness that sent a ripple of surprise through the onlookers. He lunged forward, his curved blade flashing in the light, each strike faster, stronger—unnatural.

Their shamshirs clashed with a fury that sent metal ringing through the arena, dust rising like smoke around their movements, a relentless dance of life and death. Gamal matched his opponent now, no—he was surpassing him. The Zurathi's face twisted in confusion, a glance cast to his master in the stands, questioning why the venom hadn't bound this human as it should have, how he moved with speed born of something beyond human capabilities.

It was beautiful, brutal. They moved in perfect rhythm until, with one final, flawless arc, Gamal's blade sliced through, swift as a hawk's descent. The Zurathi's head fell, severed, a silent end as the crowd roared with approval.

Gamal didn't wait to take in the crowd's praise. I watched as he staggered toward the gate, the flush of battle draining from his skin, his body stiffening as he collapsed. He would be carried off, but he would live. He had made it out—defying the nobles' bloodthirsty hopes to see him paralyzed, tortured, and then dead.

A grin broke across my face. They had wanted a slow spectacle, and I had denied them. It was my sigils work—triggered just as the venom slowed Gamal's pulse, pushing a surge of life through him, flooding him with strength that seemed almost divine.

I had broken their game.

And there, watching the nobles' confused faces, I felt something awaken in me—power, ancient and immense, a type I had not known in the guarded halls of Yueham's palace. My fingertips tingled, the sigils alive, potent with untapped potential. When I reclaim all of it—when I tear down the binding that limits me—Durathar will fall.

Azariel will fall by my hands.

·‡·⌘·ⴆ·✳

The earthy mixture was cool, a soothing balm against the fire at the back of my neck as Yuka worked it gently into my skin. Her fingers moved carefully. She leaned forward, her voice a quiet murmur by my ear. "You can't keep doing this, Kaito," she said, her tone a soft admonition, words woven with worry. "It will lead to permanent damage, and to... other things." Her hand stilled, her gaze meeting mine with quiet insistence. "My sigil limits me here. I cannot heal as I could if we were back in Yuehama. So, take it easy. Please."

There was something in her, a warmth, a patience, that reminded me of family—a sister I might have known had the spirits smiled upon my parents. I could only nod, briefly pressing my fingers over her hand in thanks.

"I'll try," I said. "I have a few days before my next fight; I'll heal by then."

She sighed, a sound woven with resignation. "Just in time to hurt yourself again." The weight of her gaze lingered, her lips pressed into a tight line.

A knock broke the gentle silence between us, and the door swung open, Azariel entered, swift and cold. Ilay, like a shadow, lurked just beyond the threshold.

Yuka's posture changed instantly; she drew back, sinking onto the bed behind me as she bowed her head in quiet submission. "Your Highness," she whispered. But I did not offer the same respect, my eyes fixed upon him, unmoving.

"Is something the matter, or did you simply miss me?" My words held his gaze, my voice level, a defiant slant to my tone.

Azariel's eyes flicked past me, cold and dismissive as he turned to Yuka. "You may take your leave." His voice held the barest edge of annoyance, as though her mere presence grated against him.

Her head dipped lower before she slipped quietly from the room, and the door closed with a dull thud. Silence settled between us, taut as a pulled bowstring, until he took a step closer, his presence pressing into mine, our knees nearly brushing as I sat upon the edge of the bed. I could feel his gaze settle on me, a sharp, probing weight.

"You tampered with the outcome of that match, didn't you?" His voice was flat, an accusation draped in an almost curious calm.

"And if I did?" I answered, meeting his challenge.

He leaned closer, his voice darkening. "No one is permitted advantages in these matches—not unless they are champions. Otherwise, you defeat the very purpose."

I couldn't help the faint smile tugging at my lips. "Were they not still entertained?"

A muscle in his jaw tightened, his throat bobbing as he swallowed. "If anyone discovers the truth, it will come back on me. They'll assume I was complicit, that I intended to insult them through your actions."

"And how is that my concern? You're the Emperor. Can you not do as you please?"

His hands braced against the bed, one on either side of my thighs, his face inches from mine. "Yuka," he said, voice soft but each word sharp as glass, "is a sweet Kamishen, is she not? Talented. A quick learner I've been told." His eyes gleamed with something darker. "Do you think she'd keep that sweetness if she was made to serve on her knees? Or perhaps, if she were buried deep in the dirt?"

He didn't need to say more. The threat was enough. A sharp, blinding anger took hold of me, and before I could stop myself, my fist crashed against his cheek.

When he looked back at me, there was no anger in his expression, only a cold amusement that twisted something in my chest. His beauty held something venomous, and his smile jagged and cruel, with his tongue pressing against the inside of his cheek.

How could something so alluring look so utterly vile?

"Don't tell me you're afraid now," he drawled, his voice low, taunting, taking note of the regret in my eyes. "You're the one who threw the punch." He edged closer, and I leaned back instinctively, my hands slipping from the bed's edge as I fell flat against the mattress. Looming over me, his face filling my vision, his voice a whisper that settled like iron in my bones. "How badly do you want to do that again? How much do you long to see the life drain from my eyes, Kamishen?"

I glared at him, but his words had rooted me. His gaze searched my face, intent, and his lips twisted in a smirk. "Where's that fire? I've grown rather fond of our back and forth."

My words came out quieter than I intended, barely a whisper as I turned my face away. "There's something wrong with you." A warmth crept across my cheeks, unbidden, and I focused my gaze to the sheets, hoping the feeling would fade.

His soft laugh chilled me, a dark, unsettling sound. "Tell me," he murmured. "The reason you had listened to that conversation was because they spoke of *him*, correct? Why is that?"

"Because... he is my friend," I said, the words as simple and true as the dawn. "You look out for the people you care about."

Azariel tilted his head, his gaze sharpening as he shifted, one hand bracing against the bed beside me, while the other came to grip my jaw with a quiet, unyielding force. His fingers commanding, turning my face so our eyes locked, his unblinking gaze holding mine captive.

"Companionship is a liability in the arena," he murmured, his voice low and edged with something like disdain. "In this place, survival requires choosing oneself. You must learn to abandon all else."

His words pressed on me, filling the silence with a weight that threatened to drown. Yet, I could not ignore the memory that rose between us—of our first encounter, the exchange where I told him I had chosen survival. That was why I was here, was it not? And yet, I felt a fire rise within me, hot and sure, as I thought of those I cared for. Yes, I had chosen survival. But I would not let that choice mean abandoning my humanity. My people.

"If my choices bring consequences," I said, my voice steady, each word an anchor, "then I will bear them. Gladly."

I pushed a hand against his chest, firm, demanding my own space back, and he relented, a faint smile curving at the edges of his mouth as he straightened. He watched me, something almost bemused in his gaze, and in that moment, I knew—Azariel would always choose himself, choose his survival. He was not fit to be a ruler.

He drifted to the bedpost, fingers toying with the gauzy fabric draped around it, his touch so deliberate it seemed almost reverent. The faint fractures of gold threading through his hand flexed as his fingers moved, catching the dim light like veins of molten metal. I couldn't help but wonder how much of his skin did those golden lines trace across? Did they feel like flesh, warm and yielding, or were they something otherworldly, like threads of stardust etched into his skin? The heat emanating from him was unmistakable, a warmth that bordered on searing when he stood close. Did he feel it, too? Did his own body burn him, or was he accustomed to such fire?

"Your first match as one of my champions is in a few days," he murmured, a note of expectation woven into his voice. "What is it you'll require to be ready? As I trust you understand, a victory is expected."

"A mirror and a needle," I replied, my tone flat and quick.

His brow arched, his fingers stilling. "A mirror and a needle?"

"Yes," I answered, unwavering. "It should be obvious that I am no warrior. If you wish for me to triumph, I need to see the sigil on my neck and use a tool other than my fingers. We wouldn't want my tampering to fail at a crucial moment, leaving me to an undignified, anticlimactic end—surely not?"

There were more tools I needed to break the sigil permanently, but I couldn't show my hand so soon. He knew I could fracture it, knew the risk that meant for him. And still, he hovered near, unafraid, composed as though he believed my leash would hold no matter how close I came. I would earn his trust, let his guard slip inch by inch until I held everything I needed to shatter his hold completely.

"I will see to it that you have what you desire," he replied, his gaze holding mine.

CHAPTER SIX

Ilay set two palm-sized mirrors onto the table. I knelt on the cushions beside it, letting my fingers skim the edge of a needle resting there, its silvered point glinting. I pressed a finger to its tip. It was sharp enough to break skin, to draw a bead of blood that bloomed against my fingertip like the first sign of dawn. "Thank you, Ilay," I said softly, reaching for one of the mirrors, its back a polished bronze etched with delicate, winding designs that whispered of an artisans' hands.

Ilay turned to go but I called him back. "Wait. Could you bring me a few more things? I'll need parchment and something to write with."

He hesitated, a flicker of concern crossing his face. "I believe... there is no harm in it," he replied, though his brows knitted slightly, as though he weighed whether he needed permission from his Emperor.

"If it's necessary, you may go ask him. I don't mind waiting," I offered, meeting his gaze.

But he shook his head. "No need to trouble him with such trivial matters. I'll be only a moment," he assured me, retreating through the doorway.

As soon as he was gone, I shrugged off the fabric of my tunic, letting it slip down my shoulders to pool at my waist. Cool air brushed against my bare skin as I picked up the mirror, angling it to see the sigils marked across my chest. It was intricate, each line and arc winding over my skin in a complicated pattern, and unmistakably Renjiro's handiwork. I traced them lightly, feeling the faint pulse of magic under my touch. This was no simple binding. Renjiro had woven it to cover nearly my entire pectoral, stretching up my neck and spilling over part of my shoulder—a meticulous cage meant to lock me in.

It was a spell for concealment, not just a binding. "My name is..." I tried to speak my true name, but the words crumbled to dust on my tongue, scattering before they could form. I watched closely, seeing which sigils stirred, which ones reacted. The shifts were so faint they were almost imperceptible if you didn't know how to look.

Holding the mirror before me, I moved to study my reflection—the misty gray of my eyes, the dark onyx waves of hair, features correctly mine, yet somehow, to my people, unrecognizable. The face that looked back seemed unchanged, yet they didn't see *me*. What did they see when they looked into these eyes? What illusion met their gaze instead of the truth?

Ilay returned quietly, laying parchment, a reed quill, and a clay inkwell upon the table. I offered him a soft, grateful smile. "Have you ever encountered the royal family of Yuehama?"

"I cannot say I have," he replied, shaking his head slightly. "I've never left Durathar, and the last envoy from Yuehama arrived long before the war—before I was even born."

I nodded, noting his youth, barely twenty summers, the bloom of his years.

"What is it like, in Yuehama?" he asked, curiosity softening his gaze.

Setting the mirror aside, I adjusted to face him more fully. "Yuehama is..." I paused, the memories rising like the mist over our mountains. "Beautiful. Serene," I said, my voice hushed with piety. "Our mountains wear ancient cedars like robes, groves of bamboo sway like whispers, and forests blush with cherry blossoms that fall like snow. The land is green, lush, veined with rivers and waterfalls, their waters as clear and pure as the spirit."

Ilay listened. "That does sound beautiful. Durathar has its own charms, but it is... different."

"Beauty exists everywhere," I said, my voice almost lost to memory. "But nothing will ever compare to home." A sadness, unbidden, bled into my tone. Ilay's gaze sorrowed as he glanced down, sensing there were no words he could offer to heal a wound that deep.

After a thoughtful silence, he said, "The palace here is... pleasant enough. Though, outside its walls lie places worth seeing—oases, scattered like hidden jewels, with their own quiet appeal."

I met his gaze, a question already forming. "When was the last time you left these palace grounds, Ilay?"

He paused, eyes distant. "I can hardly recall. I was a child. I have served here for so long."

"Then I hope," I said, voice quiet, "that one day, you may see those oases once again."

He nodded. "As do I," he replied softly, before taking his leave.

I turned my attention to the parchment, tracing the sigils my uncle had bound upon me, line by meticulous line, each curve and taper, the ink steady beneath my hand. Someday, I would claim the thrones of both Durathar and Yuehama, and I would not rise to power nameless. When I revealed myself, they would know me.

·‡·⚮·㐫·茶

My next battle had proved harsher than I'd expected. It seemed they had decided to test the limits of my endurance, the depths of my resolve. I was not so naive as to ignore that magic could wane under the press of close-quarter combat, nor so arrogant as to believe it a limitless shield.

This time, I faced a Zurathi warrior whose roots hailed from Akhsarun. I could not help but feel a flicker of kinship with the Akhsarian. Many of them were trapped in a foreign land, much like us. Though luckily for them, their culture was not so different from their neighboring kingdom.

They armed us with spears, and I felt the weight of it in my grip, the coldness of its iron. I needed to keep my distance from him, it was difficult and I found myself faltering. Yet with my magic—those blessings from the Moon—available for that match, I was eventually able to manipulate the space between us, force a distance that suited me, until finally, I emerged as the victor. I had now taken two lives, and this one felt heavier than the last. I thought, foolishly, that time would temper the weight of this killing, dull the blade of it against my heart. But it remained as sharp, as cruel as ever—perhaps because there was no anger in me for the Akhsarian.

The first time I took a life, there had been rage, a reason. But in the arena, as I looked upon the fallen warrior, I felt only emptiness and the slow burn of something that I could not name—perhaps sorrow for a stranger, kin only in fate.

The water lapped quietly against the sides of the bath, warm enough to soothe the ache in my muscles. My arms draped over the edge, chin resting on my hands as I stared ahead, taking in the dim glow of the chamber of the palace bath. Shadows danced along the stone walls and drape dividers, mingling with the faint scent of jasmine and sandalwood that lingered in the air.

A sigh escaped me, sinking into the quiet that filled the room. Normally, I would have requested Yuka's tending and would be granted it. Her presence could easily ease my tension, and her touch knew how to make even a sting of healing treatments tolerable. I'd asked, but they'd sent this Zurathi, another assistant to the High Sage instead.

He was quiet as he worked, rubbing a cool paste over the cut on my shoulder where that spear had bitten deep. His touch was clinical, practiced, and distant—a far cry from Yuka's gentle precision. The wound stung under his fingers, the earthy, bitter scent of herbs filling the air between us. It didn't stop the pang of disappointment and regret from settling deeper.

The chamber was silent, the only sounds the echo of dripping water and the low hum of the sage's steady movements. Around me, the moonlight slipped in through small, carved openings of the lattice windows, bathing the chamber in silver glow from the moonlight. Oil lamps were lit in small alcoves, adding to the soothing glow. The intricate tilework on the walls shimmered softly, and the stone floor held the faint patterns of lotus flowers and curling vines—a vision of calm that felt worlds away from the arena.

The sage's hands moved with a strange hesitance as he worked the balm into the wound at my neck, his touch featherlight yet thorough, as though to ward off the inevitability we both felt: the wound would reopen. The balm held a faint sting, mingling with the ache beneath it—a warning, as gentle as Yuka's voice had been. I could not keep testing the limits of this healing. My next match loomed in two days, a span that felt impossibly brief. My flesh craved a reprieve, and yet I knew what I had to do.

I needed the rest of the tools to break this sigil—permanently. I'd traced it enough times, mapped out the runes that chained me, studied each line with an urgency that bordered on desperation. But it would mean asking Azariel, and the idea of asking anything of him felt like stepping willingly into a snare.

"Allow the paste to settle a while before you submerge," the sage murmured before rising to leave. His robes drifted through the soft veil of white fabric draped around the pool's edge, affording a thin semblance of privacy. I watched his figure blur into the shadows, a sense of solitude wrapping around me as I shut my eyes, surrendering for a moment to the silence.

I must have drifted, lulled by the warmth and quiet, for it was the shift of water that pulled me back. My gaze snapped open to find Azariel sinking in behind me from the opposite side, the water pooling around his broad shoulders as if shaped to his frame. His head rested back against the stone, eyes closed, an unguarded expression softening the lines of his face. The water's soft ripples played over his golden fractures, tracing the strange beauty of his form.

"Will you keep staring, or do you have something to say?" he murmured without opening his eyes, the barest hint of a smirk teasing his lips.

I forced myself to turn towards him and relax against the basin's cool stone, though the sharpness of his presence made it hard to keep my tone as indifferent as I wished. "For someone who claims little interest in my company, you've chosen my bath when there are plenty others."

His eyes flickered open, a glint of mischief in their depths. "Am I not allowed to congratulate my champion on his recent victory?"

I scoffed, lowering myself until the water rose to my chin. "Does Rustam receive such invasive congratulations?"

Azariel's gaze drifted lazily over me, unbothered by my question. "I doubt there's room enough in a bath for anyone to share with Rustam." His grin lingered, as if he found humor in the thought.

My gaze traced the glow of his golden fractures, watching as they dipped beneath the surface, scattering light like stars sinking into the depths. I looked away, all too aware of the water's clarity, the way it revealed far more than it concealed. But the image clung to my mind, as vivid as the heat that now crept up my cheeks.

"If you have questions about them," he said, a slight tilt of amusement in his tone, his gaze resting where mine had lingered. "As most do, then ask them... Or was it not questions that held your attention, but a wish to touch?" With quiet purpose, he drifted closer, his frame cutting through the water's surface in fluid silence.

"I'll settle for questions," I replied quickly, my palm instinctively lifting between us as if that could halt his stride and prevent his proximity.

But he moved swiftly, capturing my wrist and bringing me closer. He guided my fingers forward until they rested against those gleaming, molten veins that marred his chest. His touch was gentle yet insistent, inviting me to trace the lines with curious fingers. I wanted to retreat, to end this contact, but my curiosity betrayed me, holding me captive to the sensation beneath my hand.

The skin along the fractures felt thinner, a tautness that seemed almost fragile, yet warm and alive, pulsing with the barest hint of energy. It felt like flesh, but of a different kind—one that strained to contain something vast and volatile beneath, like molten metal encased in a fine layer of silk.

Beneath my touch, his heart drummed a fierce cadence. *How simple it would be,* I mused, *to drive something sharp into these fragile cracks, to seize the heart that beats there.* My touch pressed a shade harder along the golden veins, but as my gaze lifted to meet his, I found him already watching, his eyes dark, his expression unreadable. The cockiness that adorned his face had vanished, leaving behind only something else.

"Does it hurt?" My voice broke the stillness that had settled between us.

"It used to," Azariel murmured, his grip on my wrist loosening just enough for me to explore the fractures unhindered. I traced the shimmering veins that stretched from his chest to the crook of his neck, following them like rivers of liquified gold set beneath thin skin.

"They first appeared when I was a boy," he continued, his voice low, threaded with memories. "It felt like something was trying to claw its way out—a force building until, finally, it burned through, forcing these cracks." His hand stayed light upon my wrist, the gentlest tether, an invitation to keep exploring. And so I did, my fingers climbed higher upon his neck, spreading across the delicate skin of his throat, feeling the pulse beneath. He let me hold him, his lack of resistance daring me to squeeze.

"They continue to grow," he murmured, his voice low. "But I've found ways to relieve the pressure..."

"And what relieves it?" I pressed, a quiet edge to my tone.

He offered no answer, only a slight curve to his lips, a glint of malice flickering in his eyes as his hand tightened firmly around my wrist. A slow, insistent warmth pulsed from his palm, each second hotter, a channel of molten light searing through my skin. I winced, yet my fingers instinctively and stubbornly tightened around his throat, feeling his pulse quicken. His throat bobbed beneath my grip as he swallowed, his grin widening as he tipped his head back slightly, basking in this twisted play.

At last, I relented, forced to release him as the pain clawed up my arm, and he let go in tandem, leaving my wrist to throb in the wake of his touch. The burn vivid, his handprint seared into my flesh, raw and red.

"Bastard," I hissed, cradling my forearm as it throbbed, the heat of his touch still echoing on my skin.

Azariel's laughter was a low murmur that drifted over the water. He stepped back, letting the distance grow between us before his form sank beneath the surface, swallowed by ripples. I seized the moment, pulling myself from the pool. The cool air of the chamber struck my skin, a balm against both the burn he left on my wrist and the simmering anger that coursed through me.

Reaching for a linen, I wrapped it around myself, holding tight to its thin fabric. Fingers clenching it as I steadied my breath.

His voice came soft but sharp, like an unseen blade. "If your magic still pulsed freely through you, would you have drowned me? Let the waters rise at your command, let them pull me under and take me down?" His fingers brushed through his white, wet hair, water trickling down his neck, catching the lamplight like searing silver.

"Yes," I answered, my words ringing out, clean and unguarded. It was foolish, perhaps, but I could not bring myself to veil the truth, to hide my disdain. I knew I should play nice, show some semblance of diplomacy toward the emperor, but in that moment, I found I could not feign it.

His gaze lit with something—satisfaction, amusement, maybe both. "Good, *Aqaynah*." He let the ancient Deva word slip, an echo of something sacred. Hearing it took me back to the songs my mother once sang, lullabies in the celestial tongue as she'd soothed me to sleep. I hadn't heard it spoken since.

"Your need to survive is... unyielding," Azariel murmured, an edge of admiration lacing his tone. "I rather like that about you. Tell me—when will you break that sigil?"

I blinked, certain I had misheard him. "Pardon?"

A shadow of a smile touched his lips. "Do not take me for a fool. If I were in your position, equipped with your knowledge, I would already be devising ways to break the seal permanently. Or," he paused, eyes gleaming, "have I overestimated you? Are you not even attempting to free yourself?"

A storm of choices unfurled before me—each answer a double-edged blade. I could not give him the satisfaction of knowing my plans, yet nor could I allow him to think I was tame, stripped of my will to escape. "I lack the proper tools to break it," I replied evenly.

"I could procure them for you."

I narrowed my gaze. "Nothing you offer comes freely. You've made that clear. So tell me—what would you demand in exchange?" The question weighed heavily in my mind: why would he want to help me, especially when I'd all but admitted that, unshackled, I would end him without a second thought. Did he not fear me? Or did he believe my magic, even at its fullest, was no match for him?

"Mm," he hummed, his eyes bright with amusement. "It seems someone has been paying attention." A low chuckle escaped him. "All I ask is that you unlock another sigil first. If you manage it, I'll grant you what you need to free yourself. So, do we have an agreement?"

Another sigil? I could barely contain the distrust thrumming in my chest as he moved, water tracing rivulets down his skin as he stepped from the pool, stopping before me. Arms folded across his chest, his muscles shifted with effortless grace, his expression one of casual demand. He looked at me as if I were a piece in some grander game he alone saw clearly.

"Do we have an agreement, Kaito?" The tone he used was soft, a whisper of invitation laced with a challenge.

I held his gaze, measuring the danger, feeling the weight of his proposal settle over me like a shroud. Finally, I answered. "We have an agreement."

.⚶·⚹·⚶·⚶

The morning light was soft as it spilled through the latticed windows, creating decorative patterns that painted the polished floors. I followed the palace bazifirs in silence, each step echoing faintly in the stillness. The scent of rose, sandalwood, and a hint of sharp cedar drifted through the air, stirring as we moved down corridors. Tapestries lining the walls depicted spirits and beasts, battles and offerings, their threads dulled by time but still vibrant enough to convey the weight of their stories.

Ahead, the Emperor's doors stood open, tall and imposing, like the mouth of a mountain cave. I felt my pulse quicken, an instinctive response as I stepped past the threshold, into Azariel's quarters.

The chamber was washed in morning light, soft and golden as it poured through the open terrace, blurring the edges of the vast room. A delicate breeze drifted in, stirring the sheer curtains that bordered the terrace, carrying with it the faint perfume of jasmine from the gardens below.

At the heart of the chamber, Azariel sat on a raised platform, surrounded by cushions of indigo and gold. He was dressed in robes of silver-threaded silk that caught the light, as if his very form glowed with the dawn. But my gaze drifted, drawn to the figure reclined beside him.

A man— Zurathi, beautiful and striking—lay sprawled across the cushions, his form lean and elegant, his skin marked with tattoos that wove down his tanned arms and across his chest, symbols of his people and the Wilds. His eyes, a shade of molten amber, were half-lidded, gaze distant yet perceptive, watching the world through a languid, detached grace.

He wore only a silver metal collar, and a drape of crimson silk around his hips, the fabric clinging low, revealing the sharp lines of his abdomen. His hair fell loose, dark and shining, framing his face as if carved by the divine themselves.

I should not have been surprised to find him in the company of a male concubine—Durathar, after all, was a kingdom known for its indulgences, and hedonism flowed freely within its walls. Yet, I had assumed the Zurathi held tighter to the bounds of pride and restraint, that such intimacies might be seen as unmasculine by their standards. Perhaps it wasn't so if you were the one forcing another to their knees. In Yuehama, such indulgences were not condemned, yet neither were they common. The Kamishen seldom pursued the luxuries of flesh and pleasure without purpose. Our people struggled to bring forth new life; to lie with another man was seen as a waste of seed.

Azariel's stone-gold gaze met mine, and he spoke my name—"Kaito"—a polite greeting, veiled and unreadable.

"I trust I am not interrupting," I murmured, my eyes shifting briefly to the concubine, who barely acknowledged me, his gaze sliding away, his focus drawn to Azariel.

"No, we were finished here." Azariel gave the concubine a silent command with a mere glance, and the man rose from the cushions, slipping from the room.

"Where is the sigil?"

Azariel chuckled a low sound. "Straight to the point." His fingers tapped a cushion beside him. "Come here."

I hesitated, but stepped forward, lowering myself beside him, sensing the weighted silence and privacy of the chamber pressing around us. He loosened the sash draped over his robe, unwinding it with a practiced grace before peeling the robe from his shoulders.

"What are you doing?" I shifted back instinctively, a flicker of wariness tightening my posture.

"Relax, *Aqaynah*," he teased, his voice warm with amusement. "If I wanted *that*, do you think I would have dismissed my companion?" He raised an eyebrow, a trace of mischief in his expression. "You wished to see the sigil—here it is."

With only his trousers remaining, he turned away from me. There, between the broad planes of his shoulders, etched into the muscles of his back, was the sigil—a latticework of symbols bound into a single form, twisting together in complicated, ancient patterns. Whoever had carved this magic upon his skin had wielded an artistry and wisdom beyond what I had seen.

Without thinking, my fingers lifted, tracing the ink as though its secrets might come alive beneath my touch. "Who did this?" I breathed, unable to temper the awe that slipped into my voice.

"Amalthea, my mother." he replied, his tone cool, unflinching.

I swallowed, feeling the weight of revelation settle like stones in my throat. This was the work of a Tenishen. Here, upon his skin, lay the craftsmanship of that fabled race—an artifact not simply of power, but of legend. The intricacy, the precision of each inked line, each coil of magic; it was almost painful to touch, knowing the rarity of what lay beneath my fingertips. And possibly just as rare, Azariel. Before me could be the last of their kind.

"Can you unlock it?" His voice was steady, unreadable.

"I... I don't know." I admitted, the humility of the truth coiling within me. "Even our Grand Shiryū have never dared a sigil so complex. I would have to untangle its purpose first, see its limits and what properties bind it. Only after that would I even begin to consider the unlocking."

I leaned closer, fingertips tracing over the sigil's shape, reverent. "It's... it's clearly a binding spell."

Azariel's brow lifted, faint amusement creasing his features. "Is that all you Celestials use sigils for? Binding?"

"Do you forget that you, too, have Celestial blood in you?" I murmured, tracing the golden fractures along his back with a gentle touch to prove my point. "Sigils aren't only for binding. They can empower one's gifts from the spirits."

I rolled up the sleeve of my tunic, baring the marks woven into my own skin, lines carefully inked over years. Leaning forward, I extended my forearm into his view, watching his gaze fall upon the patterns. "These sigils allow me to magnify my abilities. These will be the cause for your drowning the next time we bathe together," I added, allowing a faint, teasing smile.

A laugh slipped from him, soft as a sigh. "So you mean there will be a next time?" His eyes found mine, a trace of playfulness sharpening his features. The arch of his brow, the faint curve of his lips—they left me momentarily unsteady, warmth rising to the tips of my ears.

"No." I retreated, pulling my arm back, settling myself onto the cushion behind him. "Why did your mother place this binding upon you?"

"I would ask my mother as a boy, time and again, why she carved my flesh. She would always answer with one word."

"And that word?" I asked, curiosity and caution entangled within me.

"*Vitanaj.*" He paused, almost savoring the celestial syllables.

"*Vitanaj...*" I echoed, the familiarity of the Deva tongue tugging faintly at my memory, though it had been lost to me in recent years.

"Survival." His answer was plain, a truth resting just beneath the stillness of his voice.

Survival, I echoed in my mind. What a sentiment from a mother to her son.

"Have you parchment?" I asked. "I will need to map the sigil's design if I am to unravel it."

He gave me a sidelong look, brow raised. "Can you not decipher it from my flesh alone?"

I shook my head, a sigh escaping me. "This is not some simple marking. Its complexity could keep me deciphering for days, especially since I've no idea what it's meant to bind." My gaze sharpened. "Have you felt anything... absent since it was placed?"

"I wouldn't know. She marked me when I was too young to remember if I had lost something."

It was clear it wasn't to bind his celestial magic. My eyes drifted to my wrist, wrapped to shield the burn he'd left the previous night, the pain dulled but a throb still echoed beneath.

In silence, we fell to our tasks, the scratch of ink filling the quiet as I traced the pattern's curves and weaves onto parchment, capturing each intricate line as though in each brushstroke I might unearth a long-hidden key.

CHAPTER SEVEN

The arena roared like an ocean in a storm as I entered, the gate closing behind me with a low, final scrape of iron against stone. I felt a trickle of warmth at the base of my neck and reached back, fingers coming away red. The sigil was unlocked once more, a crimson line marking my skin like a key. I wiped it away, willing the pain to stay buried, at least for this fight.

My gaze lifted, drawn to the stands almost involuntarily. I shouldn't have looked, shouldn't have sought him out. And yet, there I was, scanning past the faces, the jeering, expectant crowd, as my gaze sought out and met Azariel's on the dais. He had a way of lingering even in absence, his presence as tangible as the sword at my side, even when I hated it. Hated him. My lip curled slightly at the thought, but the truth of it gnawed beneath my disdain, a thorn I could never quite pull free.

A distant creak echoed through the arena as the opposite gate lifted open, and I turned, my heart stilling as I watched a figure emerge, stepping forward into the light. He was Kamishen. One of my own. Taehyun. Recognition struck me like a blade. He was no stranger to me; I knew the way his hands had steadied a blade, the way he'd carried himself as part of the Imperial Guard. Once, he had been bound to the same soil, loyal to the same kingdom, to my family. Now, he was my opponent. My enemy because the arena demanded it so.

My mouth felt dry, the weight of the crowd's gaze pressing down, urging me forward, but my feet wouldn't obey. To cross that space meant more than stepping into a fight; it meant betrayal. The crowd surged, a pulsing demand for violence that I alone resisted. But my heart beat wildly against my ribs, each step forward feeling as if it might split me open. My feet remained rooted, refusing the call to close the distance, to raise a blade against my own.

It was Taehyun who closed the distance, each step deliberate and solemn. His hand rested on his sword, but he did not draw it until he was only a few paces from me. A moment's hesitation flickered in his eyes as he looked at me, as if my stillness had unsettled him, as if he, too, was reluctant to fulfill the crowd's brutal demand.

"Despite what they would wish to see, I will not fight someone unarmed," he said, his voice steady, carrying across the sand. "Draw your sword, brother. Fight with honor, with the Moon in your soul and Yuehama in your heart." Words that should have brought comfort, a balm between us, Kamishen to Kamishen, even as they held a promise that one of us would fall by the other's hand. Words to ease the sting of betrayal, to cloak this arena in forgiveness.

I nodded, fingers curling around the hilt at my side. The blade emerged from its sheath with a quiet ring, its weight familiar, yet heavier now than ever. I would fight him and I would face him as he deserved—without magic, without tricks.

Our swords met in a clash of steel, striking against each other with an intensity that echoed through the arena. Taehyun's form was relentless, his movements a symphony of skill honed over years, his strikes unyielding. He did not hold back, his every step a reminder of home, a memory that stirred a deep ache within me. His stance, his footwork, every fluid strike—all were so achingly familiar. He moved with a precision I had once admired, once studied, as I trained under the watchful eyes of the Imperial Guards.

Yet, as the fight wore on, anger simmered beneath the ache. I should not have to cross swords with my own men, not here, not as an enemy to those who should have been my allies. The clash of our blades was a betrayal, a perversion of all we had once stood for, and yet when Taehyun looked into my eyes, there was no glint of recognition. He looked at me not as the prince, not as someone he had walked the halls of Yuehama's palace with—but as a stranger bound by origin.

But I knew the Imperial Guard well, every strength and weakness honed through years of sparring and watching, every tactic stored away. In this moment I pulled from those teachings, and pulled from my new teachings. I moved with a swiftness I'd learned under Gamal's instructions, adapting, evading, striking when I saw an opening. At last, I caught Taehyun off guard, and he faltered as I twisted past him. My blade swept forward, biting into his leg, and he stumbled, his knee hitting the ground with a dull thud. His sword slipped from his grasp, and I stood over him, my blade poised at his throat.

He met my gaze, and there was no fear there, only a calm acceptance. Taehyun inclined his head, granting me permission, a silent offering of his life, a final honor.

I could not take it.

I drew my sword back, the weight of it slipping away from his skin. Taehyun's brows knit together in confusion, a flash of disbelief. With a flick of my wrist, a whispered command to the air, I summoned my magic. The force swept through him, knocking him to the ground, his head striking the earth softly, his eyes fluttering closed as his breath stilled. *"Sleep, brother,"* I thought, looking down at him. *"You've fought a worthy fight."*

The silence from the crowd was brittle, breaking apart as the murmurs began, low and discontented. They were not fools; they saw that he still breathed, and their disappointment grew, a wave of disapproving murmurs, scattered boos.

But I looked back at them unflinching, hiding the ache beneath my skin. I let my sword fall to the ground beside him, defiant in my silence. And then, as if compelled, my gaze drifted to the dais where Azariel sat. He rose to his feet, his expression carved in displeasure, but I held his gaze, meeting his cold eyes without a flicker of emotion.

Azariel lifted his hand, graceful as a dancer reaching toward the heavens. A sliver of light shimmered into existence above his fingertips, small at first, delicate as a spark. Yet it swelled, elongating into a lance, pure celestial light, radiant as the warmth that seemed to pulse through his umber skin. His gaze never wavered, fixed upon me with an unsettling calm, even as the golden lance hovered, poised and deadly.

Then, with a languid flick, as if he were brushing away a speck of dust, he sent the lance spiraling downward. It sliced through the air with a terrible, searing speed, a comet falling from the sky. I watched its descent, too slow to comprehend, too late to stop it. It struck Taehyun's prone form with unerring precision, plunging through his chest, a merciless arc of light piercing his heart. Blood sprayed outward, painting the sand, a brutal contrast to the glow of that divine weapon. The scent of scorched flesh filled the air, sharp and bitter.

My body stilled, locked in place, as I stared at Taehyun's lifeless body sprawled upon the ground. The crowd surged, a thunderous wave of delight, their voices rising in rapture over the emperor's pitiless act. Each cheer felt like a blow, reverberating through me, threatening to loosen something deep and fragile within. I felt the prick of tears, a sting that clawed its way forward, demanding release. But I blinked, steeling myself, forcing them back. I would not allow them the satisfaction of my grief. I would not allow *him* the satisfaction of seeing me break.

With each steadying breath, I wove my walls tighter, fortifying the silence within me. If he wanted to shatter me, he would have to try harder.

⚱ ☄ ⚕ ⚶

The portcullises never lifted, never rattled open to free me from Durathar's brutal spectacle. The crowd had long since departed, yet I was left in that blood-stained pit, a prisoner to their twisted whims, with only Taehyun's still form for company. It wasn't until nightfall, when the silver touch of moonlight swept over the sand, that they came for me—palace bazifirs, their faces as blank as the cold steel in their hands.

They led me through the silent corridors, every turn, every shadowed passage back to my quarters etched too deeply into my mind, a gilded cage I could walk in blindfolded by now. But then we passed the hall that wound toward Azariel's chamber and my steps slowed, my resolve hardening with each beat of my heart.

I glanced at the guards, daring them with my silence before breaking away, my pace quickening as the heavy tread of their boots followed, Duratharian curses echoing in the stillness. I didn't care if they dragged me back in shackles. This was a cruelty too far. I had to confront him, make him face the ruin he'd left in that arena.

Ilay stood stationed outside the emperor's doors, his brow creasing in confusion. "Kaito?" His gaze darted to the bazifirs trailing behind, but I pushed past him, my hands pressing against the heavy doors. "Wait, Kaito—the Emperor has com—" His voice faded behind me as I forced them open.

"You bastard! I won that match! You had no right to—" I faltered mid-step, my words falling to silence.

Azariel was not alone. He lay sprawled upon his bed. Its silken dark sheets and pillows left in a tangled mess. Straddling his form, a woman moved upon him with practiced ease, her fingers digging into his chest, nails pressing crescent moons into his skin as her head tipped back, releasing soft, unguarded sounds of pleasure. The soft curve of her breast moved with every thrust, a mesmerizing rhythm that moved in time with her hips. Their bodies were a tangled rhythm, a raw, unashamed unity that seemed to pulse with each breath they took.

I felt the shift in the air as his gaze met mine, dark and unyielding, amusement glinting beneath the shadows of desire. "Go on," he murmured, his voice ragged with pleasure as he continued to grip her ass, fingers dipping into her pale flesh. "No right to what?"

I couldn't meet that gaze, heavy as it was with layered meaning, so I let my eyes drift to the intricate patterns upon the floor, my tongue heavy with words that had slipped through my grasp. "I... I can wait until you're... finished." My voice was barely a whisper, as unsteady as I felt.

Behind me, one of the guards cleared his throat, his presence lingering. "Your Majesty," he began, a note of hesitation in his voice.

Azariel's response was immediate, dismissive. "He's fine... Leave us."

The chamber filled with the woman's breathless sounds, the room pulsing with a decadence I was unaccustomed to hearing so openly. I stepped over to the table at the room's edge—a waist-high slab of polished stone adorned with a silver decanter of wine, jeweled goblets, and small trays laden with delicacies. It would do. Anything would work to ground me, to draw my mind away from the scene unfolding just behind me. The Duratharians lived as beasts, their passions as wild as their battles—fucking and fighting with no regard for order or restraint.

I poured the dark, ruby wine into a glass and took a deep swallow, letting its sweetness calm the frayed edges of my patience. But even as I turned back, my gaze inevitably found him again. His attention, to my surprise, was no longer on his companion but on me, his gaze lingering, almost intimate and hungry, in a way that made my skin prickle with heat. Anger twisted into something else, something unfamiliar, a flush climbing to the pointed tips of my ears, betraying me.

She leaned forward, her long, dark slate locks cascading like silk as her hand cupped his jaw, drawing his gaze firmly back to her. He allowed it—a fleeting reprieve, a moment of indulgence—and I forced my attention back to the table. My eyes landed on the faint glimmer of a small knife lightly concealed behind a platter. Slowly, deliberately, I slid it into the sleeve of my tunic.

Then, without warning, I felt a presence close behind me—a familiar warmth that seeped through my bones as his arm wrapped around my waist, pulling me back against him. I swallowed, the closeness unsettling, the breath I took shallow and uneven. "Azariel..." His name escaped in a whisper, tinged with surprise.

He didn't respond, only tightened his hold as his other arm wound around me, keeping me in place. His breath skimmed over my skin, his lips tracing the curve of my neck with a touch so featherlight it could have been mistaken for a whisper. My body went rigid, caught between the instinct to flee and the traitorous warmth unfurling through me. I had never known any intimacy with another man, and my mind screamed that I should have recoiled. But I did not. My pulse thundered beneath my skin, every beat a reminder of the closeness. His unyielding hardness pressed against me, and a rush of confusion gripped me, tangled with a heat I couldn't name. *What is happening to me? What was I even doing here?*

Taehyun's lifeless body burned vividly in my mind, the memory igniting a storm of fury within me once more. The small knife slipped down into my waiting fingers as I gripped it tightly, the cool weight anchoring my resolve. Without hesitation, I drove the blade into Azariel's thigh. His response was a sharp hiss of pain, followed by a low, rumbling chuckle that sent a shiver up my spine. His breath was warm against my neck, a disarming intimacy that made my skin crawl.

"I take it I mistook your glances?" he murmured, amusement lacing his voice.

His grip on me didn't falter, unyielding and possessive. His free hand closed over mine, still clutching the knife embedded in his flesh. With a forceful command, he guided my hand as we withdrew the blade together, the motion deliberate, agonizingly slow. My fingers throbbed under his, crushed against the handle as golden blood seeped over the silver.

"I am neither your lover nor your plaything," I said, my voice calm though my chest roared with defiance. "You have no right to lay claim to such familiarity, not without my permission." The words sliced through the space between us, but they did nothing to loosen his hold. Instead, he turned the knife in our grasp, bringing the edge near my throat—not inward, but outward, as though taunting me.

"You really are a feisty, entertaining thing," he mused, his tone maddeningly light, as though this was all some grand performance for his amusement.

"If it's entertainment you seek," I said, steel threading my voice, "perhaps you should return to your whore." My gaze swept the room, searching for the woman he had so callously abandoned. She was gone, her naked form slipping silently through the chamber doors like a shadow fleeing the sun.

Azariel only laughed, rich and unbothered, lowering the knife to the table with infuriating ease. "You've scared off my *whore*, it seems," he said, his lips brushing my neck once more, his voice a low purr. "It only seems fair that you take her place."

It was in that moment—a revelation, or perhaps the desperate grasping of a fractured mind—that I saw it. The similarities between the pleasure slave and I. Her skin bore the fairness of unpolished ivory. Her hair a charcoal sheen, and her eyes, hauntingly light like the moon. She seemed to hold a mirrored image of my own.

Had he chosen her because she looked like me? The thought clawed at the corners of my mind, dragging the image of her riding him back to me. Each detail sharpened under the weight of realization. *Don't be ridiculous,* I told myself.

"You neglected her for something you will never have," I shot back, forcing an even tone despite the tremor of rage and confusion thrumming through me. With a sharp movement, I drove my elbow into his stomach, earning a breathless grunt. "That is your fault, not mine."

I stepped forward, breaking free from his hold. Azariel straightened, unfazed, and reached for the table as though nothing had happened. He took up a bottle of wine, pouring it down his throat in a languid motion.

"Add it to the list of things I shouldn't have done, according to you," he said calmly, the corner of his mouth quirking as though he found the entire exchange endlessly amusing.

My throat tightened as his words, a mocking reminder of what I'd spat upon entering. He'd heard every word. "You killed him," I said, my voice raw, trembling under the weight of it.

"I had to."

"No, you did not!" I snapped, anger igniting in my chest, scorching. "I had won. A death wasn't needed. I am weary of this bloodthirst, of these... barbaric games."

"And where was that mindset when you killed the Akhsarian?" he replied, unfazed. "Do you think sparing one of your own absolves you? That it erases the blood on your hands that isn't Kamishen? I see the hunger in you, Kaito. You are not so different."

"I am nothing like you," I spat, heat rising to my cheeks.

His gaze held me, probing. "So if a Duratharian stood before you in the arena, would you pull back, as you did today? Would you refrain from magic?"

My silence answered him. I felt it, deep down—the fury that would tear through me against one of his own. Against him, if given the chance. The desire to return the pain they'd inflicted, to avenge the fate of my people. Even the thought stirred my blood.

Azariel placed his bottle down as he stepped close enough that I could see the cold gleam in his eyes. "Prisoners, criminals, slaves. Those are the ones who fight. The arena does not care for bloodlines or kingdoms, only survival. But I'm afraid you've disappointed. The crowd desired a spectacle, a merciless champion, but you... you defied them."

His tone dropped, deadly calm. "You will no longer step foot in the arena."

I met his gaze, my chest tight. "What do you mean?"

"You are a fighter who refuses to kill, a champion who falters," he said softly. "The arena has no use for you. Had it been left to them, they would have watched me end you there beside your kin."

My breath hitched, a bitter taste filling my mouth. "What will you do with me now? Parade or execute me as an example?"

A chuckle escaped him, low and amused. "No, *Aqaynah*. I am not so wasteful. I've granted you a pardon. You are to be my companion for a time."

The word was a lash against my pride. I took a step back from his warmth. "I will not be your palace pet. I will not get on my knees to please you," I hissed, my words laced with barely restrained disgust. "I would rather die."

"Palace pet?" His brow arched, his expression mocking. "I don't seek another concubine, and I doubt you'd even know how to fuck like one... But that's not what I require from you."

I flushed under his gaze, the burn of humiliation only fueling my anger. "Then what do you want?"

He didn't hesitate. "Have you forgotten our arrangement?"

My pulse quickened. *The sigil.* "I can continue my work without abandoning the arena," I countered, struggling to keep my voice steady. I didn't want the false comforts of his palace, nor his protections. My place was with my people, suffering beside them. There I could be of use to them, learning information from the champion's masters, and providing aid with my magics. "There are others I want to protect, those I can fight beside."

He laughed, but the humor was gone. His expression shifted, sharp and unyielding. "I think you've forgotten your place again." His voice dropped, cold. "You are a slave, Kaito. A gift to Durathar, the price of Ashti-Yasu. You are what I say you are. Be grateful I didn't end you in that arena."

The weight of his words pressed upon me, his tone carrying a twisted sense of mercy, as if he had given me some gift. But I knew better. He needed me more than I needed him. All of this, every decision, every order—it began because he knew I could break sigils. He kept me alive for his own purpose.

My lips curved, though my heart pounded with new resolve. If I were to survive this, I would have to play his game. To understand him, to study his power. When the time came, I would need to know his weaknesses, his limits. And when I broke free, I would make him pay. Until then, I would be his docile pet. I would choose survival, as he wished.

"Thank you," I said, masking my voice with false humility. "I will serve you well as a companion, as thanks for sparing me."

Azariel raised a brow, studying me for a moment, then his mouth curved in a wolfish grin. "You may take your leave now, Kaito. Tomorrow, we have much to discuss."

CHAPTER EIGHT

"What in the name of the spirits is this?" I murmured, lifting the flimsy garment Ilay had brought.

"It is the attire of the royal concubines," he replied, resignation in his voice.

"I am no concubine."

Ilay only hummed, holding out the fabric again, his tone softening, almost apologetic. "Kaito, forgive my words, but it may be wise to... temper yourself when it comes to Emperor Azariel. Especially in the presence of the nobles who haunt these halls."

Another reminder to remember my place. "I will bear that in mind." My words came flat, detached, though I offered a stiff nod.

With a resigned exhale, I slipped out of my tunic and trousers, feeling the weight of my identity left behind with them yet again. The new fabric clung to me like a reluctant second skin as I wound it around my waist, adjusting the rich silk—a dark blue deep as midnight with silver threads lining its hem. It barely covered me, grazing the tops of my knees.

Ilay approached with a silver collar, similar to the one I'd seen around Azariel's favored concubine that night a couple moons ago.

"I mean it," he continued, his gaze solemn as he lifted the collar. "The Emperor's hold on the throne may seem unshakable, but it is not. Many in these walls are only too eager to unseat him."

"If they wish him gone so badly, why not challenge him openly? Isn't that the way of your kind—to brawl for the crown?"

Ilay's face tightened, a flicker of something—offense, perhaps. "Our politics are not as savage as you imagine. Fear and strength, yes, they are part of it, but the path to power here is tangled in silks and shadows. The royal council can deem a ruler unfit, strip them of their power. Regardless of how... being dethroned only leads to death."

"So his rivals lack the spine to face him. Instead, they weave a net of lies and smoke, plotting like cowards," I sneered, letting the venom slip into my tone.

"Yes," Ilay replied simply, fastening a silver cuff just above my bicep to match the collar. "It is no secret the Emperor bears blood not purely Zurathi. They see it as tainted—a threat to the bloodline." He adjusted the cuff, glancing up as he continued. "They fear the stain of his heritage, despite his strength."

The world of Durathar was like a viper's nest, striking at the heels of its own ruler. Here, legacy was everything; Rohan and Darius commanded respect by name alone. The Pahlavan bloodline signified strength, power. Azariel, though fierce and unyielding, lacked one thing they valued above all else—unbroken Zurathi blood. To them, he was a conqueror unworthy of their legacy.

Ilay's gaze lingered, earnest. "Just... do not give the court more fuel with your antics. Despite what many believe, Durathar has seen darker rulers. And should Azariel fall..."

A plea lingered there, one I hadn't expected. I gave a small nod. "I will... strive for my best behavior." My eyes met his, catching a trace of loyalty, a hint of respect. This bearer knew Azariel more deeply than he let on. There were secrets within him, knowledge of the nobles here that might prove useful. But I would have to tread carefully, lest he run back to Azariel with suspicions.

I reached for the collar around my neck, fingers tracing the cold metal. "Is this like the others?" My gaze drifted to the golden collar encircling Ilay's own throat.

He shook his head, then knelt, his hands smoothing the folds of silk against my waist. "The black ones, like those on the arena fighters, sever them from the spirits of the Wilds. They taint, repelling the spirits' blessing. The golden ones, like mine, are mere symbols—a mark of servitude. But at times, they're laced with a black metal, caging those that are..."

"Are like me?" I cut him off, meeting his gaze. "A leash for servants who might bite?"

He swallowed, nodding. "Yes. But you... you are Celestial-born. The collars have no power over your kind. For Kamishen slaves, it was your own magics that were twisted to cut you off from your spirits. Our collars on a Kamishen would merely be decoration. Silver marks you as one meant to please. Just as gold marks me as one who serves."

"Silver marks you as one meant to please." Ilay's words lingered, curling like smoke through my mind, and I drifted back to that night with Azariel. My fingers slipped from the collar, tracing the crook of my neck, as though his breath still ghosted over my skin, a warmth that hadn't fully faded.

Was this his plan all along? Was it more than just the sigil? Did he want to bind me in silks, not chains—to claim me as his concubine, to draw me close, to touch as he pleased. If he wanted to keep me alive and close, there were countless roles I could serve within these walls, none of them so intimately tethered to him.

"What is next?" I asked, my fingers finally dropping from my neck as I pushed the thought away.

Ilay inclined his head, his voice soft. "Now, I will take you to the Emperor."

At first, I thought I was being taken to Azariel's chambers. But as the corridor turned, a cold realization struck. This was the path to the arena, yet this time I wasn't led down to the fighters' level—I was being guided to Azariel's side.

When we reached the dais, I found him seated on a throne-like chair, one of carved ebony and inlaid gold, radiating the air of a king among commoners. Beside him sat the

Empress Soraya, his father's widow. Around them sprawled plush cushions, spread for those kept like delicate birds in a cage—royal pets. I'd never seen him with his concubines here before. Yet here I was, made to sit before the nobles like a gift, like an adornment. Why had he summoned me here, to this place of judgment and spectacle? Was it to make a silent declaration to the court—that the fates of slaves rested in his hands alone?

Azariel's gaze drifted from the sands below, catching on me with an unreadable glint. Other nobles turned as well, their glances heavy with judgment, curiosity, disdain. I felt laid bare under the weight of it. The fallen champion, now the emperor's prize. What tales would they spin tonight?

A gentle pressure on my back from Ilay, a silent command, and I bowed low. Azariel flicked his fingers toward a cushion by his feet, then resumed his gaze on the fighting below. A match was already underway, blood darkening the sand.

I lowered myself onto the cushion, sinking into the softness as my eyes shifted past him, toward Soraya. Her skin held a warm olive glow, her eyes a fierce emerald, and her dark hair tumbled with a softness that spoke of both power and restraint. Darius had her features—the same quiet beauty, the same fire simmering beneath.

What would they feel, I wondered, if they knew the man responsible for their beloved's death was now seated at their side, eating their food, draped in their silks? How would Soraya look upon me then, or Azariel, if she knew he kept me close?

The crowd's roar pierced my thoughts, a visceral wave of noise that pulled my attention to the sands below. Another death, another victor.

I turned back to Azariel, catching his profile as the arena floor was cleared in preparation. "You mentioned we had matters to discuss today," I prompted, a subtle edge in my voice.

"Did I?" His brow arched, a smirk tugging at his lips. His elbow rested upon the arm of the chair, head lazily propped upon his hand, watching me with the faintest flicker of amusement.

"Yes, you did." My face hardened, the words leaving my lips tight and unforgiving. "Why am I here, Az—" The name died on my tongue as I caught Soraya's gaze lingering on me, and Ilay's reminder to behave rang through me. "Your majesty." I corrected, the title curdling in my mouth like sour wine.

A distant groan of iron rang out as the gates of the arena yawned open once more, pulling a renewed cheer from the crowd. Azariel extended his hand, pressing a finger lightly to my cheek, redirecting my gaze to the sands. "This, *Aqaynah*," he murmured, voice a low, mocking purr, "is why you are here."

That insufferable name—crafted, I was certain, to belittle and mock me—coiled like bile inside me. I wanted to bite back, to snap at the finger that dared graze my skin, but before I could give in to the urge, my gaze focused on the arena's next fighters. I felt my blood drain, my heart clutch tight in my chest.

Rustam and... Gamal.

The roar of the crowd became a distant thunder as dread twisted inside me, silent and suffocating, binding me to the scene below. The sands had claimed another fight, and this time, it held someone I did not want to lose. Someone I wished to protect.

My chest rose and fell in slow, deliberate breaths as I watched them—Gamal, with his familiar steadiness, and Rustam, looming like a living shadow, his presence amplified by the fearsome bear spirit, Dubkhers.

"If you're ever put against Rustam, it means someone wants to see you dead." Gamal's words, once spoken in passing, now rang with a haunting truth. I swallowed hard, forcing composure to settle over me like a mask. "What is this?" The words slipped from my lips, my hand reaching to clasp his calf, fingers curling tightly around it. The muscle beneath my grip tensed, and I let my fingers dig in, tethered by the silent fury roiling within.

"Companionship is a liability to survival," he replied, his voice woven with that taunting malice I'd come to recognize. I didn't need to look up to know he was smiling; I could hear it curling in every word. "You were wanting to stay in the arena for him, weren't you?"

I clenched harder. Were it not for the fine fabric between us, my nails would've pierced his skin.

Below, the arena's sands grew still, the anticipatory hush a heartbeat before the storm. Rustam—towering, feral, channeling Dubkhers' essence—was a wall of flesh and might, a brute bound to crush anything in his path. Gamal was no match in strength, his figure small, nearly inconsequential, beside the Zurathi champion. Yet he moved with swift precision, weaving through Rustam's advances with the finesse of a serpent. His dual blades gleamed, catching light as they danced in his grip, gliding through the air in an intricate rhythm of feints and strikes. For a breath, it seemed even—Gamal's skill honed by survival, darting in and out with strikes aimed at Rustam's exposed moments.

But the illusion of balance shattered as Rustam surged, one bear-like paw swatting aside Gamal's defenses. The crowd's roar swelled, a beast of its own, as Gamal staggered, thrown off balance. Rustam advanced, relentless, with a hunter's ferocity, a wall of muscle and spirit. I watched helplessly as the gap between their power became insurmountable, the arena sands swallowing each brutal blow, each desperate step.

Gamal lay hunched across the sands, his arms raised in a futile shield, each blow from Rustam's fists battering flesh and bone with sickening finality. Blood sprayed like mist under the onslaught, darkening the ground beneath him. His swords lay discarded, mere inches away, yet worlds beyond his reach, as the hulking Zurathi bore down, relentless. My heart twisted painfully, each beat like a silent scream. The crowd's roar rose and fell in waves around me, a tide of hunger that devoured the last edges of hope.

I forced myself to look down, unable to bear witnessing the inevitable, not again, not when the sands readied to drink another life so freely. But then I felt it—the tight grip at the back of my head, Azariel's hand winding through my hair, tilting my gaze back to the carnage.

"This could have been you," he murmured, each word a thread of malice woven close to my ear. "In fact, wasn't this exactly what you wanted? Begging to remain down there, to forsake the safety my companionship could offer?"

Rustam stepped back, the bloodlust in his eyes dimming as he surveyed Gamal's crumpled form. The air stilled, save for the hum of breath held across the arena. Gamal was still, yet not lifeless enough for the arena to declare a victor.

Azariel's hand tugged more forcefully, his breath grazing my ear. "I thought I saw something in you—a spark to survive at any cost. But I see there's a weakness in you, a folly of attachment. But I will tear it from you, Kaito. In time, I'll make you—"

"What is survival without others? Loneliness is not surviving." I bit back, the words sharp on my tongue. His needling obsession with me was a thing twisted and vile, something I could no longer bear. *I am nothing like you,* I thought, *you cannot make me like you.* Before reason could steady me, I reached up and seized his hair in my own grip, tugging hard enough that he had to tilt his head back. His dark chuckle spilled out, mocking and low.

"Done playing docile, are we?" he sneered, fingers tightening in my hair.

Around us, the Duratharians cast quick glances and muttered, their attentions flickering our way, but soon, another cheer ruptured through the crowd, loud and wild. I released

Azariel, and he loosened his hold just enough that I could look back to the arena. A tremor of awe moved through the gathering.

This wasn't the cheer of finality. This was something else. Against all odds, Gamal had risen to his feet, one of his blades once more in his grasp. His other arm hung at his side, clearly broken, but his eyes glinted with a tenacity I recognized—the refusal to yield. The refusal to die here.

Rustam loomed, frustration bleeding into his movements, and charged again. Gamal sidestepped, swift as a shadow, his blade finding the crevices between armor and spirit. He moved with a precision that defied his broken form, each dodge drawing blood, each step shifting the balance of the fight. Murmurs roses around me, a palpable shift, as the undefeated Rustam faltered.

Gamal's strikes, small yet deliberate, began to wear down the giant, reshaping the very sands beneath them. Rustam's blood mingled with the earth, his powerful form staggering beneath the relentless, unyielding precise fury of Gamal's blade. Each motion of Gamal's was a testament—a fierce, furious refusal to fall.

I felt Azariel's hold on me loosen as I pried his hand from me. Leaning forward on my cushion, I watched, entranced by Gamal's fierce beauty, the terror and splendor bound together in every desperate motion. His stubbornness, his determination to defy death, made something deep within me twist with admiration.

The heavy steps of a guard thudded beside us, accompanied by a low grunt, broke through my concentration on the fight below. "Your Majesty, should we remove him?" he asked, his voice colored by hesitation.

Azariel waved him off with a sly grin. "It is fine. Just foreplay," he quipped, casting me a sidelong glance that I met with a glare. He only chuckled, placing a finger to his lips in a mocking gesture of silence, then pointed back to the arena below.

It was then that Gamal struck his final blow. His blade found its mark, slicing through Rustam's abdomen with brutal precision. The massive Zurathi staggered, his insides spilling forth, and then he collapsed—a lifeless mountain on the blood-streaked ground. The crowd erupted in a thunderous roar, their voices raised in victory, in awe, chanting Gamal's name. Rising to my feet, I joined them, feeling an unfamiliar lightness, a genuine smile breaking across my face. Gamal's gaze drifted upward, seeking the Emperor of Durathar, exhaustion shadowing his face. But then his gaze found mine, and beneath the exhaustion he let satisfaction and triumph slip through.

A warmth pressed against my side as Azariel's arm wound possessively around my waist, pulling me onto his lap. My body went rigid beneath his touch, the elation and relief slipping as his grip tightened.

"If you insist on keeping your whore at your side," Express Soraya murmured sharply, her voice low, so only Azariel and I could hear above the crowd's jubilant applause, "then see that he knows his place. Especially when the envoy from Lunrae arrives. Do I make myself clear?"

"Understood," he replied, his tone as plain as polished stone. "Let me savor his defiance a while longer before he's broken," he added, a faint thread of irritation weaving through his words.

Lunrae? What would an envoy from Lunrae be doing here, of all places? They were Yuehama's allies. I turned my gaze to Azariel, the question sitting silently in my eyes. He met it with a look of pure impassiveness, his hand reaching to grasp my jaw, pulling me toward him until our faces were close enough to feel his breath, a thin veil of false intimacy. His lips brushed over mine—cool, restrained, a whisper of a kiss that held no heart. Then, slowly, his lips traced the line of my jaw, a feigned lover's path, stopping at my ear.

"Play nice, and I'll reward you," he murmured, the words drenched in performative affection. I felt the hollow in them. This was for Soraya's benefit, a display for her eyes and theirs, a pretense of possession, of desire. It was all a careful illusion—a game he played to show control. He didn't want them to see the truth behind this dynamic we had. He didn't want them to question why I am in this position when it was clear I was not meant for it. He didn't want them to know the real reason he kept me alive.

For a moment, I held his gaze, studying his expression until I let it soften and gave a quiet nod. He didn't know he'd already given me a gift. In his arrogance, he'd let a piece of his plans slip. So I relaxed into his lap, playing the docile pet he desired, feeling the weight of every gaze upon me, letting them see what he wanted them to see, hiding the silent rebellion that burned beneath.

CHAPTER NINE

"Ilay, have you heard why someone from Lunrae is expected in Durathar?" I asked, dipping my quill into ink before tracing the sigil on the parchment. I focused, drawing on my magic, willing the sigil to stir to life as I traced its form to match the movement of my own reflected mark in the mirror Ilay held for me.

In time, I had come to build a quiet camaraderie with the Emperor's Bearer. I'd come to know fragments of his lineage—a legacy as twisted and torn as his role here. His mother had served in these halls, her blood mixed from the western continent—Vorynthia—a pleasure slave, born from conquest. A prize. His grandmother had been taken as a prisoner of war, brought here like all beautiful things Durathar desired, to be possessed and shattered. Ilay was blood of the Veil—the ancient spirit of night, death, and shadow. Once feared for their sorcery, their powers inside him lay dormant, diluted, mingling with the blood of human and Zurathi.

Despite their stations, Ilay and Azariel had formed an unlikely bond in youth—a connection, I assumed, strengthened by their shared half-blood, by the fact that neither was purely anything, not fully Zurathi or fully other. So, when Azariel ascended after Darius' death, he appointed Ilay as his Bearer—the only soul he dared trust within these treacherous walls.

Ilay spoke, his voice barely above a whisper. "As you know, Ashti-Yasu—the Rite of Rest—is but a temporary state. Lunrae believes Durathar will rise against Yuehama once it expires. They fear the ruin, the bloodshed, the pride of your people. Emperor Renjiro will lead to a swift downfall," he added gently, dropping his gaze as if expecting me to take offense. "Lunrae does not want its land tainted by war like Yuehama's. They come seeking a treaty, a truer alliance."

So Renjiro's alliance would go unsupported; Lunrae would not send aid as they once did under my father's rule. My uncle's failure to maintain their trust had left us isolated in our time of need. He should have used this time to gather strength, to prepare for the inevitable storm, perhaps to strike first. But his silence—what did he intend to accomplish by leaving our land vulnerable?

"Will Azariel accept such an alliance?"

Ilay's gaze grew distant. "I cannot say. His predecessors would not. Darius, Rohan—they sought submission, not alliances." A small, wry smile ghosted his lips. "But what his highness wishes matters little for now."

"He's the Emperor, is he not?"

"Yes," Ilay replied with a careful pause, "but until he is vowed to another, he does not have full reign. Empress Soraya rules as regent; all decisions, particularly political ones, ultimately lie with her."

And there it was. My father's teachings drifted to me like a distant echo—how he'd always said power did not rest solely with crowns and titles. Respect was due to all our people, he'd taught, because real power coursed through the unseen hands, through voices that slipped like shadows in palace halls and streets. It was those who swept, served, and toiled who carried the true unfiltered truths. Words that wove from noble to commoner, from throne to slave and back again. Ilay had given power here like no other could, he had given me more knowledge about my enemy.

The reed quill slipped from my hand, resting alongside the mirror as I turned to Ilay, my curiosity woven with caution. "Why has Azariel not yet bound himself in union? How many summers has he seen?"

Truly I am not one who should judge traditions and the age at which one was vowed to another. I was promised, though not yet wed. Mine was no more than a placeholder, as was the custom in the northern kingdoms. It was not required for ascension, only an agreement to be fulfilled after. A promise waiting in the wings of duty, dormant until the throne was mine.

Ilay, too, set down his mirror, his gaze steady as he answered. "Twenty-four summers," he replied, the words carrying a certain weight. He stood, crossing the room with calm poise. "In truth, there was never any expectation that he would need to vow himself to another. That duty belonged to Darius. Only the Emperor himself is bound by tradition to ensure the bloodline's endurance."

I scoffed faintly, shaking my head. "Azariel doesn't seem... suited for such a bond."

"Attachments do not come easily to his highness," Ilay replied with a slight, knowing smile, a glimmer of old friendship in his eyes. He lifted a swath of silk from the bed—a delicate black drape, shorter, somehow thinner than the last. "Enough idleness, Kaito. The celebration awaits, and he has asked for you."

I accepted the fabric, my fingers brushing over its edge with faint resignation.

When he had finished with me, my skin was soft with the lingering scent of floral water, a fragrance that clung like a gentle veil. The fabric Ilay had brought lay in delicate folds against me, thin enough see the contours of my lower half. Jewels glinting from beneath the silver collar and upon my wrists. He gave me a black mask adorned with intricate silver filigree, designed to veil the upper half of my face. Once again, I had been adorned to please his gaze, a spectacle for him to present to his court.

The festivities had been set in the palace gardens, a place I'd glimpsed only from afar, looking down from the terrace of Azariel's quarters. Now, in the embrace of twilight, I wandered through it, each step unraveling a fresh tapestry of beauty I had scarcely imagined could exist in Durathar.

Lush green arbors and flowering vines spilled over marble paths, their colors ablaze under the dying light. Gardens like this were a rarity here—a delicate defiance against the harshness of this land, flourishing under the careful hand of those who had tended it. A place only available to the Duratharian elite. It was a glimpse of what I might have found back home, the closest I'd come to it in what felt like an eternity.

My fingers lowered to brush against the soft petals of a jasmine shrub, their sweet fragrance stirring something deep and familiar within me. They were pale as starlight, delicate and pure, and for a moment, I could almost imagine them as cherry blossoms—the ones that swayed in gentle waves outside my family's palace. Their fragrance, too, was lost to me, like a breath left lingering on the edge of memory.

All around me, the garden unfolded with the grandeur of a dream. Sunset poured over the blossoms, staining the leaves and flowers in shades of fire and honeyed gold. Ivory drapes hung from carved archways, their fabric moving softly in the evening breeze, as if the garden itself sighed with a life of its own. Lamps, each suspended from slender posts or held in delicate wrought-iron frames, began to glow with warm light as the last of the day faded. Their carved designs cast patterns onto the grass below, so that the ground itself seemed decorated for the solstice.

Everything about this place felt extravagant—more so even than the starlit chamber of the last feast. It was a world set apart, a haven of beauty crafted for those who could afford to live untouched by the harsh desert beyond the palace grounds.

Here, in the midst of silken drapes and flickering lights, it was as if the very air breathed luxury, a paradise conjured to please the emperor and his guests.

I wandered deeper along the winding garden path, shadows lengthening as the low murmurs of voices grew closer, joined now by the faint strains of music drifting through the dusk. The delicate tune carried an alluring melody, as though plucked from some distant and forbidden dream, mingling with the scents of jasmine and something richer, headier, laced through the cooling evening air.

This gathering bore little resemblance to the last event I had attended—a tribute to prowess and skill. Here, indulgence reigned. Wine flowed like rivers of garnet, and the air was thick with smoke and scents meant to stir passions. Lush silk blankets lay strewn across the grass, littered with bodies entwined, tangled in varying states of abandon.

The faint sound of string instruments carried over the gardens. A celebration of the solstice, Ilay had warned me, murmuring of "heat and endurance" as we walked through the palace corridors. But I had not fully believed him until now.

The servants moved like phantoms among us, stripped of all but plain masks that veiled their faces, their anonymity like a half-offered invitation. One glided to my side and extended a crystal goblet, offering it with a silent smile before disappearing into the crowd. I brought the glass to my lips, tasting a sweetness that was almost too cloying, with a delicate floral note I couldn't place. Despite the richness, I sipped, letting the unfamiliar flavors anchor me, calming the flicker of nerves that tugged at my senses, whispering that I was being watched.

Setting the glass aside, I scanned the expanse of the garden, seeking the fires where Azariel was said to be. But before I could slip past the clusters of lingering guests, warm fingers grazed my bare back, tracing their way around to my front in a possessive sweep.

"I always knew you'd be better suited as a concubine," a voice murmured, low and familiar, the kind of voice that seemed to claim without permission. I met her amber eyes glinting behind her mask, recognizing the gaze that roved over me, sizing me up as if I were hers to claim.

"Nayila." My tone fell flat, a chord of cool disinterest. "Weren't you warned not to touch me?"

"Your master is otherwise occupied, I doubt he will notice your occupancy." Nayila murmured, her voice a hushed purr as her hands wandered along my sides, trailing up over my chest, her body pressed flush against mine. I felt the peaks of her breasts through the fine veil of fabric she wore, her nipples brushing against me. "Or will you run to be rescued by him?"

"I need no rescue," I replied, letting the words escape with the quiet restraint of my patience.

"Nor would I dare harm you, so there is no need indeed." she continued, her fingers weaving through my hair as her lips hovered close, the scent of wine and faint florals mingling on her breath. "I only seek the pleasure of dancing with someone as handsome as you... Dance with me and then you are free to run back to your half-breed master." She entwined her fingers with mine, tugging me gently toward a fire, casting light across the assembled revelers who swayed, lost to the enchantments of spirits, music, and each other's warmth.

Nayila turned, pressing her back to my front, her hips beginning to sway, following the pulse of the music. Her hands lifted mine, guiding them around her waist, and I found myself mirroring her rhythm, allowing my fingers to trace along the curves just above the layers of silk. Her body against mine stirred something I struggled to ignore, the thin silks between us proving an inadequate guard against her brazenness.

"Do you not fear your Emperor?" I whispered, leaning close, my breath hot against her ear. "Your words belittle him, and your touch encroaches on what he claims as his."

Her laughter was low, indulgent, laced with the arrogance of one raised close to power. "My father is vizier, a voice on the council. Here, the council's whispers can outweigh the crown." Her fingers drifted to the fabric at her chest, tugging it down to reveal bare, supple skin. She took my hands, placing them over her exposed flesh, leaning back with a satisfied moan as her ass was pressed against my groin. I felt my body react, the silk over my hips tightening and shifting as my desire betrayed me. I gave her breast a firm squeeze before her hand slid one of mine lower, guiding me under the delicate folds of fabric to the heat of her skin between her thighs.

"Tell me," she whispered, lips brushing my jaw. "Do you submit to him, or do you take from him?"

"Neither." A voice, flat and cutting, sliced through the haze.

My gaze lifted, and there stood Azariel, watching us with an amused annoyance. The firelight flickered over him, glinting against the golden bands on his arms and the white silk draped low on his hips, a white and gold mask that failed to obscure his expression, his eyes gleamed with something close to mockery.

"Neither?" Nayila's voice faltered, her hand on mine frozen in surprise, halting her guidance to her heat below.

"I do not care for men," I said, fixing my gaze on him as I pressed my lips to Nayila's neck, feeling her sigh against my skin as my fingers tightened over her breast, drawing another quiet moan from her.

Azariel's grin curved, all satisfaction and idle threat. My demeanor struck a nerve. "How disappointing. I had planned a gift for your good behavior, but if it's unwanted, I'll simply send your human away."

My human? "Gamal is here?" I could feel my control slip as I stepped forward, moving past Nayila, whose hand reached out, catching my wrist.

"I'm not done dancing with you, Kaito," she insisted.

Azariel's gaze shifted past me to her, detached, with only the hint of disdain. "There are many partners here to sate your needs. Perhaps he'll find you later, adrift among all these willing souls." He turned away, and I slipped from her grasp, drawn after him.

"Why is Gamal here?" I pressed, keeping pace.

Azariel's gaze flickered over me, landing with pointed interest on the evidence of my arousal beneath the thin fabric at my hips. "So eager over any touch, so easily stirred," he mused, half-smiling. "You should know your worth, Kaito. Don't make yourself so... accessible."

"Know my worth, know my place," I snapped, my steps quickening to close the space between us. "Why don't you tell me what else I should think, what to feel, *master*?"

He stilled me with a firm grasp on my hip, his touch anchored and assured, stopping our tracks. "Where's the thrill in such easy surrender, *Aqaynah*?" He leaned in close, lips a breath from mine. "If you're so eager to lose yourself in the softness of borrowed affection, then by all means, indulge. But do not forget the shadows that gather at the edges of pleasure, nor the teeth that lurk there." His hips pressed against me, our bodies close, and I felt the unmistakable heat of him, the unmissable heat between us that burned in the coldness of night. Desire stirred, a low warmth in my groin, remnants of Nayila and I amorous moment still lingering.

"Do you think you've rescued me once again?" My voice, sharpened with defiance, matched his intensity. "That I'm still so helpless in a den of vipers?"

"Yes," he said simply, his tone low, words edging dangerously close. "She would've devoured you whole if I hadn't stepped in." His lips brushed mine, a taunting promise.

I held my ground, refused to pull away or yield, meeting his challenge in kind. "Take me to Gamal."

Azariel inhaled, taking in the air that lingered between us, his hand sliding upward to rest on my throat, his thumb tracing my pulse before tightening slightly. "Is that her scent... did you let her lips touch yours? Or..."

"No—" My denial was silenced as his mouth crushed against mine, his tongue demanding entry, a forceful, unapologetic taste that stole the breath from me. His kiss was deep, searing, every inch of it intended to claim and devour. My body responded against my will until, finding strength, I shoved him back.

"Don't do that again," I spat, the words raw.

He chuckled, a sound laced with a casual cruelty, as he withdrew. "Did you drink the wine?"

I said nothing, but my eyes narrowed, suspicion rising.

"There's aphrodisiacs in it, subtle but potent. That might explain why it lingers..." His gaze dipped downward, a smirk playing at his lips, and mine followed, finding the evidence undeniable. The ache, the heat—everything still pulsed within me, a need that refused to ebb.

Then realization hit with chilling clarity, a sense of violation. I hadn't been able to quell the desire that had pooled low within me, ever since Nayila had pressed herself against me. Would I have surrendered to her, let her guide my hands, if I hadn't tasted that wine? And worse yet—would I feel this relentless pull toward him?

"If you want both heads to remain clear, then avoid drinking or eating anything at gatherings like these," Azariel said, turning his back to me as he continued down the path.

Ahead, a pavilion rose, elegant and isolated, framed by draping silks and guarded by watchful palace bazifirs. It was a space unmistakably reserved for the Emperor himself. No one else dared linger, save for one figure standing at its center—Gamal. Maskless, his garments were simple yet refined, his arm bound and braced, a reminder of the fight that had nearly shattered it two moons ago.

"What's the point of masks when some of you are still so unmistakable?" Gamal remarked, his gaze drifting between Azariel and me with an uneasy smile. He wasn't wrong; Azariel was impossible to mistake, his skin veined with golden fractures like lines drawn in sunlight. And as for me, among the Kamishen, I was the one marked most heavily, sigils etched deep across my skin.

I couldn't hold back a smile as I stepped beneath the pavilion. "I'm more curious as to why you are here."

Azariel followed languidly, leaning against the pavilion's post as he spoke, his tone cool and measured. "I forgot to mention—Gamal killed my former champion, so he must take his place."

"First human to be champion." Gamal's words were directed toward Azariel now, a subtle challenge in his voice. "Your champions are usually Zurathi. Why is that?"

"Children of the Land are not gifted with blessings from the spirits," Azariel replied, nonchalant, though his gaze was sharp. "Unless one counts the tenacity of cockroaches and the knack for multiplying like ants. What advantage would you offer, besides the choice of an opponent easily bested?"

"Do you not see how unfair your bloodsport is?" Gamal pressed, a thread of defiance in his tone.

Azariel's gaze darkened as he closed the distance between them. "When did I ever claim it was fair?"

Gamal's voice did not waver. "How can you allow it, knowing this?"

Azariel scoffed, casting a dismissive glance at me. "Your companion is just as bold as you are. Fitting," he said, rolling his eyes. "This is a celebration, and I have no interest in ruining my mood. Enjoy your gift, *Aqaynah*." And with that, he turned, leaving us in the muted glow of the pavilion.

Gamal glanced at me, his eyes clouded with a flicker of confusion at being called a gift.

"It is just how he refers to you now. I'm sure he thinks that making you a champion will make it so I owe him something in the end." I said, "Though it was not him that made you a champion. That was yourself." It was Gamal's skills that had made it so he killed Rustam and became the victor of that match.

His hand reached out, fingers grazing my forearm. He leaned close, his voice no louder than a sigh between us. "Be wary of him, Kaito. They prefer their pets obedient. He indulges your defiance now, but once he tires of the novelty... his cruelty is not so easily tamed."

A flicker of a smile curved my lips, even as his warning clung to the air between us. "I am well aware. But so long as I am of use to him, I am safe. And if that fails, I'll see him fall before he lays a hand on me."

He gave my arm a gentle squeeze, something unsaid pooling in his gaze. "I am glad you live. Make sure it stays that way."

"And I am glad you're still breathing too," I laughed softly, lowering myself onto a pile of cushions scattered across the floor.

He exhaled, a wry smile easing across his face as he took a seat beside me. "Well, then... this is a celebration, after all. Should we not indulge?"

I cast a wary look at the low table spread before us, overflowing with delicacies and drinks gleaming in shallow bowls, each laced with the now unmistakable scent of aphrodisiacs. "Indulge, yes. But perhaps not too freely and cautiously."

Gamal's gaze drifted past the pavilion, his finger toyed idly with the stem of a grape before plucking one free. "You are aware he thinks we are bedding each other, right?"

The words struck so suddenly I almost choked on air. "Pardon?"

A faint curve tugged at his mouth, neither amusement nor mockery. "Perhaps I am wrong... perhaps not. Still, he does not like me. And it is not merely because I am human." He pressed the grape between his teeth, his tone light. "Nor is it the crimes that condemned me to the arena."

"Perhaps," I murmured, though the back of my neck grew warm despite myself. "I think it is more likely he fears you might sway me, convince me to withhold my aid. He is ever on his guard."

"My brother once told me they just needed his aid, his service. To not worry. To not think too much into it." He said, his voice softer now. "But the Duratharian court devours those who imagine they can change it. Giving a false upper hand.." His gaze met mine, a warning left unsaid but yet loud.

"I digress.." His head tilted to the side with a casual ease before his gaze dropped. A chuckle escaped him. "What are you wearing?"

The question turned the air lighter, the weight of our talk giving way to something easier, something we both needed. Our words weaving through the haze of incense and laughter around us, each sip of wine sparking stories and talks of the arena. The moments passed, slipping like water through my fingers, until I began to realize Azariel had granted me something after all—a reprieve, perhaps, in Gamal's presence. A friend, even in this gilded den of snakes. Though I would never admit that aloud.

When Gamal rose to leave, a servant arrived to guide him through the corridors, ensuring his injured arm would be tended to once more before the night's end. He gave me one last look, a fleeting glimpse of relief, before he vanished beyond the silk-draped entrance.

I couldn't just stay seated alone, my pulse slow and languid, fingers grazing the emptied rim of my glass as I watched the gardens. With the wine fogging my mind, I stood and drifted from path to path, searching for Ilay, though the winding trails blurred, each step folding the world in upon itself.

"You're the Emperor's pet, aren't you?" A Zurathi voice slithered from the shadows of a path leading deeper into the garden. His figure prowled toward me with the grace of a hunting cat. "Strayed far, have you? Need help finding your master?" His tone dripped with false playfulness, his eyes hungry as they traced over me, savoring the way his words left their mark.

"I have no master," I retorted, though my mind warned me to hold my tongue. His attire—rich silk wrapped in jeweled finery and lack of collar— revealed his rank as one of wealth, a noble in station.

A smile curved his lips as he drew closer, fingers hooking beneath my collar and drawing me toward him until our noses nearly touched. "You look like you have a master." His voice was a low whisper. "Show me how he likes it, pet. On your knees."

Marked as I was—a concubine, a slave meant for pleasure—perhaps I should have expected such treatment. Azariel's status had offered me a measure of protection, a shadow of safety in his name. But I was learning, night by night, that his people held his claim in disdain, that the mere mention of his title fell on deaf ears among those who served their own purpose.

A cold smile spread over my lips, feeling his hard arousal press against my hip. "I can show you exactly how he likes it." I slid my hand down his abdominal, tracing the hard plane of muscle beneath his garments, my touch soft, until my fingers closed around his testicles with bruising force.

"Stupid whore!" he snarled, his fist colliding with my face. Pain burst like fire, blood trickling warm from my nose, but I held my grip, squeezing tighter. Another blow rocked me, a snap of bone, but still, I laughed bitterly. "Not what you expected? His majesty loves this."

His hand raised to strike again, but suddenly he was yanked backward, dragging me with him as his grip held fast to my collar.

Azariel's voice, soft but lethal, slid into the space between us. "Does no one understand the meaning of not touching what isn't theirs?" His hand twisted the Zurathi's arm, wrenching it painfully behind his back.

"Your highness... forgive me, I-I didn't know—"

"Didn't know what?" Azariel's smile was a dagger's edge. "That he was mine?" Azariel's fingers tightened, and the air filled with the sickening scent of burning flesh.

The noble whimpered, his jaw clenched as he trembled. "This is the part where you let go," The malice in Azariel's voice was a cool, deadly caress. "Or I'll melt the flesh from your bones."

The Zurathi released me instantly, and Azariel released him in turn. Stumbling, the man fled without another word, vanishing into the foliage.

I opened my mouth to speak. "I don't want to hear that you had it under control," Azariel cut me off, a cold disappointment shadowing his gaze. "You didn't." His words lodged in my chest like thorns, prickling with a shame I couldn't explain. "Do not stray from me or my men again. Is that clear?"

My anger flared, breaking through the small remnants of fear, and my voice spilled out before I could stop it. "Was I meant to sit in the pavilion all night, waiting for you to summon me like a dog?" I spat, each word a shard. "You requested me here as company, but I've hardly seen you. Am I to be your companion or not, Azariel? Or am I simply a trophy for when it pleases you?"

His expression tightened, but he stepped close, his hand rising to cradle my face. His thumb brushed the blood from my split lip, lingering just a moment longer than necessary. "I had matters that didn't concern you," he murmured, his tone steadying.

"Such as what?" I hissed. "Burying yourself in another?"

A languid chuckle escaped him. "I think you've been nearer to that than I tonight." His fingers moved to my nose, testing it carefully. "Hold still. This will hurt."

Before I could draw breath, he snapped it back into place, pain flashing white-hot, making my eyes blur as I gritted my teeth. I let out a hiss as tears were brought to my eyes.

His gaze softened, just slightly, watching as I brought a trembling hand to my nose. "I should find him and kill him for that," he said, his voice chillingly casual.

Azariel moved to leave, but I grabbed his arm. "Save the spectacle," I murmured, exhaustion soaking through every word. "Just bring me back to my chambers. My head aches."

Together, we walked back in silence, the night folding heavily around us. All I wished for was to shed this evening like a soiled cloak, to let water wash away the blood and perfumes, and with it, the unwanted touches of this night.

CHAPTER TEN

"How is it that you're no longer a fighter, and yet injuries still find you?" Yuka chided softly, her thumb sweeping balm over the cut on my lip, the faint scent of herbs lingering between us.

"It was worse last night," I murmured, my gaze drifting up to her face, tracing the softness in her expression. The swelling had faded, leaving only the faint bruising on the bridge of my nose and the thin, half-healed line on my lip.

She sighed, her fingers lingering a moment. "The nobles here hold little respect for servants—especially those in pleasure. It's best to avoid the ones who come seeking to claim it." There was a shadow in her eyes, a sorrow that told me she had known this truth well. "No offense, your majesty," she added, glancing over at Azariel, who lay sprawled across his bed as though he were the sun and the world revolved around his whims.

He merely waved a hand, unaffected, as if the cruelty of his people was a familiar companion.

"In Yuehama, servants, whether bound to labor, the sword, or the body, are seen as vital to the kingdom. They're given respect." She spoke with quiet pride, a faint gleam of distant memories in her voice.

"Are you treated well, Yuka?" I asked, studying the lines that traced her brow.

"Now, I am." She gave a small, wry smile. "At first, I wasn't. But when they saw what I could do... Well, sages are valuable. You don't want to anger the hand that can save your life."

Azariel's voice slid into the space between us. "It's always wise to remind them who holds the threads of their fate." His tone was cool, almost reminiscing.

Yuka stood, carrying the small wooden bowl of salve, and crossed to him, sitting by his side. "Empress Soraya insisted there be no mark upon you for the banquet with Lunrae's envoy tomorrow," she said.

"It's just my hand," he replied dismissively, offering it to her as if the wound were trivial. She traced the balm over his knuckles, bruised and raw as if they'd met with something rough repeatedly.

"You didn't have that last night," I remarked, watching her work the balm into his skin.

"I found a snake in the gardens after I returned from escorting you." He spoke lightly, though his eyes sparked with an edge. "A nasty thing that refused to be still."

Yuka's brow arched, mirroring the skepticism rising in my own. "This is from a garden snake?"

"Yes," he replied, his smile unexpectedly charming, yet unsettling in its ease.

She merely hummed, shaking her head as she rose. "Try to keep out of trouble, Kaito." Her hand drifted through my hair, a touch both comforting and fleeting, and then she was gone, leaving us alone.

Azariel straightened, crossing the room toward me, a determination in his gaze. "Shall we continue?"

He had gathered all I needed to break the chains of his sigil—a finer needle, a sharp blade, charcoal, and chaparral. The pieces lay before me, the puzzle on his back I had nearly solved, yet there lingered a fragment of mystery, a piece that kept slipping from my grasp.

"Azariel... are you truly unaware of your mother's purpose in this?" I asked, letting the question hover in the rays of sunlight between us.

He paused, the barest flicker of hesitation crossing his eyes. "Perhaps I know a bit more than I've let on."

"Then explain it to me."

"She wanted to suppress my celestial side," he began, a coolness in his voice. "She wanted me Zurathi through and through, to make sure I could survive here. She knew her blood in me would lead to scrutiny. Bastards are common here—indulgence is practically our customs—but the dilution of our connection to the Wilds? That's different. That's an unforgivable weakness."

I listened closely as he spoke, my fingers grazing over the lines of his sigil, searching until I felt something I'd overlooked before—a subtle fissure, a quiver in the magic beneath his skin. Amalthea's intent was clearer now. She wanted him Zurathi. His story held truth, but there was more, something deeper, tangled into his very magic and bound by her hand.

Gently, I reached around, lifting his arm and cupping his tricep. "Summon your light for me," I murmured.

Obediently, he conjured a thin thread of light, hovering above his palm—a flicker of the same force that he had used to form the lance that had struck Taehyun down. "Hold it," I instructed, my voice soft but firm. "Do not let it fade."

I released my grasp and focused on his back once more. The sigil trembled under my touch, the light straining against the lines of ink and magic etched into his skin, a trembling barrier holding back something vast and untamed.

This sigil... it was not just a failed lock to seal away his celestial essence. It was a reservoir. Amalthea had not wanted him entirely powerless in the event that Durathar might yet betray him. She had stored his gifts within, thinking perhaps that he could wield it if pressed, if he had to strike back. But I doubted she had counted on the strain—how his body, being only half Shen, could not bind his gifts without damage. The fractures—those golden veins shimmering under his skin—were the marks of power trapped too long, breaking him from the inside out.

"Release it," I commanded softly, and in an instant, the room erupted in blinding light, a flash so intense it melted the air. The blast ripped across the chamber, a surge that scattered fruits and shattered glass, the table itself splintering beneath the force. The sigils calmed, and the golden cracks in his skin faded slightly, dulled but still ever glowing.

If I unlocked the sigil completely, letting his full power flow freely, he would be unstoppable, a weapon of Durathar that no kingdom in Tairasa could stand against. But if I didn't... I had no idea when I would get the next chance to unlock my own.

My gaze lingered on the tools resting on the table, fingers hovering, brushing the blade's edge. I reached for it, but in a swift movement, he caught my wrist, his touch both a challenge and a warning.

"Does this mean you're finally ready to unlock it?" His voice was level, though his eyes watched me with a dark curiosity.

"No," I lied, masking my intent beneath cool indifference. "I missed something because you withheld the truth. I'll need more time."

"You have until the day after the envoy arrives," he said, each word a reminder of time slipping away.

I couldn't allow him his full power. I didn't need magic to destroy him. I could wait until he was at his most vulnerable, slip past his defenses and bring him to his knees. Then, I could unlock my own power, leave him dead at my feet. It would require patience—a calculation of setting, timing, even his mood.

My mind flickered to the moments he'd let his guard fall, to those rare glimpses of odd warmth that had wormed their way into my memory. I'd play into his twisted affections, act as if I understood my place, let him believe he had bent me to his will.

"Let us bathe," he murmured, casting a lingering glance at me from over his shoulder. His words held an invitation, softened by something unspoken. "I have a gift for you."

"Another gift?" I asked, arching an eyebrow.

"It's more of an apology... for last night. You were to be my guest, and you were right—I was absent."

Remorse in someone like him? It was hard to reconcile, yet his sincerity felt real, disarming. For a moment, I simply watched him, unsure if I'd imagined it.

"I accept your apology," I replied, letting only a hint of surprise lace my tone.

We walked through the winding corridors, though this time he led us down an unfamiliar path. The palace baths had felt grand enough—communal pools draped in gauzy veils, scattered with flowers, perfumed by herbs. But this chamber was another world entirely. At its center lay a vast, singular pool, adorned with intricate tiles that gleamed beneath the light streaming down from an open ceiling and arched walls. Sunlight poured in like liquid gold, spilling over immaculate floors and casting dappled reflections onto the water's surface, strewn with petals. Divans and low, cushioned seats were arranged around the basin, low tables piled with exotic fruits and delicacies, lush greenery lending warmth to the air. Everything about the place whispered opulence.

"My gift is a private bath?" I ventured, watching as he slipped the silk from his shoulders and waded into the water.

"No," he replied with a subtle smile, glancing toward the chamber's entrance. "She is."

I turned, and there in the doorway stood a woman—a vision carved from the same breath as Nayila. The pleasure slave's auburn curls cascaded down her back, her body a sculpted silhouette, skin kissed lightly by the sun. He had chosen someone to reflect what he assumed was my taste, as if he'd carefully arranged her image to pull from me a response he already anticipated. And he wasn't wrong.

"Your Majesty," she greeted him with a graceful bow, then turned her gaze to me, her voice a soft whisper as she said, "Kaito."

With a slow, deliberate motion, she began to unravel the sheer robe from her shoulders, the delicate fabric slipping to reveal her beauty fully. She was a sight designed to stir desires, a stunning apparition conjured to entice, to draw me closer—or perhaps, to draw me in entirely.

She took my hand in hers, her fingers soft yet certain, and led me to the pool's edge. There, under the hazy veil of sunlight filtering down, she began to undress me with a care that felt almost sensual. "Let me bathe you," she said, guiding me into the warm embrace of the water. She reached for a cloth at the basin's edge, wetting it and lathering it with a fragrant soap that rose in the air, as heady as incense.

As she began to wash me, her body brushed against mine, her breasts grazing my skin with each gentle motion.

"You're tense," she noted, her voice a low, soothing hum. "Do you not enjoy this?"

I glanced across the pool to where Azariel reclined against the other edge, watching, his gaze veiled and unreadable.

"No, I do," I replied after a pause, trying to steady myself. "It's just that... I'm used to bathing myself." I forced a small smile, though unease twisted beneath my skin. Perhaps such gifts were commonplace in Durathar, but I felt suspended between expectation and uncertainty. Did he want me to lose myself in her, to take her under his watchful gaze? Or was his offering simply the luxury of not lifting a finger to bathe?

"You can touch me, if you like." Her voice dropped, rich and velvety as she lifted her breast, the water's sheen coating her as her nipples peaked in the cool air. She wrung the soapy cloth over her bare chest, letting the suds trickle down her skin. Slowly, she ran the cloth over her skin, her lips parting in a teasing smile.

She took my hand, guiding it to her chest, pressing her softness into my palm. I traced my thumb over her taut nipple, feeling its firmness against my skin, yet something within me remained still, untouched by the desire she offered.

"If it is my presence that holds you back, I will look away," Azariel teased from across the pool, tilting his head back and letting his eyes fall shut, an almost playful dismissal in his tone.

Whatever this game was, I would play into it. Accept this twisted form of comradery to earn his favor.

I responded with a firmer touch, my hands sliding down to grip her hips, drawing her closer until she gasped softly. "You missed a spot," I said, flicking my gaze to the cloth she held, and she responded with a knowing smile. Leaning in she pressed her chest fully against me as she reached up to rub the cloth over my neck and shoulders, the suds seeping beneath my collar.

My hand drifted lower, fingers tracing the curve of her ass, and I squeezed, relishing the fullness of her body underneath my touch. She let out a soft, breathless sound, her eyes half-lidded as the cloth slipped from her fingers into the water. Her arms rose, winding around my neck as she leaned up to press her lips to mine, her touch tender and pleading.

For a moment, my gaze wandered over her shoulder to where Azariel sat reclined, his eyes closed, face composed as though we were nothing more than shadows in his presence. The thought lingered, but her breath brushed against my skin, pulling me back.

One hand released its grip on her, trailing over her curves, down to the softness of her thigh, until my fingers found the warmth waiting there, slick and ready. My fingers slipped between, gliding over the tender warmth, tracing slow circles around that delicate pulse of her clit, coaxing her need to rise with each gentle stroke. She moaned against my lips, the sound muffled, her forehead dropping to my chest as I pressed gently inside her pussy.

I pushed deeper, feeling her shiver as I moved to match the rhythm she set, her hips pressing forward in quiet, unspoken need against my hand. Her hand came up to brush my cheek, guiding my gaze back to hers. I hadn't realized I was looking toward Azariel again. I felt the weight of her expectation to match that feeling within her gaze and the gentle pleading of her touch. I found myself unable to hold it, unable to look her in the eyes and fall into the intimacy she offered. So, I lowered my head, kissed her with a softness I didn't feel, and let my hands guide her through motions I barely registered.

From below the water, my cock finally stirred, a faint hardness taking shape as my body responded out of habit, an unthinking rhythm taking over where desire could not. Her body trembled against mine, pressed so close I could feel every shiver, every silent plea for my attention. She was beautiful, her moans soft and angelic as they mingled in the humid air around us. I tried to focus on her. I wanted this. I wanted to lose myself in the contours of her body. I wanted to revel in the delicate way her lips parted against mine as she whispered my name.

But an unsound part of me kept forcing a thought to surface in my mind: *how would my name sound spilling from his lips?*

At last, her body arched in final surrender, shuddering around my fingers, and I let my touch fall away, leaving her breathless as she rode out her orgasm. Soon her hand found mine, a gentle yet insistent pull, there was a sultry glint in her eye as she led me from the pool. She took me to a nearby divan, easing me onto its softness before she knelt between my legs.

Her hands found my cock, warm and tentative, fingers curling around its half-hard shaft, attempting to make it rise beneath her touch. She leaned close, her breath warm against my skin, her lips parting as her tongue flicked over me. I let out a low sound, an approximation of pleasure. Her touch was firm, eager, yet something in its urgency felt almost desperate, as though she were trying to coax something from me that lay beyond her reach.

She murmured something in Duratharian under her breath. *"Impotent"*, I caught it, the word biting more sharply than her hand. My gaze shifted instinctively toward Azariel, searching for any sign that he'd heard. But if he had, he gave no indication, his posture relaxed, as though this moment held no sway over him.

"Am I not to your liking?" she asked, her gaze lifting to mine, her hands pulling back, doubt clouding her once-brazen eyes.

"It's not that..." I began, but the words faltered as Azariel's voice, low and unyielding, cut through the silence. "Leave," he said as he rose from the pool, water cascading from his frame as he crossed the room, stopping before me. His voice was a low command, and she obeyed without a word, slipping from the room.

"Allow me." He ran a hand through his white, damp hair, his gaze piercing, unreadable as it lingered on me. Azariel knelt, his hand finding the base of my length, confident, unhesitating.

"Azariel," I whispered, the name escaping my lips unbidden.

He held my gaze, a faint smile tugging at his lips. "Clearly, my gift was not to your liking. Allow me to make amends." He leaned down, his mouth grazing my cock, his tongue tracing a line along my shaft that left me helpless to resist the thrill that shot through me. I drew a sharp breath, fighting to maintain my composure.

"Look," he murmured, a glint of satisfaction in his eyes. "Already, you're hard for me."

A faint protest rose within me, half-formed, as I struggled for control. I was torn between stopping this and giving in. "Surely an emperor shouldn't defile himself this way..."

"Do I seem like one who cares?" he replied, voice dropping to a warm, velvety whisper. His tongue flicked over my tip before pressing the flushed head to his lips, lingering at the seam, his mouth poised yet withholding and teasing. A spark of desire flared within me, quiet yet consuming, as I fought to still the urge to push my hips forward.

"Do not tease me," I said, the words slipping through clenched teeth, sounding rougher than I intended. I gripped the divan's fabric beneath my fingers, the tension holding me taut. If he wished to debase himself, to take me in such a way, I would not stop him. Though my impatience grew wary of his games.

"Always so vexed," A smirk curved his lips as he met my gaze, his eyes dark with wicked mirth. "Keep looking at me like that... it turns me on." His voice was a low hum, and then his mouth lowered once more, tongue flicking along my length, circling deliberately over the sensitive tip where my arousal beaded and pooled.

I inhaled sharply, my restraint fraying, but forced my retort. "Do you ever stop talking?" I barked, though a soft, unwilling breath escaped me, slipping past my parted lips like a confession.

"Show me how you like it then." There was a challenging glint in his eyes as his hand moved slowly, languidly up and down my cock. "Fast, slow, deep, teasing. Show me, shut me up." He leaned forward, drawing my tip into the warmth of his mouth, engulfing it in a searing heat that made my breath catch. In this moment, I felt I could bend to his will, a dangerous yet magnetic force pulling me under.

My fingers threaded through his hair, urging him deeper, my breaths becoming shallow as his throat tightened in response. He struggled to take me fully but didn't pull away, his mouth sliding down, the press of his tongue teasing my sensitive underside.

My eyes fluttered shut, and I let my head fall back, surrendering to the weight pooling low in my balls. "Faster," I whispered, my voice rough with need, driving him to quicken his pace.

The grip in his hair tightened as he moved, each motion intensifying the tension coiling inside me. I could feel the heat gathering, the weight growing heavy, ready to burst. "Az," I breathed, my gaze falling to him. He looked up, meeting my eyes with that unwavering, intoxicating focus. He looked so striking in this state. Where anyone else might seem submissive or vulnerable, he embodied the very opposite—poised and powerful, even now.

I couldn't hold back any longer. My thighs tensed, and a release surged through me, spilling warmth that he accepted without flinching. His throat tightened, swallowing, drawing out each pulse until I was spent. Finally, he pulled back, the remnants of his touch lingering like a ghost.

"Do you only care for men when your cock is inside them?" His eyes met mine with a teasing glint, a faint smirk dancing on his lips.

I brought a thumb to the corner of his mouth, gently wiping away traces of his saliva. I hesitated, choosing my words carefully. "Fucking and being fucked by a man... is different from what this was."

"Is that so?" he asked, one brow raised with a knowing smile. Perhaps I was in denial, unwilling to let him be the reason I accepted that my lust could not be bound by gender.

Rising to his feet, his own arousal clear, he held my gaze, unyielding. But I didn't dare look down. Not fully that is. "Soraya expects your presence at the banquet with Lunrae tomorrow," he remarked, almost dismissively, as though nothing at all had transpired between us just moments ago.

I shifted in my seat, feeling unexpectedly vulnerable under his calm gaze and the abrupt shift of his words. "And why does she want me there?"

"A symbol," he replied, twisting a damp lock of hair between his fingers, letting drops fall as he wrung it dry. "To remind them Yuehama lies collared and subdued beneath our heel. Do make sure you're... presentable."

The implications were clear: I would stand as a warning, a living display of submission to Durathar's will, and a shadowed promise that Lunrae would soon suffer the same fate.

As he turned to leave, I couldn't stop myself from blurting, "Where are you going?"

A wicked smile crossed his lips. "I have matters to attend to, and you need to finish your bath," he said, his voice trailing off as he walked away.

CHAPTER ELEVEN

I adjusted the sash at my hips, the fabric pulling slightly tighter than I'd have preferred, but I was grateful for the concession—a tunic with sleeves, trousers that provided modesty. My form was cloaked, for the most part, aside from the open drape of my tunic, which hung like a light coat, baring my chest and upper abdomen. "Are you certain this is what I'm meant to wear?"

Ilay glanced at me, a faint smile ghosting his lips as we walked through the corridor. "Why? Does it not suit you?"

"It's fine," I replied, tugging at the edges of my tunic. "I just assumed, as I am to be put on display, it would be more revealing."

"This is what the Emperor requested."

The palace bazifirs stood sentinel by the council hall doors, their burnished armor catching the mid-afternoon sunlight spilling through the arched openings of the corridor. Without a word, they parted, swinging open the towering doors with practiced precision.

Inside, the council hall stretched wide and magnificent—a vast space, ornately adorned, with vaulted ceilings that curved upward, every inch embellished with intricate carvings and gilded patterns. A banquet table stretched along the length of the room, laden with fruits, roasted meats, spiced rice, and delicacies that would tempt even the most sated guest. Goblets of fine wine, jeweled pitchers, and dishes heaped with fragrant herbs lined every inch, places carefully set for each noble who would attend.

At the far end, just short of the grand throne room's splendor, was a smaller yet no less opulent throne area. There, Empress Soraya reclined on a carved seat of ivory and gold, speaking in low tones to a Zurathi I recognized immediately—Vizier Sulqadir, a figure as commanding as he was calculated. Not surprising, he truly bore so much resemblance to Nayila, his daughter.

Guests were already filtering in, Durathar nobility arrayed in sumptuous fabrics and adorned with gemstones that caught and reflected the hall's golden glow. They mingled with the nobles who had come to reside at court to bask in Durathar's power, their laughter low and subdued. A quiet sigh slipped from my lips as I took in the scene before me, steeling myself for the performance that would follow. I scanned the crowd but saw no trace of the Lunrae envoy or Azariel.

I felt the weight of hands settling on my waist, a soft familiar exhale warming the curve of my ear. "Were you looking for me?" Azariel's voice was little more than a whisper, threading through the quiet tension between us.

I breathed a sigh, my reply as quiet as his, yet edged with a wryness I couldn't help. "You know nothing of boundaries."

"Ah," he murmured, unbothered. "You didn't seem to mind my disregard for boundaries yesterday." A smirk graced his lips as he let go, sliding to my side with a graceful ease that spoke volumes. I clenched my jaw, feeling warmth spread treacherously across my cheeks, tingling up to the tips of my ears.

"Walk with me." He said it softly, and without waiting for my answer, began moving through the hall. I followed, our steps soundless as we passed through the murmur of courtiers, their conversations weaving with the rhythm of drums and lute strings. A fire dancer, luminous in the flickering firelight, twisted and turned in graceful arcs, her movements like poetry in motion. I found myself momentarily captivated, her form bending and flowing as though she was part of the flame itself. But when I glanced back, Azariel had already stepped out onto the terrace.

The warm air wrapped around him as he leaned against the railing, the muted strains of music softened by distance. His attire, reminiscent of the finery worn by nobles of Durathar, was rich and layered—dark fabric draping over his shoulders, cinched with gilded bands, highlighting the taut lines of his form. A slender crown rested upon his head, the delicate metalwork and small gemstones glinted softly against his snowy locks, which lay subdued beneath its graceful weight. He looked like a prince—beautiful, elusive, and veiled in mystery.

He broke the silence, voice thoughtful as he looked past the horizon. "I don't know what exact place you held in Yuehama, but you seem... refined. Educated. You carry yourself with a poise uncommon for one of low birth. And you worked alongside the Grand Shiryū, you must have been close to the crown." His gaze didn't shift, yet I felt the weight of it. "What do you know of the alliance between Lunrae and Yuehama?"

He had no qualms assuming that those outside the nobility in Yuehama were ignorant of our politics, but I met his question without hesitation. "The alliance was formed after Durathar seized Akhsarun," I said, my voice even, concealing the bitterness that lingered on my tongue.

We had long known Durathar's gaze would fall on Yuehama first, and from there they would push through to Lunrae. The plan was simple: if Durathar's men breached our most populated territories, Lunrae would send aid. But war is rarely kind to plans, and the tide rose faster than we had feared. Their aid came too late to halt the fall of our capital—too late to keep them from storming our palace.

Azariel nodded, a slight curve to his lips. "And what was each side to gain from such an alliance?"

Besides being protected from you? I thought to myself.

"Yuehama would gain Lunrae's men, their forces standing with ours in a time of need," I answered. "And Lunrae... Lunrae would finalize the crown prince's hand for their princess before his ascension."

"They would have become one kingdom."

"Just as Durathar and Akhsarun had supposedly become one." Though, in truth, it would be naive to call what happened a unity—Durathar had merely swallowed Akhsarun whole. They brought them to their knees and seized the land.

"Did Durathar truly remain blind to the alliance's purpose?" I asked, my voice a quiet question.

Azariel let out a low chuckle, a sound edged with bitterness. "More likely Soraya kept me in the dark, just as she does with all matters of Tairasa's politics," he replied. "I understand, though. She never believed I would sit upon the throne. That honor was always meant for her precious Darius. Why burden the half-breed bastard with knowledge of kingdom affairs when he's been relegated to managing slaves and prisoners?"

"But you're Emperor now," I said, raising a brow, testing the defiance in his gaze. "Would it not serve her to share this knowledge with you—especially when you're expected to face diplomats from other kingdoms?"

"One would think so," he replied, a trace of amusement flickering across his lips before vanishing.

A respectful throat-clearing from behind broke the moment. "The envoy from Lunrae awaits, Your Majesty," Ilay announced, bowing slightly. "Your presence is needed."

Azariel drew himself up, a subtle tightening in his shoulders and an imperceptible stillness settling into his expression. The Emperor's mask fell into place, a calm yet impenetrable veneer that I had once only glimpsed from the arena floor. Back then, it had seemed unbreakable, distant, as though carved in stone. But now, up close, I recognized it for what it was—a mask layered with duty, a burden laced with expectations he had never been groomed to bear, and yet one scrutinized by every gaze that fell upon him.

I was directed to wait alongside Ilay, just off to the side, watching as Azariel approached the throne and took his place beside Empress Soraya. She sat poised, draped in majesty, her presence a sharp contrast to the barely-contained weight Azariel wore. Before them stood the envoy, an older man clothed in the ceremonial robes of northern Tairasa—his attire not unlike our own in Yuehama, richly woven and layered, with patterns embroidered across the silk folds. His ears, pointed like those of my people, bore jeweled adornments that glittered in the light—a reminder of the Kamishen heritage we shared, though separated by borders.

He approached the thrones with measured steps, two Lunraean guards trailing behind at a respectful distance, their eyes sharp and ever-watchful. I recognized him immediately: Councilor Jiro Asahi, a familiar face from the Lunraean royal council. I had met him once, years before, in the palace hall during a tense meeting with my father. His presence then had been formidable; now, it was tempered by the weight of diplomacy and the bitter knowledge of what he could lose.

Councilor Asahi bowed low before the thrones, his gaze lifting only as he spoke, his voice a blend of respect and restraint. "Thank you for granting this meeting and for the honor of such a gracious banquet."

Empress Soraya inclined her head, a languid gesture of acknowledgement, and motioned for him to rise. He straightened, his eyes unreadable, fixed upon the rulers of Durathar.

"As is customary for such visits," Asahi announced, turning slightly as if to reveal something precious from behind. His guards parted just enough to allow a woman to step forward. She moved with a quiet elegance, her form cloaked in layers of fine silk that shimmered under the lights, her face half-concealed behind a delicate veil, yet I could still see the gleam of her eyes beneath. Resting upon a silken pillow in her hands was a dark scabbard—a gift forged by Lunrae's master artisans.

With a solemn grace, Asahi accepted the scabbard and knelt before Empress Soraya and Azariel once more, lifting the blade high in both hands, an offering of fealty and artistry. Soraya cast a sidelong glance at Azariel, who then rose to receive it, his movements deliberate as he wrapped his fingers around the hilt and drew the blade free. The metal caught the light, revealing a gleaming, obsidian edge darker than the night, the surface etched with intricate sigils, symbols of power and protection meant to ward off all manner of threats. Lunrae had poured its mastery of metallurgy and mysticism into this weapon, and for a brief moment, even I felt its pull.

Azariel's gaze softened as he ran a finger down the blade's length. "It is... exquisite," he breathed, allowing the awe to flicker in his expression.

"We thank you, Counselor Asahi," Empress Soraya replied, her voice measured, though her eyes gleamed with an interest of her own.

Asahi rose, his duty not yet complete. "This is but one of the gifts our kingdom offers," he said, a subtle note of intrigue in his voice. The woman who carried the sword stepped forward, raising her veil with delicate fingers to reveal a face that was both beautiful and fierce. "This is Reika, one of the most revered sword dancers of Lunrae. She would be honored to offer a private performance for your majesty, a demonstration of her skill, a display of beauty... and a taste of Lunrae's own spirit."

Her voice was soft, demure. "It would be a pleasure, Your Majesty." She bowed, the hint of a promise lingering in her words.

It was clear—Lunrae's envoy sought to seduce Azariel with gifts of metal and flesh alike, to sway him before ever mentioning their proposed alliance.

Azariel, his gaze fixed on Reika, extended his hand and helped her rise. "I would be more than honored to witness your talents, Reika," he said, his voice smooth as velvet.

I rolled my eyes, the movement small, hidden.

Empress Soraya rose, her expression serene. "Let us feast, and we will speak of politics when we are well-sated." Her smile widened as she made her way toward the banquet table, her attendants quickly moving to clear her path. The nobles and dignitaries followed, each finding their place around the table's grand expanse.

Azariel turned to me, his expression now softened with a hint of mischief. "Come, you are to sit beside me."

I hesitated, feeling the weight of unfamiliar stares, the kind of attention that clung too tightly. To sit at the table for a banquet such as this—even in Durathar—was nearly unthinkable for a slave. I let my gaze wander, realizing then that I was the only one without title or freedom in this circle. Servants moved about, pouring wine and setting trays of jeweled fruits, musicians played their melodies, and dancers swayed in delicate silks. Yet here I was, placed among nobles and dignitaries, an outlier in their glittering midst.

"Are you sure this is wise?" I whispered, glancing at Azariel as he guided me to the head of the table, just opposite Soraya, to a seat at the corner beside him. His hand pressed firm against my back, urging me forward.

"Trust me, it's fine," he murmured, his voice too smooth to hold worry.

But I knew better; I knew the language of courtly stares and unspoken slights. Empress Soraya's narrowed eyes confirmed the wrongness of it. I sat at the table among men, though I was no more than a dog granted a seat it did not deserve. A stray intruding on a feast meant for masters, when I should have been at their feet, silent, unseen, and forgotten. Just as Soraya would have preferred. Her gaze lingered on Azariel with barely concealed irritation before flicking toward me, a simmering disapproval in her eyes. I sank back, trying to make myself smaller, to blend into the silhouette of the courtier beside me, yet I could feel her gaze still, cold as a drawn blade.

Azariel's hand fell to my thigh, firm. "Stop looking so uncomfortable," he said through a barely visible smile.

"I can't help it," I replied under my breath. "I feel as though you're using me as a piece in a game I don't understand."

"Of course you're a piece," he whispered, his tone laced with dark amusement. "But now you're mine, not hers." His hand retreated as he leaned forward, speaking easily to a courtier across the table, leaving me with the uneasy realization that I was both shield and weapon in this silent war.

The banquet proceeded, a performance in subtle glances and half-formed smiles, with Soraya casting me fleeting looks, as though to remind me of the unbroken hierarchy that only Azariel seemed intent on disrupting. She soon turned her attention to her conversations, laughing softly with Durathar's council and courtiers, and with Asahi. But her amusement felt brittle, her eyes too sharp as they returned now and then to Azariel, her discontent veiled but unmistakable.

When Soraya came to Azariel's side, hand touching his shoulder, her tone held the soft authority. "It's time we speak with Counselor Asahi in private," she said. "Leave your pet here."

Azariel turned, feigning surprise, his brow arching just slightly. "But I thought you wanted him present for this?"

She barely held back a sneer. "That was before you dressed him like a courtier and seated him as an equal."

"He comes with." Azariel's expression barely shifted as he rose, his hand lifting to me. "Come, Kaito."

I muttered under my breath, "I am no one's pet," but I rose regardless.

We walked as a small group toward a private chamber adjoining the council hall, the murmurs and sounds of the banquet fading behind us as the heavy doors closed. Soraya's robes flowed like a dark river as she led the way, her posture regal, her irritation hidden beneath layers of courtly grace. Asahi followed, beside him his Lunraean guard walked. Vizier Sulqadir drifted silently alongside Azariel and I.

Inside we gathered around the low table, Azariel drawing me close beside him until I nearly sat upon his own cushion, my place nearly indistinct from his. No bazifirs accompanied the Durathar royals, as if the councilor's presence posed no threat against the trio of Zurathi.

"Councilor Asahi," Soraya's voice fell like silk across the table as a servant poured black tea, the delicate fragrance curling into the air around us. Her words were smooth, disarmingly cordial. "I understand Lunrae seeks alliance with Durathar. Let us hear your petition."

Asahi straightened, clearing his throat. "Yes," he began. "It is no secret that Durathar wields unmatched strength. You conquered Akhsarun in a mere few summers. You have breached the borders of Yuehama, and soon—after Ashti-Yasu runs its course—you will likely claim it as well." His gaze brushed mine, an apology barely veiled within it.

"Lunrae does not possess the forces of Yuehama or Akhsarun," he continued, voice steadier. "We are neither naive nor stubborn enough to believe we can hold our own against a growing empire the size of Durathar." His words hung there, unvarnished, baring his kingdom's submission. I could not blame Lunrae for bending, but a subtle, bitter disdain tightened within me. How easy it was to concede, to yield before the threat even materialized.

Azariel's voice cut through the councilor's solemn appeal, his tone coolly inquisitive. "For all you know, Yuehama's forces could yet rebuild during Ashti-Yasu, could press back against our advance. Even more so if Lunrae's armies had aided them as intended. Does your heart not tremble with shame for turning against your allies even before their fall?"

A flicker of surprise crossed Asahi's face as he struggled to hold Azariel's gaze. "We do feel shame, Your Majesty," he replied. "But we must protect our own people before sacrificing for a kingdom that cannot hold its ground."

Azariel tilted his head, an almost mocking bemusement softening his features. "So you would rather both kingdoms fall? Your alliance could have secured survival for both, yet you've chosen otherwise." He paused, voice edged with a feigned innocence that barely masked his contempt. "Did Lunrae send even a single soldier to aid Yuehama? Did they not call upon you as we breached their borders, or did you simply choose not to answer?"

Asahi's lips parted to respond, but Azariel continued with the precision of a blade. "You request alliance with us now, yet you could not honor one so close. If you would betray those who share your borders and blood, why should we trust your fealty?"

"Azariel," Soraya's tone sharpened. "He is our guest; allow him his words."

The councilor's composure wavered, yet he nodded. "It is a fair question. Yet sometimes survival demands difficult choices. We must prioritize the lives of Lunrae's people, even if that means withdrawing support from a kingdom already lost." His eyes, dark with reluctance, strayed from me despite my presence beside Azariel and in his peripheral, refusing to linger where the weight of his betrayal might find reckoning. Would he speak so freely if he knew the rightful emperor of Yuehama sat before him, hearing his every cowardly word?

"So survival alone has driven you here, to forsake Yuehama?" Azariel's voice was a quiet, unsparing blade.

"Yes," A faint flush of shame colored Asahi's face, and I felt my fingers wrap and tighten on Azariel's thigh, anger hardening my grip. "If you fear that aligning with us will bring Durathar to ruin like Yuehama—"

"We hold no such fear," came a low chuckle from Vizier Sulqadir.

"Durathar is without rival," Asahi pressed on, head bowing as he sought to maintain dignity. "There is no other kingdom in Tairasa formidable enough to turn us against you. We ask for nothing but a peaceful submission, Your Majesties." He inclined his head, a symbol of deference that cloaked cowardice in humility.

I gritted my teeth, fingers digging deeper into the fabric of Azariel's trousers, imagining that I could cut through the absurdity with mere will. I could feel his calm presence, his fingers subtly prying mine free beneath the table, his gesture unseen but solid, tethering me to his control as he gripped my hand tightly.

"I admire your honesty and your will to see Lunrae thrive," Azariel replied, voice smooth, unreadable. Asahi's shoulders eased, the tension slipping as he released a subtle breath.

"Is peaceful submission your petition, then?" Empress Soraya said.

"Not quite. We seek a true alliance. One forged of permanence and purpose," Councilor Asahi replied, his eyes glinting with cautious hope. "As you may know, Princess Meiyuna was promised to Prince..." His gaze lingered on me, and for one terrible instant, it seemed as though he recognized me. My pulse stilled, and instinctively I leaned closer to Azariel as if proximity would make me disappear, a movement I detested even as I made it.

Azariel glanced down at me, a subtle furrow creasing his brow as his carefully guarded expression softened, just for a heartbeat. His grip slackened, his fingers threading through mine in an unspoken offer of solace, before his gaze returned to Asahi.

Perfect. He thought I was leaning on him for comfort. The more he believed me tamed, the better I supposed. I let him think it, settling into the illusion he cradled so willingly.

"Prince... the late prince of Yuehama," Asahi continued, glancing away, his face betraying no memory. Yet, as I looked down at my chest, I caught the faint stir of the sigils, restless as if disturbed. Then it hit me, my mere presence had been the cause for me to be forgotten from others' memories.

"Are you proposing an alliance through marriage between Lunrae and Durathar?" Soraya asked, her voice barely veiling the amusement that twisted at its edges.

"Why would we dilute our crown further with Celestial blood?" Sulqadir cut in, voice as sharp and unforgiving as the desert sun.

"Marriage has long been the emblem of true unity," Asahi replied, his tone pleadingly earnest, clearly unaware of the Duratharian obsession with the purity of their Zurathi lineage.

But Azariel's voice surprised me. "Let us not dismiss the idea too quickly."

Soraya's gaze flicked to him, emerald fire sparking in her eyes. "Azariel, do not indulge such notions."

"I will entertain whatever I wish in matters of *my* marriage," Azariel retorted, his smile a brittle, cutting thing. "You wanted me married anyway, did you not? Is it not the last condition before I ascend fully to the throne?"

"To a Kamishen? If your father and brother were alive—"

Azariel's smile sharpened, his words dipping like venom into the space between them. "It's fortunate, then, that they are not. And fortunate, too, that the choice of marriage rests with the crown alone. Not even a regent may intervene. Do not forget yourself, Soraya."

The Empress's jaw tightened, her eyes locked onto him, seething with restrained fury. A silence hung over the gathering, weighted and thick. Then she spoke again, softer, a barely contained storm. "All I ask is that you consider the consequences."

I studied Azariel's face. What was he doing? Did he grasp nothing of the delicate, volatile politics woven through his own people? To propose an alliance of this kind was to dare his council to rise against him. A union with Lunrae, a nation devoid of Zurathi blood—what sense did it make? Better to claim Lunrae's submission, enslave them, and take their land as their own.

"If I may interject," Sulqadir's voice cut smoothly into the tension, an attempt at soothing the unspoken conflict. "Your Majesty, we should convene with the council before moving forward. A decision of such magnitude demands careful thought, and the full consideration of all possible outcomes."

"Indeed," Azariel replied, voice as cool and impassive as ever. "I am not one for reckless haste. Councilor Asahi," he continued, turning his attention back to Lunrae's ambassador, "I shall provide *my* answer by week's end. Durathar extends its hospitality; you may remain at the palace as our guest." He looked to Soraya, finality glinting in his gaze. "I believe we are finished here. Enjoy the remainder of the banquet."

CHAPTER TWELVE

Azariel's humoring of Lunrae's proposal had, perhaps, been a calculated risk, one I'd dismissed as foolish bravado—a gift-wrapped invitation for Durathar's council to sharpen their blades against him. And yet, as I made my way to his chamber for the second time that day, summoned once more to study his sigil, I wondered if he grasped the stakes more than I'd given him credit for. Perhaps he understood his own vulnerability and sought to anchor his power in that celestial blood he bore, a shield against those who might strike him down.

No more delaying. I'd exhausted every plausible excuse, and if I were to forestall an alliance with Lunrae, I had to act swiftly. Ending Azariel now, before any treaty sealed Lunrae's fate, felt like a mercy—an unearned grace for allies who'd already abandoned Yuehama. The chance to grovel and beg for forgiveness might yet be open to them, for the sake of my people and what remained of Lunrae's honor. It was a kindness, however undeserved.

I fingered the small pouch concealed beneath my garbs, its weight a reminder of the half-truths I'd spun to Ilay. I'd told him I was learning my place, preparing to surrender fully to Azariel's will. That much, he'd accepted with a quiet nod, procuring for me the dried aphrodisiac leaves once mixed in the solstice wines I had requested for such submission. Not enough to rob me of my senses entirely, but enough to dull restraint, to make the pretense of submission that much easier to uphold. There was nothing more vulnerable than a man laid bare with his cock out, and that was when I would strike.

I slipped a pinch between my lips as the bazifirs led me through winding halls, each step pulling me deeper into the trap I'd set for myself.

When I entered Azariel's chamber, he was seated on that raised platform of cushions, engrossed in parchments spread over a low table, the painted lines of his sigil half-hidden beneath his idle hand. His gaze flickered, distant, as he lifted a glass to his lips, his fingers tracing absent patterns over his mother's craft.

"It is beautiful," I murmured, allowing softness to lace my voice as I approached. "Your mother's sigil work." I slid closer, fingers skimming the edge of the parchment. "Even our Grand Shiryū could not shape such grace. She made it an art."

He sighed, a flicker of something—memory, perhaps—passing over his expression. "She had a gift for making things beautiful." His voice was quiet, yet edged with loss.

"What became of her?" I asked, reaching for the parchment, though my attention was half-rooted in his words, half-awaiting the slow tendrils of aphrodisiacs spreading through my veins. "I thought the Tenishen were extinct." I shifted the parchment, letting it fall just so, obscuring the glint of the knife lying on the table. My other hand slid slowly, fingers curling around the hilt with deliberate care, lifting it in silence. In one fluid motion, I slipped it beneath the cushion I sat upon, hidden and within easy reach.

A pause lingered, hesitation woven into the silence before he spoke. "My father found her when he went to Vorynthia, in a court that claimed to have discovered the remnants of the floating isle of Simurgh. They captured her people, killed the men, and took the women. She was... a gift, offered to my father." His gaze turned inward. "He called her his little dove. Obsession overtook him. Soraya was pregnant with Darius when he returned with Amalthea. He was indifferent to his marriage, enamored with his prize. In a twisted and sick way, he had loved my mother."

A shadow crossed his face, settling in the furrow of his brow. "In time, Amalthea yielded to him, and she bore him a son. I was six when the council grew uneasy—fearful that my father's desire for her would overshadow his duties to his wife, that he would continue to sully the Pahlavan line with Tenishen blood. So they had her killed. Soraya made certain I watched. It was a lesson to remind me of my place beneath her and Darius." His voice thickened, edged with dark amusement. "But the spirits proved to have a sense of humor. Rohan's wife could only bear him one child. And I, not her son, now sit upon his throne."

A solemnness settled over the room, and I felt a pang of pity buried beneath my disdain. "Duratharians destroy beauty as easily as they seek it," I said softly, the words slipping from me before I could temper them as I turned my attention to his back. "They take what they covet, without thought of consequence."

Azariel turned slightly, his eyes meeting mine, and I let my fingers linger on the inked lines along his back. "Tell me of your family," he asked, his voice a quiet command.

"Children of the Celestial Bodies live long, but at a cost—fertility. I was the only child they were able to bear before their death."

"You have no one, then?"

"Would it matter if I did?" I replied, a note of bitterness slipping through. "They would not be here."

"You once said loneliness is not survival. I had assumed you were surviving for someone."

A quiet chuckle escaped me, the irony weighing heavy. "I can see how you'd think that," I did have a reason for survival... It was all for Yuehama.

My hand found the quill, fingers brushing its stem with a deliberate slowness. The black sheen of Asahi's sword glinted from across the table, catching my attention. "Did the sword dancer perform her private dance for you?" I asked, voice smooth as I traced unneeded lines onto the parchment, filling the silence with movements I hoped seemed idle.

"Yes."

"Did you enjoy it?" I murmured, my tone steady.

He looked at me, his gaze sharpening, and said without restraint, "You mean, did I fuck her?"

My fingers paused mid-stroke at his crass words. I forced myself to continue. "Did you?"

His smirk deepened, eyes glinting as he lifted his glass to his lips, sipping slowly. "Are you jealous, *Aqaynah*?"

I hadn't intended for jealousy to spill into my words, hadn't meant to sound as though I cared. But this was the opening I needed to nudge the evening into different waters. "What if I was?" I let a hint of bitterness slip, gaze fixed on the parchment like a wounded lover, avoiding his eyes.

"Then I'd tell you she tried to seduce me, and failed."

"I don't believe you." My words were barely out before he caught my wrist, his grip firm and unyielding, the quill slipping from my hand and blotting ink across the parchment.

"Then I'll show you." He pulled me toward him, taking my bait, guiding my hand to his abdomen, his skin taut, warm and bare. Slowly, his hand traveled up, trailing mine over his chest with a languid insistence. "She touched me like this... and then came closer." He grasped my thighs, shifting me effortlessly onto his lap, until I straddled him, every inch of space between us dissolved. "And closer," he whispered, his hand cupping my face, pulling me toward him.

"What are you trying to prove?" I asked, fixing him with a glare as I turned my face away, breaking the pull between us. "All you've shown me is how much she clung to you."

But beneath my practiced disdain, a flicker of genuine jealousy simmered unexpectedly. The aphrodisiacs must have finally begun to work, clouding my thoughts with a warmth I hadn't intended.

"I want your touch to replace hers," he murmured, his fingers gripping my jaw, firm but not unkind, tilting my face toward his. He leaned in, his breath warm and close, his lips hovering dangerously near mine. "Will you erase her touch for me, Kaito?"

Yes.

I leaned in, letting my lips brush against his, tentative yet fierce, as though this moment held a fragile power. My hand drifted to the nape of his neck, fingers threading through his hair, pulling him closer, drawing him deeper into this fevered embrace.

Azariel's hand slipped from my jaw to rest lightly on my throat, his fingers tracing a tender line along my skin underneath my collar. He tilted his head, deepening our kiss, his breath mingling with mine. The sharp edge of his nose grazed my cheek, and then his tongue slipped between my lips, tentative, exploring. I met him in kind, our tongues entwining in a languid, unhurried dance, each of us daring the other to surrender.

There was something dizzying about him—warm and intoxicating, as though he carried a heat that could sear me down to my bones. I let myself drown in it, in him, the soft press of his lips against mine, teasing, daring. I caught his lower lip between my teeth, felt the subtle curve of his grin before he reclaimed my mouth, fervent and wanting. His arm wrapped around my waist, a tether, and then he pulled me down with him as he sank into the cushions.

His hands slipped away, each settling on my thighs, his fingers tracing slow, deliberate paths upward, stopping just shy of the fabric's edge. Beneath me, I felt the hardness of his cock, straining against the fabric. For a moment, my mind dulled, the warmth of his hands and his closeness pulling me into a haze. But reality broke through like a blade, sharp and cold. My heart hammered as I pressed one hand to his chest, feigning passion as my other hand groped for the knife hidden beneath the cushion.

My pulse surged when my fingers brushed against the cold metal. In an instant, I seized it and brought it to his throat, my lips pulling back, leaving only the steel between us as I stared down at him. His eyes held no shock, no fear—only a disturbing glint of amusement that made my skin prickle.

"What is that? Mint, violets?" he murmured, purring as one of his hands moved to the back of my neck, drawing me down with a force that burned. "If you wanted me to fuck you, you wouldn't need to drug me. I thought my affections were clear."

Mint and violets? The taste on my tongue—it in fact was wrong, an unfamiliar concoction that belied my intent. *Ilay.* Of course, the loyal dog would have betrayed my request. I'd been the one deceived.

"It was for me, not you," I hissed, my words laced with venom.

His hand roamed higher, slipping beneath my garments, his grip rough as he clasped my ass with a possessive hold. "I can feel the hardness of you pressing against me. It seems you had no need for it."

"Shut up," I growled, steadying my hold on the knife, pressing it firmly against his throat as if to silence his taunts, though his smirk never wavered.

"I knew you were plotting something," he murmured, amusement lacing his tone. "You're not a good liar, *Aqaynah.*" His low chuckle rolled through the air, as I pressed the blade harder to his throat, watching as a bead of golden blood rose, gleaming beneath the edge. It was as if he relished the sting. "You are ambitious," he went on, his voice soft and taunting, "but your sense for self-preservation lacks refinement. You haven't thought this through. You lead with your emotions, not your head. Tell me, what happens when you kill me? Do you think my kingdom would bend a knee to you?"

A laugh, dark and bitter, slipped from his lips. "They barely wish to bow to me—and I carry Zurathi blood. You, a Kamishen, are unwanted on their soil. They would hunt you down before you could step off Durathar's sands alive."

I held my breath, the weight of his words settling like iron in my chest. He was right. Though I had thought this through, I had not been thorough. The politics here were sharp and vicious despite its barbarics. I was still their enemy, an outsider. And I had no army to keep them in line. All I had was... *him.* I needed him alive.

"But I won't stop you." His hand slid from my backside, gripping my wrist and pressing the knife deeper. Golden blood pooled and slid from his skin, his eyes gleaming as the blade bit further. "Go on," he whispered, his voice threaded with a dangerous kind of thrill, "and see what you bring upon yourself."

He was a masochist, that much was clear. He drank in the moment, the edge of the knife dancing against his skin as his throat rose and fell against its edge, each breath steady, confident.

"Silent again?" he taunted, his voice a purr. "Tell me, why do you want my crown?"

"I don't want your crown," I replied, my voice low, gritted. "I want mine. Yours is simply the bridge to claim it." With a sharp inhale, I drew the blade away before stabbing it into the cushion above his head. Exhaustion seeped into my bones, and I rolled off him, sinking onto my back beside him.

Azariel shifted to his side, his eyes probing mine with an unreadable intensity. "What do you mean?" His fingers glided over the fresh cut on his neck, a faint glow radiating from his touch as his celestial light seeped into the wound. Heat blossomed beneath his fingertips, sealing the skin and halting the flow of blood

"It doesn't matter." My fingers traced the intricate, binding sigils my uncle had marked me with. "Even if I wanted to tell you, I couldn't." I paused, the weight of the words pressing down on me. "It forbids me."

He drew the knife from its place within the pillow, holding the blade delicately, his fingers tracing the cold steel before turning it toward me, handle first. "Then rid of it, and enlighten me."

I hesitated, the weight of his gaze pressing on me as I reached for the handle, feeling the coolness of steel that was meant to kill.

"It is too soon for me to reveal that," I murmured, words woven with a thread of caution. If he had no inkling of my identity, or even my likeliness to the prince of Yuehama, others surely would if I unlocked Renjiro's sigil. Asahi, Soraya—each knew my name and could upend the advantage I held in the shadows. Anonymity had become the last weapon in my possession now.

His brow lifted, almost imperceptibly. "You do not trust me?"

I held the knife between us, a space of uneasy truce. "I hardly know you. And what I have seen of you—" The words caught in my throat, the warning rising like a serpent within me, reminding me of the mercy he'd shown after my attempt on his life. I owed my survival to his whim. "You are..." The truth snagged in my mouth, and I forced it down, lest I provoke him.

"So you do not trust me. And," A flicker of something unexpected shadowed his gaze, a glimmer that could have been hurt or worry. "You fear me too?"

"I do not fear you," I answered, perhaps too quickly, as I set the knife back upon the table. *I could never truly fear someone like you.* I thought bitterly, the words sharp and biting in the silence of my mind. *You're just a brute, preying on those you deem weaker.* But that thought stayed caged behind my teeth, unspoken.

"Perhaps I should though. You are everything they say—volatile, cruel, barbaric. My instincts constantly tell me to flee from you, yet I always remain." I held my breath. "Perhaps out of some stubbornness, or foolishness."

I hadn't finished my thought before his hand was upon my cheek, his warmth trailing to the nape of my neck as he drew me toward him. Our lips met, his breath mingling with mine, and my body stilled as if suspended over some precipice.

"Why?" I whispered, the question trembling between us. "Why do you always need to push it?"

"Because you do not hide your hatred," he replied, his words a soft murmur, laced with a strange fondness. "In a place where I question every motive, every glance, you are a rarity. You don't seek to flatter or to cower. When your walls fall, they fall genuinely alone."

He paused, a dark humor twisting his smile. "And that is why I cannot leave you be, that is why I push boundaries. Pretend, if you like, that there's nothing between us. But remember—" he chuckled, a low, resonant sound, "you are a terrible liar."

A flood of warmth rose within me, a realization unsettling yet irrefutable. I had thought his pursuit a mockery, another cruel game until I was useless to him. But perhaps that cruelty had been tempered by something else, something closer to kinship, a reflection of the same defiance that burned in both of us.

I reached up, my hand finding the nape of his neck, and I pulled him back to me, our lips meeting once more. We lingered in that fragile silence, as if one misstep, one sudden word, could shatter whatever brittle understanding bound us in that moment.

Azariel's body pressed against mine, steady and unyielding, sinking me further into the embrace of silken cushions as he loomed above. His lips brushed along my jaw, trailing lower, lingering on my neck, stopping just above the collar that bound me. "Let me rid you of this." he murmured, his voice laced with an edge of impatience, fingers grazing the iron clasp. "Remain still," he ordered, hands firm on either side of the lock.

"Ilay has the—" I began, but before I could finish, I heard a sharp snap as he broke the lock with a strength that only Zurathi blood could wield. I sighed, caught between exasperation and awe, watching as he tossed the collar aside. "I suppose brute force has its uses," I muttered, lips curving into a thin line.

Azariel only grinned, triumphant, and lowered his head to my now-bare neck. His lips hovered, tracing the sensitive skin, a ghostly touch that sent a shiver through me before his tongue slipped out, a warm flicker against my pulse.

A ragged breath left me as I clutched the firm muscle of his back, my grip tightening, unable to ignore the heat and tension that pooled low within me. I felt his hand drifting up my thigh, fabric sliding under his fingers as he moved with a hunger that left me breathless. Then his touch settled on me, fingers tracing along the curve of my hips, his grip unyielding as he moved to cup my backside.

Instinctively, I pressed a hand to his chest, my fingers splaying across the hard planes of his body, stalling him. "Wait..."

He pulled back, his gaze steady, studying me with a quiet patience that felt wholly out of place against his usually relentless nature. "Have you really never been with a man before?" he asked, voice a low murmur as he searched my face.

Heat flushed across my cheeks, and I knew that was all the answer he needed. A soft, knowing smile tugged at his lips as he took my hand from his chest, bringing it to his mouth, pressing a kiss against my palm.

"There are other ways," he whispered, his voice softer now, edged with something close to reverence, "to find pleasure without penetration." He held my gaze, his lips brushing over my wrist in a silent promise. "Will you let me show you?"

My pulse hammered in response, an erratic rhythm that seemed to echo through my entire body. I nodded, unable to trust my voice to carry the weight of my consent.

His lips curved into a soft smile, but his hands moved with deliberate purpose. "Then this must go," he said, his fingers toying with the hem of my fine garments. Slowly, as if savoring the act, he knelt between my legs and tore the fabric apart, baring me fully to his gaze.

A flicker of boldness sparked within me, and I leaned up, my fingers reaching for the layers that shielded him from me. "I will not be the only one laid bare," I whispered, my breath brushing against his skin as I undid the bindings of his trousers. My hands urged them down, stripping him of the last barriers between us.

Azariel eased me back into the cushions, his hands steady and firm as he lifted my legs to rest around his waist and pulled me down against his front. My breath hitched as my gaze trailed down the length of my body, to where his cock rested beside mine, flushed and glistening.

He took us both in hand, his fingers curling around the hardened shafts, pressing them tightly together. The simple contact sent a shiver through me, and I watched as he parted his lips, a bead of saliva slipping from his tongue to drip onto us. The heat of it sent a tremor down my spine.

His thumb traced languid circles over our tips, spreading the slickness with an artistry that felt as reverent as a prayer. Slowly, achingly, his hand slid down, binding us together in his grip, before gliding back up with the same deliberate pace.

I couldn't hold back the gasp that escaped me, my head tipping back into the cushions as pleasure unfurled, warm and relentless, through my veins. My fingers curled into the soft fabric beneath me, grasping for some anchor to keep me grounded. Another moan slipped free, unbidden but impossible to suppress, as his movements stoked the fire building low in my groin.

"See how good I can make you feel, Kaito," Azariel murmured, his voice dipping into a husky, seductive drawl. His half-lidded eyes brimmed with desire, his lips parted as though caught mid-breath, and the shallow rise and fall of his chest betrayed his own unraveling control.

Heat rushed to my cheeks, spreading until it reached the tips of my ears. I could feel it— feel him—and I couldn't deny how easily my body surrendered under his touch, how effortlessly he unraveled me. The warmth pooling in my chest, the hardness stirring at my core—it all responded to him, as though his very presence commanded my body.

I want to be the one that makes you feel good, my thoughts stirred.

My hands trembled slightly as I brought them down, fingers wrapping around our lengths and clasping them tightly against my palms. Azariel's own hand relented, giving way to mine as I slid downward, drawing slow and deliberate strokes to the base of our cocks. His hands shifted to brace on either side of my shoulders, his body leaning over mine.

Our faces were so close I could feel the ghost of his breath against my lips, hear the ragged moans that fell from him, low and guttural. His lashes fluttered closed as his hips jerked involuntarily into my touch. "Don't stop," he whispered, the words escaping him in a breathless whimper that sent a thrill through me.

Then, his lips found mine. The collision was both tender and frantic, his broad shoulders curling inward as he pressed down, consuming me in the kiss. My hands never faltered, sliding back up in a slow, teasing stroke, my thumbs brushing over the slick, swollen tips of our arousals before gliding down again.

I quickened my pace, each stroke firm, unrelenting, and precise. My thighs clenched around him, my entire body taut with the tension of desire and pleasure. Azariel's breath hitched, his broad frame shuddering above me as his lips broke from mine. His head fell to the crook of my neck, and I could feel the heat of his breath against my skin, the quiet tremors that betrayed how close he was.

"Az," I breathed, the syllable catching as pleasure lanced through me, sharp and unrelenting. "Cum with me," I whispered, my strokes steady and unyielding, a silent plea laced within the command.

And then it happened, the crescendo of everything we'd built together. His body tensed against mine, a guttural moan spilling from his lips as his release spilled between us. My own climax followed in an instant, a blinding wave of euphoria that stole my breath, left my body trembling, and my mind adrift.

The warm evidence of our pleasure coated my hands, pooling between our bodies as my movements slowed, every lingering stroke a shiver of aftershock. Azariel's lips pressed gently against my temple, his breaths heavy and uneven, and in that moment, the world faded to nothing but the sound of our shared breaths and the steady rhythm of our hearts.

CHAPTER THIRTEEN

The first light of morning poured through the open terrace, bathing the room in a golden glow. My eyes blinked against its brilliance, adjusting slowly. The bed beneath me was unfamiliar—its frame carved of polished wood, draped in cascading white and gold fabric, creating a canopy that swayed faintly in the breeze. This was not my bed.

I shifted, and there he was. Azariel.

He lay on his stomach, one arm tucked beneath the pillow, the other draped carelessly across the mattress. His face, unguarded in sleep, was free of its usual sharpness—no malice, no arrogance, no veiled intentions. Just serenity. Strands of white hair, unruly from the night, fell across his face in soft disarray. In that moment, he looked impossibly beautiful, impossibly touchable.

I shouldn't have been here. Not in his bed. Not so close. His words from the night before lingered in my mind—his confessions of affection, his claim that my sincerity drew him in. But sincerity was a luxury I couldn't afford. He didn't know the truth of me, the weight of my name, the motives that tethered me to him like a spider's thread. If he knew, would he still reach for me? Would he still hold me between his warmth and the gilded world he ruled?

Would I even want to remain at his side in a few weeks? His armies would soon march upon my kingdom, and there was nothing I could do to stop them. Yuehama was slipping through my fingers, and I lay here beside its conqueror. I could not simply abandon it or my people for the sake of this fragile, selfish indulgence. My life was never meant to be lived in the throes of desire, untethered from duty. This—whatever it was—would shatter eventually, and I knew the pain would be as inevitable as the rising sun.

I reached out before I could stop myself, brushing aside the pale locks from his brow. His nose scrunched faintly at the touch, and the softest chuckle escaped me. For a moment, the weight on my chest lessened, the present pulling me from my spiraling thoughts.

"It's too early," he murmured, his voice thick with sleep, his face turning to burrow deeper into the pillow. "Go back to bed, *Aqaynah*."

I threaded my fingers through his hair once more, unable to resist teasing the soft strands. "What does that mean? Aqaynah?"

His voice was muffled, lazy but tinged with faint amusement. "Your people... forgotten Deva?" His hand reached up, curling gently around my wrist, stilling my touch. He shifted onto his side, his eyes half-lidded as he brought my hand to his lips and pressed a languid kiss to my knuckles.

"We know fragments—words and phrases passed down in old tales and songs—but few are fluent enough to hold a proper conversation," I said softly.

In Yuehama, our tongues shaped the flowing cadences of Yueyan, our native language, while Tairan, the universal tongue of the continent, was our second. Any time devoted to learning another language was spent on the tongues of neighboring kingdoms—practical knowledge for diplomacy or survival—rather than the ancient, fading words of the Celestial Bodies.

His lips curved faintly, a secret half-formed as he guided my hand to his cheek. "It means... temptation of the water. A water nymph." His eyes closed shut for a moment, as he leaned into the warmth of my palm.

I raised a brow, attempting to mask the heat rising in my cheeks. "Clever," I muttered dryly, though the corners of my lips betrayed me.

A lazy smile curled on his mouth as he pulled me closer, his strength effortless. My body pressed flush against his, his unnatural warmth seeping into me.

His arms wrapped securely around me, and for a moment, I gave in to the illusion. I rested my cheek against his chest, my own arms slipping around his waist, holding him as if he could anchor me here, in this fragile calm.

His heartbeat thudded against my ear, steady and strong, and I wondered—when his celestial magic could flow freely through him, would his touch still feel like this? Would he still feel so warm and calming?

I closed my eyes, letting the moment stretch just a little longer, even as the world outside this bed threatened to tear it all apart.

The stillness of the bedchamber was broken by his voice, low and deliberate. "Are you able to unlock my sigil?" Azariel's words were like the first ripple on a glassy pool, shattering the quiet intimacy that had briefly settled over us.

"I am," I replied softly, though the weight of my answer was anything but.

He shifted his head to face me, his stoney-gold eyes piercing as his hand tilted my chin upward. "I don't wish to ruin this moment, but the deadline I gave you was not for show. Before I move forward with my plans, I must have access to what my mother saw fit to bind within me. Whatever it is, it could give me leverage today with the council."

I could hardly blame him for pressing the matter. The fragile bubble of time we shared here meant little in the grander scheme of Durathar's machinations. Outside this chamber, decisions were being made, alliances forged or fractured, each one with the potential to undo him.

"I can do it now," I said, my hand pressing gently against his chest, guiding him to lie back beneath me. The sight of him yielding, even in this small way, sent a ripple of something unspoken through me. "But as you've said yourself, everything comes with a price."

His brow lifted, his lips curling into a knowing smile. "Negotiating? Now? Need I remind you, we already have a deal. You unlock my sigil, and I grant you the same. What else could you possibly want?" His fingers brushed a loose strand of hair from my face with such ease, such familiarity.

I held his gaze. "I wish to be present for your meeting with the council today."

"Do Durathar's politics intrigue you so deeply?" His tone was amused, but his eyes searched mine.

"They do when they concern northern Tairasa," I replied. "Please."

This was no idle request. The council—Durathar's most powerful and dangerous assembly—offered an opportunity no Yuehaman spy could ever dream of. To observe, to listen, to learn. It was a chance I could not squander.

Azariel sighed, the weight of it brushing against my resolve. "Very well. But you are not to speak. Not a word. You are not even to look anyone in the eye. Is that understood?"

I nodded, though the words settled heavily in my chest. It felt wrong to manipulate his affections, wrong to use this fragile thing between us for gain. From a political standpoint, bringing me to the council was reckless—no more than a pleasure slave in their eyes, and yet far too dangerous a distraction for the watchful Soraya and her venomous glares.

"I understand." I slipped from the bed, gathering what I needed. The fine needle, the blade, charcoal, chaparral, and a bowl.

When I returned, I poured the dried herb into his hand. "This needs to be ash. Could you...?"

He chuckled softly, the sound warm and unhurried as he closed his fingers over the shrubbery. A faint glow seeped from his palm, and the scent of chaparral—earthy and sharp, tinged with sunlight—wafted into the air. He tipped the ashes into the bowl, and I ground the charcoal alongside it, adding water from a chalice to create the thick, ink-like paste.

"Lie on your stomach," I instructed, and he obeyed, stretching out with the slow grace of a panther.

"You don't realize how fortunate you are that I was brought here," I began, dipping the needle into the ink and pressing it against his skin. The muscles in his back twitched under the touch, but he said nothing.

"Not all celestial children possess the knowledge or skill to unlock a sigil, let alone read one. It is a rare art," I continued, my voice steady as I worked. "We call those who can create and break them: Shiryū."

"Boasting, are we?" he teased, his tone light despite the sharp sting of the needle.

"Perhaps." I smiled faintly. "But this is no idle claim. Your sigil wasn't just locking away your potential—it was forcing it to store itself within you rather than flow freely. The fractures on your body, the strain you feel... I fear, Azariel, that if not a sword or fist, this would have killed you in a few summers."

The room fell silent, save for the quiet rhythm of my work.

At last, he spoke, his voice quieter now. "Then I suppose I owe you my life." He glanced over his shoulder, his expression unreadable, though the faint curve of a smile lingered at the corner of his lips.

"I'm sure you'll find a way to repay me someday," I said, letting a faint smile curve my lips. My hand hovered briefly over the needle before setting it aside, fingers brushing the knife's hilt instead. "This part will hurt—but then it will be over."

My gaze traced the sigil etched into his back. I let my fingers glide over the grooves, feeling for the place where the binds hold was weakest. When I found it, I paused, the moment hanging heavy between us like a breath not yet exhaled.

This was it—the moment my enemy would gain the power to conquer not just this continent, but perhaps others beyond it. And yet, what more could I do? A twisted part of me, one I loathed to acknowledge, had humored the idea that I could mold him into *my* weapon, that I could wield his strength to serve my own ends.

But now, the weight of that ambition pressed against my chest, an ache that felt like it might tear me apart. He believed I was genuine—that my affections were born of sincerity. But they weren't. And the bitter truth of that realization left a hollow, unrelenting pain in its wake.

The tip of the blade kissed his skin, and I pressed. The golden blood—a result of the pent up celestial magics in his vessel—welled up, warm and luminous, pooling around the incision as his flesh dimpled under the pressure.

Slowly, deliberately, I dragged the knife across the sigil's path, carving through its binding lines. His body tensed beneath my hand, his breath catching in his throat as his fingers gripped the sheets, twisting them as if the fabric could anchor him.

When I finally pulled the blade away, the blood had begun to spread, shimmering like molten sunlight as it seeped into the inked lines. It moved with purpose, as though drawn by the sigil itself, tracing its patterns in a final act of defiance. Then, with a soft, soundless pulse, the sigil vanished, leaving only the wound I had made.

Reaching for the sheets, I tore a strip of cloth to staunch the bleeding. But before I could press it to his back, his hand lifted, a silent command. He stretched his arm backward, and from the tip of his finger, a faint, radiant light flickered to life. The warmth of celestial magic coursed through him as he guided the light to the wound, sealing the cut as effortlessly as he had his neck the night before.

He was practiced, I realized—far too practiced at mending his own wounds. It seemed like a skill born not of convenience, but of necessity. And as the light faded, leaving only a faint scar in its wake, I found myself wondering how many times he had been forced to do this before.

"Do you feel different?" I asked, tilting my head as Azariel pushed himself upright.

"Not particularly," he replied with a quiet chuckle, the sound carrying an intimacy that brushed against my senses. "Your turn." He extended the needle to me.

I accepted it, collecting the mirrors Ilay had procured earlier. "Hold this," I said, handing one to him. "Aim it at my neck." Adjusting the second mirror before me, I angled it to catch the reflection of the sigil etched into the back of my neck.

This one was trickier—not for its complexity, but for its placement. The skin there was delicate, the flesh beneath far too vulnerable.

The needle was laid aside, its purpose unneeded for this, as the blade was chosen without hesitation. I steadied myself, the knife cool against my skin as I pierced into the sigil. Pain bloomed sharply, and my jaw tightened as the warm bead of blood surfaced. Like before, it didn't trickle down but was drawn to the intricate lines of the sigil, tracing them like veins of liquid fire before dissolving entirely.

Azariel moved instinctively to grab the sheets as the remaining blood began to drip. But I stopped him, catching his wrist and guiding his hand to my neck.

His brows furrowed, the faintest shadow of hesitation crossing his face. "Are you certain? It will hurt."

"I want to know how it feels."

He studied me for a moment, his gaze softening. "Then at least allow me to distract you from the pain." His words were low, a tender murmur before his lips found mine.

As his fingers grazed the top of the cut, warmth spread from his touch, searing and intense. My lips parted with a sharp gasp, the sensation burning far deeper than I'd anticipated. How had he endured this without even a flicker of pain?

My fingers tangled into the back of his hair, gripping tightly as his tongue swept over my lips, coaxing and commanding all at once. His scorching touch trailed downward, pressing into the wound, and my body arched involuntarily, caught between the ache and the pull of his kiss.

"There," he whispered, his voice a breath against my skin. He drew back slightly, enough to press his lips to my forehead in a gesture so soft it sent a pang through my chest.

"Thank you," I breathed. My gaze fell to the chalice on the table, and a quiet thrill rose within me. I raised a hand, willing the water inside to rise. With a flick of my wrist, it leapt free, scattering both liquid and chalice across the room in one fluid motion. The magic was intoxicating—a river that once flowed freely by the grace of the celestials, only to be dammed by the sigil. Now, the gates were shattered, and the currents roared back to life.

"See *Aqaynah*," Azariel said, his laughter soft, carrying a note of admiration.

I smiled faintly, shaking my head. "Are you saying you find that seductive? That was a parlor trick, something even a child could manage."

"Anything you do is tempting," he replied, his voice low and warm as he nuzzled into the crook of my neck. The closeness of him, the weight of his words, sent my pulse racing anew.

A knock at the door broke the spell, Ilay's voice followed, muffled but audible. "The council will be joining shortly. Are you ready to prepare for the morning, Your

Majesty?" The door cracked open just enough for his words to slip through. Instinctively, I reached for the sheets, pulling them over myself in a futile attempt at modesty. The heat of Azariel's bare skin still pressed against mine, a reminder of last night's shared intimacy.

His head tilted, a soft sigh escaping his lips. "Time to prepare for the day," he murmured, his voice low and unhurried. Then, turning his gaze toward the door, he called out gently, "Enter, Ilay."

.‡·🕸🌀🌾

We were escorted to the same council chamber as the one where Councilor Asahi had proposed his alliance with Azariel nights ago. Yet tonight, the room felt different—heavier, as if the weight of eight bodies gathered around the table bore more than mere flesh. Vizier Sulqadir sat among the other five council members, their faces a tapestry of age and judgment. Some I recognized dimly, relics of my father's lessons on Duratharian politics. But the years had stolen their names from me, leaving only fragments of memory. At the head of the table sat Empress Soraya, her expression carved from stone. Azariel and I took our places at the opposite end.

Soraya's sharp voice was the first to cut through the silence. "Azariel, have you finally come to your senses regarding Lunrae's proposal?"

His face betrayed nothing, his tone colder than the marble beneath our feet. "I have. I will marry Princess Meiyuna."

A stillness fell, one so complete it felt alive.

A councilor spoke, his voice low and deliberate, tinged with an elder's condescension. "Darius' vision—and that of his forefathers—was to unite Tairasa under Durathar's rule. Do you understand what such an alliance will signal to the kingdoms of the eastern and western continents? You risk diminishing the very legacy your father and brother built."

Soraya's restraint frayed as she leaned forward, her words steeped in venom. "Lunrae folded without a fight. Their blood is weak, their leadership spineless. Aligning with them will make us appear just as fragile. Does your mother's blood blind you so completely, Azariel? That you simply wish to be with your own kind?"

Azariel's fist clenched against the table, his composure slipping as her barbs struck true. "Your obsession with conquest blinds you to reason. This hunger will leave us vulnerable, but you are too arrogant to see the cracks beneath our feet."

His voice rose, uncoiling with the force of a storm. "Yuehama and Akhsarun's siege. Lunrae's surrender. You call it victory, but it's an illusion. Our armies grow hungry for more, but who will stand beside us on enemy soil when you decide to take the other continents? Will the slaves we've stolen fight for us when their loyalty is tested? What if the other continents come here? Numbers dwindle throughout Tairasa, men die without time to create life to replace them. Do you not see the future you're forging? It is a blade pointed at our own throats."

Azariel straightened, his voice steady but brimming with an authority that silenced even the oldest in the room. "I have played the part you set for me. I've entertained your whims, stayed out of Darius' way, punished your prisoners, and stained my hands with blood for your amusement. But now I am your Emperor. You will listen to me."

The air thickened, charged with a tension so fierce I dared not even breathe, lest it spark an eruption. His words pressed against my chest, leaving no room for sound, only the thrum of my racing heart.

"As Emperor, I declare an end to this endless war. We will no longer force Tairasa to bow to Durathar. Instead, Lunrae and Durathar will unite through marriage, preserving trade and stability. I will negotiate a real alliance with Emperor Renjiro. With Lunrae on our side, Yuehama cannot afford to retaliate for the war. Peace will be their only choice."

Azariel's voice carried conviction, and I saw then how deeply I had underestimated him again. He was no forgotten prince, lost in indulgence. He had been watching, waiting, strategizing. This declaration had not been created on a whim—it was created in the years spent in the shadows, watching the inevitable downfall of Tairasa due to Durathar's insatiable hunger for more.

Soraya rose. Stepping past a Bazifir as she crossed to the window, her back to the table, and spoke in a low, dangerous tone. "You insult your brother's memory. Do you think he would approve of forging an alliance with the kingdom that spilled his blood?"

Azariel didn't flinch. "And how many Yuehamans have we slaughtered in return? Most of their land is tainted, their people broken. What is the point of conquering ruins? Do you not see the futility?"

She turned, her gaze alight with something dark and accusing. "Are you a sympathizer, Azariel? Has your... pet softened you? Don't think I haven't noticed the absence of his collar."

Her words struck like a whip, and my hand drifted to my neck instinctively. I had forgotten—Azariel had removed it. And in that moment, as her eyes bore into mine, I felt the room's judgment settle over me like a shroud.

Her voice dipped, low and venomous, like a serpent poised to strike. "I think it is time I remedy this problem of yours—this blindness that clouds your judgment." With a measured flick of her wrist, she extended her hand, and the Bazifir standing at her side presented her his spear.

Before I could react, the air itself seemed to split. The spear whistled with a deadly hum, a blur of gleaming steel slicing through the space between us. Its aim was precise—me.

A sudden force wrenched me sideways, and the world plunged into darkness. I was pressed tightly against Azariel's chest, his arm unyielding around me, his breath hot and steady against my ear. A sharp wetness slicked my skin, a scent I recognized all too well. *Blood.*

The veil that had swallowed me dissipated in slow, shifting tendrils, like a storm breaking at dawn. Feathers vast, unyielding, white as sunlit bone, marbled with rich streaks and speckles of earthen brown. They unfurled around us, their edges catching the chamber's light with a sharp luster.

"Tenishen," someone whispered, a councilor whose voice trembled with awe and dread. The name hung in the air, heavy with recognition.

I turned, my breath catching as I looked up at Azariel. His wings—otherworldly and immense—arched protectively around us, the feathers rippling as though alive. My gaze dropped to the streaks of golden blood running in rivulets down their pale expanse, pooling at the tips before falling in slow drips onto the marble floor.

"Az..." I whispered, the word catching in my throat. My hand lifted on instinct, trembling as it brushed against the wet feathers. My skin was untouched. His blood, not mine, coated me.

But Azariel neither flinched nor turned to meet my eyes. He stepped away, his movements deliberate, every step ringing against the stunned silence that gripped the room. The calmness in his posture was more unnerving than rage—a stillness that heralded something far more terrifying.

He walked toward Soraya.

The Empress, who had wielded power and fear like weapons, stood frozen, her composure cracked and fragile. The shadow of his wings fell over her like an omen, and the air thickened with a palpable, suffocating tension.

"It would be distasteful for me to kill my father's wife," Azariel said, his voice smooth and cold as steel. He pressed her back against the window's edge, one hand braced against the glass near her shoulder, the other reaching for the Bazifir who had dared to arm her.

There was a sickening thud as Azariel's palm collided with the guard's head, slamming it against the wall beside Soraya, his helm crashing to the floor upon impact. The Zurathi struggled, his hands clawing at Azariel's wrist, but it was futile. Light, blinding and wrathful, burst from Azariel's hand.

The Bazifir screamed—a raw, primal sound that echoed off the walls—but the councilors dared not intervene. One by one, they turned their faces away, their hands rising to shield their noses from the acrid stench of burning flesh. Smoke curled in thick tendrils as the Bazifir's skin began to melt beneath Azariel's celestial light, his body convulsing in agony.

Soraya, trapped between the unyielding glass and Azariel's unrelenting strength, paled. The color drained from her face, leaving her ashen and frozen. Her gaze flickered between the melting remnants of her Bazifir and the gleaming, golden blood still dripping from Azariel's wings.

The Bazifir's screams gave way to silence, replaced by the grotesque crackle of melting bone and the low, humorless chuckle that rumbled from Azariel's throat. His laughter was not a sound of mirth but a chilling reminder of the power he wielded—a power they had all underestimated.

"I didn't know I could do that," he murmured, his voice laced with dark amusement as he released the lifeless body, letting it crumple to the floor in a heap of smoldering ruin. His gaze flicked to Soraya, his lips curving into a smile that held no warmth. "Did you?"

His hand, streaked with the remnants of the Bazifir's flesh, slid against the wall, leaving a grotesque smear as it came to rest against Soraya's cheek. She flinched at his touch, her breath hitching, but she dared not move.

"Terrifying, isn't it?" Azariel laughed, the sound echoing with a cruel satisfaction. His other hand rose to cradle the other side of her face, boxing her in entirely.

"Azariel, don't," she whispered, her voice cracking, the commanding empress reduced to a woman begging for mercy. Her resolve, once sharp as a blade, crumbled under the weight of his presence.

"Beg," he said simply, his tone a velvet threat as his fingers pressed gently into her skin. His golden eyes burned with an intensity that left no room for refusal.

My gaze shifted to the other councilors, their fear thick in the air, an almost tangible presence. They feared what lay beyond their grasp, what they could no longer bend to their will. And what they could not control was the monster they had forged from the fires of their hatred. They feared Azariel.

Perhaps I should have feared him too, as any sensible person would. But fear refused to find me. Something deeper stirred within—an inexplicable force that urged me forward. I could not say what compelled me to close the distance, to draw near the monster that Durathar so deeply loathed. Nor could I explain why I wished for her life to be spared, even as she stood deserving of his wrath. Yet, against all reason, I did.

"Azariel," I said, my voice steady, though it took effort to keep it so. My hand found his wrist, a fragile tether against the rage that brewed within him. "Do not descend to their level. You are more cunning than that—more than they could ever comprehend."

His jaw tightened, the golden glow in his eyes burning against Soraya like an unspoken promise. For a moment, I feared my words had slipped past him, unheard. But then I released my grip and stepped back, leaving the choice in his hands.

"Thank my *pet* for saving your life," he said, his tone cool, detached, and razor-sharp.

"Thank him?" Soraya hissed, her pride flaring even as fear ghosted across her face.

"Did I stutter?" His voice dropped, lethally soft. The acrid scent of burning flesh rose as his hand pressed deeper to her cheek, flesh beginning to singe and turn red.

"Th-thank you," she bit out, her teeth clenched as if the words themselves were poison.

Azariel released her with deliberate slowness, stepping back as though she no longer warranted his attention. The air felt heavier in his wake, laden with unspoken threats.

"Sulqadir," he commanded, his voice once more that of an emperor, cold and absolute. "Draw up the documents for the union between Durathar and Lunrae. Summon Asahi and me when they are complete."

Sulqadir inclined his head, his eyes carefully fixed on the polished floor. "At once, your majesty."

The room remained silent as Azariel turned, his movements graceful but unyielding, like the tide pulling away after a storm. And as the councilors lingered in that oppressive quiet, I couldn't shake the feeling that they were realizing, perhaps for the first time, the full breadth of what stood before them.

CHAPTER FOURTEEN

"Your Highness, I should send for a sage," Ilay said, his measured voice breaking the taut silence as he walked alongside us through the corridor. His gaze lingered uneasily on Azariel's injured wing, the pale feathers bent and bloodied, hanging slightly ajar while the other was tucked away neatly. "What exactly happened?" he pressed, though he kept a cautious distance.

"It is nothing, truly. I am fine. Everything is fine," Azariel replied, his tone clipped, brushing aside the chaos that had only just unfolded as though it were of no consequence. His words, dismissive as they were, hung hollow in the air. Ilay turned to me then, his dark eyes searching mine for answers. But I met his gaze with a pointed look—a silent warning that this was not the time to explain. And it wasn't.

I had no measure yet of what Azariel's wrath truly entailed. Based on his reputation, this display of violence might have seemed typical, but the councilors' stunned expressions earlier painted a different story. Whatever they thought they knew of him or his power, they had not anticipated this—the raw, unbridled fury he had unleashed upon them. I, too, was still grappling with what I had witnessed. The monster they had feared into being had exceeded their imaginations thanks to me unlocking his sigil.

"It's already beginning to heal," Azariel said, extending his wing as we walked. His voice held a detached calm, as though the glistening blood and jagged, broken feathers were merely an inconvenience. But he was right. Before our eyes, his wounds were knitting themselves back together slowly, flesh mending, feathers smoothing. A gift of the children of the stars. Without his sigil unlocked, the events in the council hall might have ended differently—for him, for both of us.

"I just wish to rest for a moment before my meeting with Councilor Asahi," Azariel continued, stepping past the threshold of his chambers.

"Then we will leave you to rest," Ilay said, his tone careful. "Come along, Kaito. I will bring you back to—"

"No." Azariel interrupted, his voice edged with quiet command. "Kaito will remain here."

My steps faltered, and I turned to face him. The air between us seemed to grow heavier. I glanced back at Ilay, whose expression betrayed a carefully masked tension. He was concerned, I could see it, not only for his Emperor but for what storm might soon follow. I wanted to go with him, to tell him everything, but there were more pressing matters I needed to address with Azariel.

"As you wish," Ilay said, bowing slightly before retreating. The door closed behind him, the finality of the sound reverberating in the stillness.

Azariel's gaze shifted to me, dark and inscrutable. "You have been uncharacteristically silent since we left the council hall," he said. "...Do you fear me now?"

"Of course not," I replied, though the words felt too quick on my tongue. I forced my voice to soften as I stepped closer to him. It wasn't fear—not entirely. I did not fear Azariel himself, but the volatility that seemed to smolder just beneath his skin. I worried for him, for myself, for the court's retaliation. Would the Duratharian nobility ever bow to a ruler they couldn't control? Would the alliance he envisioned ever stand if his own kingdom sought to tear it apart?

"Then why are your lips silent? What storm brews in your mind?" Azariel's voice, low and deliberate, filled the stillness between us. He leaned back against a table, hands braced on its edge, his piercing gaze locked onto mine. There was an unspoken question in his eyes, as if he sought to measure the distance between us, to discern whether the chaos of the council chamber had shifted something irreparable.

"Do you truly desire peace between the kingdoms?" I asked, my voice steady despite the tempest churning inside me.

"Yes," he answered. "They may not see it, but survival often demands compromise, not conquest."

"I agree with your vision," I said, the words deliberate as I stepped closer. My fingers grazed the healthy feathers of his injured wing, soft as silk, yet trembling beneath my touch. His body shuddered, and for a moment, the impenetrable mask he wore cracked, revealing the man I woke up to this morning.

"War has drained the manpower and resources of Yuehama and Durathar. If it continues, it could do the same to Lunrae. With dwindling populations, fewer soldiers, and instability, Tairasa becomes vulnerable to outside threats. Durathar needs allies, not adversaries." I said, my gaze flicking to meet his.

His lips curved faintly, though his narrowed eyes tempered the smile. "You understand politics better than I expected," he murmured.

"Marry me," The words fell with all the weight of inevitability. "Not Meiyuna."

His reaction was instant—a low, startled chuckle. "What?" he said, his voice teasing, though there was an edge to it. "Are you afraid I'll neglect you once I have a wife? You've nothing to worry about." He reached for me, his hand cupping my cheek with a tenderness that felt more like a knife to my chest. I pulled away, the heat of his touch still lingering on my skin, a testament of my guilt. "Besides... Such a thing is unheard of—two men ascending the same throne as equals."

"You are the Emperor," I replied, my tone quieter but unyielding. "Decree that it be heard of." I paused, letting the tension coil between us, my mind running through the consequences like sand slipping through my fingers. The pros and cons of unveiling myself spun in a silent storm.

"Azariel, there is something you must know. I am the—" The words caught in my throat, seized by the cruel grip of my sigil, silencing the truth I so desperately needed to voice. Frustration burned through me, and without another word, I turned away. My hands moved with purpose, gathering the tools I needed. The needle trembled only slightly as I brought it to the intricate lines etched into my chest, disrupting the sigil that bound me, unspooling its power thread by thread.

The knife followed, its edge cold and unforgiving as I pressed it to my skin. The sharp bite of the blade sent a jolt through me as I cut, blood welling to the surface as I finally released myself from my uncle's chains. Crimson stained linen as I pressed it against the wound, desperate to stem the remaining flow.

"Let me help you." His voice, steady yet tinged with something unreadable, came from behind me. I didn't have time to respond before Azariel stepped forward, brushing aside the cloth with a gentleness. His fingers found the wound, and a searing light emanated from them, heat scorching the skin as he sealed the cut. Pain lanced through me, but it was dulled by the rush of adrenaline coursing through my veins, by the weight of what was about to be revealed.

His fingers lingered, and his gaze, sharp and unwavering, held mine. "You look..." he said, his voice quiet, almost distant, as though he were piecing together a memory long buried. "It's as if I've found a piece of something I didn't know was missing."

"I am Prince Kyo Seiryu," I said, my voice low but firm as the words were finally allowed to slip out. "The rightful heir to Yuehama's throne."

His breath hitched—a subtle shift, almost imperceptible. "Kyo," he murmured, his hand drifting upward, his fingertips brushing my collarbone before curling around my neck. His grip was firm, his thumb pressing against the hollow of my throat. "Yes, that's right. Prince Kyo. Son of the late Ayame and Emiko. Murderer of Emperor Darius Pahlavan of Durathar."

The air grew heavy, suffocating, as his hand tightened. My own hands shot up, grasping at his wrist, but his strength was unyielding. Warmth seeped from his fingers, a warning of the celestial light he could summon at will. His smile was crooked, almost lazy, but his eyes blazed with dangerous intent.

"My people fear me," he said, his voice a low rumble, filled with dark amusement. "But do you know what would make them respect me? Delivering my brother's killer to them on his knees." His gaze bore into mine, sharp as a blade. "Give me one reason," he hissed, his grip tightening, "why I shouldn't end you here, *Aqaynah*?"

"Speak to me like a civilized man, not a brute," I said, my voice hoarse, the strain clawing at the edges of my composure. One hand slipped from his wrist, curling into a fist, and I drove it into the center of Azariel's face.

His head snapped back slightly, a sharp intake of breath preceding a low, unimpressed, "Ow." His grip on my throat loosened as he rubbed his nose, his gaze cutting back to mine, unreadable. "Go on," he said, voice like smoldering embers. "Give me your reason."

My hand drifted to the faint burn on my neck, the ache sharp against my skin. "I am your best tool for peace," I said, my tone unwavering. "Renjiro and my people will never bow to you. Lunrae's submission is no guarantee that Yuehama will follow. The hatred between our kingdoms runs too deep, especially with my uncle at its helm. And even if he did submit, you could never trust him. He is the reason I am here. If he could betray blood, what makes you think he wouldn't betray you?"

"Marrying you could jeopardize my alliance with Lunrae," he said, his voice colder now, his wings shifting faintly in agitation.

"Lunrae has already submitted. They'll continue to do so without a marriage tying them to you. And do you think Meiyuna truly wishes to be wed to a man such as you?"

"What makes you think your kingdom would serve me—accept me as their Emperor? My own people scarcely tolerate my rule. What hope do you have that yours will bow to me?"

"Because I know they will." The certainty in my tone lingered like a blade unsheathed as his gaze searched mine, looking for deceit or naivety, but I offered him neither. Only my truth.

"I will ensure it," I continued, my breath steady as if whispering a vow to the stars. "I will bend them to your will, Azariel. I will force every kingdom, every throne, to its knees for you. You want unity across the continent—an unshakable alliance. I can give you that."

Azariel's gaze darkened, the edges of his features hardening as though carved from stone. "Do you even care for me?"

"Of course I do, Az." The words escaped me so easily before I could process the reasoning behind his shift.

A hollow laugh escaped his lips, low and bitter. "Do you?" he asked, though it wasn't a question. "I scorched the flesh from someone's face, Kyo. Reduced their bones to ash, and then tried to kill the regent. That is not normal—there is something broken within me to have done that." His laugh sharpened, cutting deeper than his words that rang true. He was cunning, tactical, and what he did was anything but. "And yet, the first thing you did after all that was talk about politics." His lips curled, though his eyes betrayed nothing but cold disappointment. "I have been a fool. The reason you don't fear me is because you think you can control me. You've been using me this whole time—using my affection as a leash to drag me in any direction you wish."

"That isn't true," I said, though it felt like a lie on my tongue, guilt coiling in my chest like a serpent.

His expression cracked for a moment—hurt, raw and unguarded. It was a look I hated, one that softened him in a way I wasn't ready to face. "You've lied to me," he said quietly, though the accusation struck like a thunderclap. "Manipulated me. You used me to your advantage at every turn. And now you want to use me again. Tell me, Kyo—what is the real game here? Unity of the continent is not what you want out of this marriage. You want your throne back, and you intend to use my army to claim it. And my power to keep it."

"You make it sound as though I am the only one guilty here of playing a game," I said, my fists clenching as I fought to keep my voice calm. "You saw me as a pawn the moment you witnessed me break that sigil. Don't act as though you've been above manipulation yourself."

"And don't act as though you revealed the truth out of guilt," he said, his tone edged with quiet resentment. "You did so because you saw an opportunity. Because it was convenient."

The silence between us was a blade poised to strike, heavy and unrelenting. Finally, I let out a breath. "Then let it be mutual. We both seek survival, nothing more. That way, there will be no need to question each other's motives."

"Nothing more," he echoed, the words cutting sharper than I anticipated. He took a step back, and then another, his gaze drifting past me. "I am not the only one who learned your face for war, Prince Kyo. I suggest you remain here where it's safe, until I return."

"And where are you going?" I asked as he turned toward the terrace. My feet carried me after him, unwilling to leave the conversation unfinished.

Azariel stepped into the sunlight, the sharp scent of desert air filling the space between us. His gaze avoided mine, fixed instead on the sprawling sands stretching beyond the palace gardens. "I need space to think," he said at last, his voice quieter now, taut with restraint. "Before I do something I'll regret."

His wings spread wide, feathers unfurling to catch the golden light. They were impossibly vast, their shadows casting jagged shapes across the stone balcony. With a single motion, his muscles tensed, and he launched himself into the air. The sight struck me like a revelation—he was beautiful, fierce and untamed, like a creature finally freed of its cage.

I didn't let myself linger. The space felt emptier without him. I turned away, the unfamiliar weight of something unspoken settling over me. My hand drifted absently to my chest, the ache in it sharper than it should have been.

⸱🜚🜟🜏🜨

Ilay returned before Azariel did. I sat slouched on the divan, my head cradled in one hand as I wrestled with the weight of my thoughts. The silence of the room offered no solace, only the echo of my own rashness. Words had spilled from me like water from a shattered vessel—unrestrained, careless, and tainted with ambition. I had allowed my emotions to wield me, leaving behind the careful eloquence I prided myself on. An apology might mend what had begun to bloom between us, fragile and uncertain as it was. Yet, perhaps it was better that it withered now, before its roots could grow too deep.

"Servants of the palace talk, and the bazifirs are no exception," Ilay said as he crossed the chamber toward me, a measured calm in his voice. In his arms, he carried a neat stack of folded fabrics. "Word of what he did has already spread. He told me himself as well what had happened. His body, his mind—they are both in turmoil. He believes it has to do with the sigil—or the absence of it." His words faltered slightly as he came to stand before me, holding out the garments with both hands. My fingers brushed over the fabric, its weight and texture unmistakable. The weave was fine, the embroidery intricate—a design distinctly of northern Tairasa, of Lunrae.

"Emperor Azariel requested something more befitting your station, Your Highness," Ilay said, his head bowing slightly. "These were provided by Councilor Asahi's entourage."

I let out a quiet sigh, setting the garments aside. "Do not bow to me, Ilay, nor address me with such formalities. We are far beyond that now." Rising from the divan, I let the Duratharian pleasure-slave attire slip from my shoulders, pooling at my feet in a dark, silken heap. "So he told you everything?"

"Yes," Ilay replied, stepping aside to give me space. "The Emperor tells me all things."

"Then I assume you know of our plan." I lifted the first piece of the ensemble—a deep crimson underrobe that shimmered faintly under the light—and began to drape it over my form.

"I do." Ilay moved closer, his hands deftly assisting me with the unfamiliar fastenings.

The northern garb was elegant, refined. The underrobe clung softly to my frame, its fabric a blend of silk and linen, lightweight yet substantial. The color deepened to shades of rust along the hem, where delicate embroidery of golden thread traced curling like a vine. Over it came a sleeveless surcoat of ivory, its surface adorned with a subtle damask weave that caught the light in rippling waves. A high collar framed my neck, and its edges were trimmed in burnished copper, the same shade as the thin chain belt Ilay fastened around my waist. The fabric was faintly perfumed with Lunrae's signature sandalwood and citrus, the scent stirring memories of courtly festivities when courtiers from Yuehama would travel to Lunrae in peaceful celebrations.

"Come," Ilay murmured, extending his hand toward me. "I am to bring you discreetly. We do not know who in the court may know your face. Emperor Azariel wishes for your identity to remain concealed for now."

His words held a new calm authority, but still, I hesitated. My hand hovered above his, my brows furrowing. Trust did not come easily, not in Durathar. But I never questioned Ilay's loyalty to Azariel. Slowly, I slipped my hand into his, the warmth of his palm grounding me as we moved deeper into the chamber.

He led me toward a shadowed corner, the air thickening as we approached the wall of cool, unyielding stone. Without warning, Ilay pressed me against it, his movements swift yet deliberate. My back met the hard surface, and he stepped closer, his chest brushing against mine.

"What are you doing?" I demanded, tension coiling through me as his presence loomed nearer.

His gaze met mine, steady and unwavering. "Did I not tell you that I am of the Veil?"

"You did," I replied cautiously, searching his face for answers.

"Then trust me, Kyo." His voice was low, almost tender.

His hand repositioned with mine, his fingers intertwining with my own. The other braced against the wall beside my shoulder, caging me in, yet his proximity did not feel threatening. Around us, the shadows began to stir, moving as though they obeyed some unspoken summons.

"Close your eyes," he instructed, his voice soft but firm. "Do not open them until I tell you."

Reluctantly, I obeyed. The darkness behind my lids deepened, and then an icy chill wrapped itself around my body, seeping into my skin like winter's breath. The air seemed to warp, muting every sound until even our breathing became distant and muffled, as though we had plunged beneath still waters. My heartbeat thrummed louder in my ears, a steady reminder of life in this strange, liminal space.

Then, as swiftly as it began, it ended. The chill dissolved, and the world seemed to right itself.

"You may open them," Ilay said, his voice pulling me back to the present. He released my hand and withdrew slightly, granting me space.

I blinked, the light returning in fragments as I took in our surroundings. We now stood in the corner of an empty corridor, its silence undisturbed by the movements of guards or courtiers.

"Does Azariel know you possess this power?" I asked, my gaze locking onto his.

Ilay's lips curved into a faint, knowing smile, softening his features in a way that made him alluring and youthful. "Did you think I was kept around simply because we shared similar childhood upbringings?" His tone carried a hint of playful reproach, though his words were tinged with something heavier. "In the end, we are all pawns in someone's game—whether for power, protection, or even companionship."

The shadows around him seemed to retreat, being called back to the corners from whence they came, leaving only the man before me. With a final glance, he stepped back, the momentary closeness between us dissipating.

I realized then that the Ilay I had come to know was but a carefully crafted facade—a mask of the dutiful Bearer, loyal and unassuming. In truth, he was far more than he appeared. To Azariel, he was not merely a servant but an extension of the Emperor's will, wielding power in ways the court would have never cared to have learned or acknowledge.

"Come," he said, his voice turning pragmatic once more. "Let us move before a patrol passes and sees you."

.♯·㊎·㊐·♯

"You wish to return north with us?" Councilor Asahi's voice was steady, though his brow arched in mild incredulity. "Under the guise that Emperor Azariel journeys to Lunrae to retrieve his bride?"

"Yes," I answered, letting the weight of my words settle. My gaze shifted to Azariel and Vizier Sulqadir, silently inviting objections, though none came.

Asahi took the revelation of Azariel's rejection of the marriage proposal with a surprising grace. Relief, even. His stoic mask betrayed a flicker of ease once we explained our reasoning. The proposed alliance offered far more security for Lunrae than a forced union. Yuehama and Durathar would find peace not through conquest but through the marriage of their Emperors—a unity that would bind Lunrae to both kingdoms as an ally.

Still, the larger issue loomed heavy. Yuehama believed me dead. Renjiro sat on my throne, ruling in my stead, his grasp tightening with each passing day.

"Renjiro must have no inkling that I am alive or that my identity has been unveiled," I said, my voice firm. "For this plan to succeed, not only Yuehama but all of Tairasa must still believe that Prince Kyo Seiryu perished."

Azariel leaned back, his arms crossing over his chest in that effortless way that exuded command. "When I depart from Durathar the kingdoms must believe my absence concerns Lunrae alone," he said, his tone measured and unbothered despite the fragile tension between us.

Sulqadir's sharp gaze flicked between us as he spoke. "So that Yuehama remains unaware you intend to breach their borders?"

"Precisely," I said, my fingers trailing over the map of Tairasa splayed across the polished table. "This cannot be treated as a conventional siege. Such aggression would sow panic and deepen the resentment my people already feel toward Durathar. If this is to work, Azariel and I will travel north with only a small retinue. This must be seen not as a conquest, but as a quiet reclamation."

I studied the map beneath my hands, the rivers and borders that divided Tairasa suddenly seeming smaller, more malleable. My hand stopped at a small village nestled along a winding river that cut through the land like a serpent's trail. "We'll accompany you until here," I said, tapping a small village on the map. "From there, continue to Lunrae as if Azariel remains within your company. Meanwhile, we'll take the Tianze River northward. Its route leads directly to Yuehama's capital. By the time anyone realizes Azariel is no longer in your ranks, we will already be at the Imperial Palace."

"And your uncle?" Asahi's voice was careful, hesitant. "Are you certain you'll be able to... do what is necessary?"

I hesitated for a moment, though I already knew the answer. The truth sat heavy in my chest. "It is for the good of Tairasa," I said quietly, my gaze steady on Asahi's. "Renjiro will never bow to Durathar, nor will he agree to true peace. He betrayed me to consolidate his power, and his pride will drive Yuehama to ruin. He would send countless of our people to their deaths in a futile attempt to resist Azariel's rule."

Sulqadir's voice, sharp and cutting, broke through. "And what of your people? What will they believe when they see you return from the dead, side by side with the man who invaded their lands? Won't they assume you abandoned them?

That this is merely a ploy to deliver Yuehama into Durathar's hands?"

The question hung in the air. I faltered. It was a risk I could not deny, and one I had not yet fully accounted for.

Azariel stepped in. "That is why we marry before we set out," he said, his deep voice steady as stone. "We will do it in secret, and I will place Kyo on the throne as my equal. To the people of Yuehama, it will appear that he secured Durathar then went to Yuehama to retrieve what is rightfully his."

"This is no siege," he added, his gaze locking with mine. "It is not a takeover—it is a rightful claiming. We will prove this by leaving the armies behind, keeping our intentions veiled, and sparing as much Yuehaman blood as possible." He restated for emphasis.

"Do you intend to keep this entire plan from the Empress and the council?"

Azariel leaned forward, his forearms braced on the table as a cold smile spread across his face. "Revealing it would mean handing Kyo's identity to the most venomous vipers in my empire," he said, his tone calm but laced with menace. "No one is to know of him or this plan. Should anyone inquire about his absence, tell them I brought my *pet* along to amuse me during the journey."

His gaze hardened as it fixed on Sulqadir, the air between them thick with unspoken threat. "I trust you'll keep your lips sealed? It would be such a tragedy if your daughters woke to find their father reduced to a pile of ash upon their beds."

I nudged Azariel under the table, my irritation flaring at his cavalier cruelty. He turned to me, his expression softening into something almost boyish, as if the words he had just spoken were as harmless as a jest. "What? You are not Emperor yet. Until then, I may deal with my court as I please."

I let out a measured sigh, reigning in my temper. "Sulqadir, your discretion will not go unnoticed. Your loyalty to your Emperor will be rewarded handsomely," I said, my tone steady but firm. "The fewer complications in our absence, the smoother this plan will proceed. We cannot afford whispers in the shadows or schemes unraveling what we've set in motion."

But I knew well that the greatest threat to our plan lay not in Yuehama, but in the serpentine halls of Durathar's court. They believed Azariel's marriage to the Princess of Lunrae was already a betrayal of their pride. If they discovered the truth—that their Emperor intended to wed the man who had slain Darius, the man they believed put into motion Azariel's ascension—their retaliation would be swift and merciless.

I glanced at Azariel, his confidence radiating like the heat of a desert sun. For all his bravado, he underestimates the fury of those who are scared of him. If it came to it, I would make them kneel. I had promised Azariel they would all yield to him, and I intended to keep that promise—even if it meant matching Durathar's darkness with my own.

At that moment, as I studied the map spread across the table, I realized how far I was willing to go. For him. For this fragile, fractured alliance we were daring to build. Even if it cost me the remnants of my soul, I would ensure his throne was secure. And they would bow—to him, and to me.

Azariel rose from his seat with the air of a predator moving in for the kill, his dusky wings unfurling just enough to command the room's attention. "So, Sulqadir," he said, his gaze sharp and expectant. "Marry us."

Sulqadir blinked, startled, his furrowed brows betraying his hesitation. "Here? Now?" His voice wavered under the weight of the moment as he rose to his feet.

Azariel's gaze was steady, expectant. "You have the documents prepared already, do you not? Let us not waste another breath."

I felt his eyes shift to me, the weight of his expectation settling heavily on my shoulders. I hesitated, the thought of what we were about to do knotting in my chest.

"Don't tell me you've developed cold feet, my beloved?" he murmured, the words laced with condescension, as though daring me to falter. His hand extended toward me, steady, unwavering.

With a slow inhale, I placed my hand in his. It was colder than I remembered, as though his touch mirrored the hollow practicality of what this union represented. Marriage had never occupied my thoughts in earnest. It was always a duty, a certainty tied to the crown I once bore—a means to secure alliances, to uphold the expectations of a kingdom. But this felt... different. Abrupt. Hollow. I had never imagined it would be sealed in a dimly lit chamber with no familial witnesses and no ceremony for my kingdom to take part in. But this is what I had wanted, wasn't it? This was my idea, after all.

Azariel led me toward Sulqadir with a commanding stride. When we stopped, he released my hand without ceremony, his focus shifting fully to the vizier. Sulqadir cleared his throat, his gaze darting between us as if searching for the right words, but Azariel cut him off with a single raised hand.

"Spare us the theatrics, Sulqadir," he said with casual disdain. "We know what this is—a political arrangement, nothing more. Speeches and blessings will not alter its purpose." Without waiting for a reaction, he turned to the table where the marriage contract rested. His movements were deliberate as he picked up the quill, his signature quick and confident, marking the parchment with finality.

He passed the quill to me, his gaze lingering. I lowered my eyes to the document, scanning the words. They were standard, exactly as expected. But as I traced my name onto the parchment beside his, my hand wavered—only for a moment—before the ink set our fate in stone.

Sulqadir watched us both, his lips pressed into a thin line. At last, he spoke, his tone formal despite the lack of grandeur. "By the will of the Spirits and the laws of Durathar, I declare you husband and... husband. Emperor and Emperor of Durathar."

Before I could even process the words, Azariel turned back to me, a flicker of mischief glinting in his eyes. "I believe this is the part where we are supposed to kiss," he said, his hand lifting to cup my cheek.

I opened my mouth to respond, but he gave me no chance. His lips met mine, cold and precise, devoid of tenderness or warmth. It left a hollowness in my chest, a reminder of all this union was and was not, and what it could have been.

When he pulled away, his voice was low, meant only for me. "You've taken my throne," he whispered, his breath brushing against my lips. "Now let us go take yours."

CHAPTER FIFTEEN

For two days, I had been confined to the Emperor's wing of the palace, an opulent cage gilded with secrecy. Azariel had dismissed the guards and servants, forbidding them entry lest my face be seen and whispers ripple through the court. Only Ilay and Gamal were permitted access. The latter, once champion, had been elevated to my personal guard.

When I revealed my identity and intentions to Gamal, his response was a sigh, heavy as stone. Yet that sigh had carried with it an unexpected loyalty. He accepted my request to join our small, clandestine group bound for Yuehama. "Group," however, felt an exaggeration. Beyond myself, there was only Azariel, Ilay, and Gamal. Azariel's paranoia would allow for no more.

"Do we truly need anyone else when we have me?" he had said with a smackable condescending grin.

I sank beneath the waters of the royal bath, letting the stillness press against me as I hovered above the stone floor of the basin. For the first time in days, I had been granted true solitude—or at least as much as could be allowed with Gamal stationed just beyond the chamber doors. The water cradled me, muffling the distant world, before I surfaced, leaning back against the smooth edge of the pool. Above, sunlight poured through the open roof, giving the surface a soft glow.

I raised my fingers, and the water answered. It spiraled upward, thin and jagged like blades. With a flick of my wrist, the liquid daggers shot skyward, slicing through the light before gravity reclaimed them, sending droplets scattering like rain back into the pool.

"Is this your idea of training for the coup?" Azariel's voice shattered the stillness, smooth yet edged with bemusement. "You should practice with something that can move—or better yet, fight back."

I didn't turn to him, my wrist already flicking in his direction. A wave of water surged from the pool, drenching him from head to waist.

"Apologies," I said dryly, my tone feigning innocence. "I was startled... You shouldn't sneak up on those bathing."

He shook his head, droplets clinging to his light hair as a lazy smile tugged at his lips. With one fluid motion, he peeled his soaked shirt over his head, tossing it aside.

"When was the last time you used your magic against an opponent?" he asked, his wings flexing once before dissolving into nothingness.

"Not since Yuehama," I muttered, watching the ripples in the water instead of him. "And I don't plan to start with you."

"Then you're content to be the weakest among us? Your inexperience will be a liability," he said, his tone calm, though the taunt within it was unmistakable. "Or is it that you fear I could still best you in your own element, *Aqaynah*?"

I groaned, rolling my eyes. "The bazifir better not be summoned when I drown you, then."

His grin widened, a predator sensing victory. "You wouldn't drown your husband, would you?" he teased, shedding the rest of his clothing before stepping into the pool.

"I'm not sure what you hope to accomplish with this." I asked, already regretting the inevitable.

"Simply offering you something to challenge your waters," he replied, his tone calm yet laced with an edge of provocation. He moved closer, the pool rippling in his wake, the waters yielding effortlessly to his broad frame. He stopped in front of me, his dark eyes gleaming with challenge.

"Imagine, for a moment, someone was foolish enough to strike at you like this," Azariel murmured, his hand snaking to the side of my neck, his thumb brushing lightly over the hollow of my throat. Beneath the water, my fingers tensed, the currents already stirring at my command, curling unseen around his legs.

"What would you do?" His fingers slid to the back of my neck, tightening their hold. It wasn't painful—yet. His gaze lingered on my lips. He leaned in closer, and before he could press further, the waters obeyed me, surging upward to drag him to his knees.

His grip tightened, unrelenting, and he pulled me down with him. Water surged around us, my lungs burning as the sudden submersion stole my breath. I exhaled sharply, forcing the water from my lungs with practiced ease, but his hold didn't falter.

Azariel's hand shifted up, fingers tangling in my hair, anchoring me beneath the surface. His strength was unyielding, his grip firm. Fury flared within me, and I willed the waters to coil tighter around him, dragging him down, holding him flush against the basin floor. My fingers clawed at his, desperate for freedom, desperate for air.

He should've been struggling. I could feel his body straining for oxygen, and yet, his expression was maddeningly smug. His smile dared me to push further. What did he truly hope to gain from this? My chest burned with the ache of withheld breath, my pulse pounding in my ears.

And then his free arm broke the water's grasp, wrapping around my waist and pulling me against him. Heat radiated from his skin, searing and unnatural, the golden fractures along his body pulsing with an intense light. My skin flared with pain where it touched his, as though pressed against molten metal.

I tried to pull away, to twist free, but his strength outmatched mine. The water was my ally, but his defiance bent even that to his will. This wasn't a fight—it was a contest, a test to see who would succumb first. Who would drown in the depths of their own resolve.

With a surge of desperation, I reached for the surface. The water obeyed me, folding over itself to carry a pocket of air to my lips. It encased my mouth and nose, and I inhaled deeply, savoring the triumph. I turned my gaze to him, smirking through my exhaustion.

But his eyes blazed with something darker, something untamed. The water began to seethe, the heat rising to an unbearable degree. My smirk faded as my skin now burned where he touched me, the temperature rising as if he meant to boil us alive.

"Azariel, stop!" My words were useless here, drowned in the silent depths.

The searing heat intensified, pain lancing through my body where his golden-fractured flesh pressed against mine. I could endure no more. Releasing my hold on the water, I let him go. In turn, his grip loosened, and I surged upward, breaking the surface before I scrambled for the pool's edge.

The room was stifling, the air thick with steam. My skin, reddened and raw, throbbed as I tried to steady myself.

Seconds later, Azariel surfaced with a gasping breath.

"Are you insane?" I shouted, my voice trembling with fury as I sat on the pool's edge, water streaming from my skin. "You could have killed us both!"

He said nothing at first, his expression unreadable as the steam curled around him. And then, with maddening calm, his lips curved into that infuriating smile once more. "I could have, but I didn't. We both still breathe, do we not?" His voice was calm, almost amused, as if the near-death moment had been nothing more than a game. "You would have killed me before that happened anyway—I saw it in your eyes. Besides, I could tell you enjoyed it... don't deny it."

He wasn't wrong. A part of me had enjoyed it. There was a dark, heady thrill in knowing his life had been in my hands, the waters obeying my command with an almost sentient ferocity. Even when the tides shifted, and I felt the control slipping through my fingers, a dangerous rush still coursed through me. But with anyone else, would I have felt the same? I doubted it. There was something about Azariel that made chaos feel... intoxicating.

He closed the distance between us, water cascading from his skin as he stepped between my legs as they hung limply over the basin's edge. His hands found my thighs, fingers pressing with a weight that felt more possessive than steadying. "We're not done," he said, his voice low, his stoney gaze pinning me in place. "Neither of us won."

I exhaled, the tension in my body refusing to ease. "I don't think either of us will ever win against the other," I said.

"You could have won," he countered, his tone devoid of its usual edge. His thumbs traced small, deliberate circles on my thighs, a gesture both calming and tantalizing. "I knew you wouldn't let yourself die. Not like that."

"You confuse me," I admitted with a sigh, the words spilling out before I could stop them. Ever since our union and my reveal nights ago he had barely spoken to me. He avoided me as though I were a shadow cast too long in the sun, relying on Ilay to act as the buffer between us. And yet here he was now, acting as if nothing had happened, as if we were still Kaito and Azariel, locked in a volatile rhythm that neither of us dared break. "I thought you were angry with me."

His lips twitched, not quite a smile. "You mean because you lied and manipulated me?" He tilted his head, snowy hair plastered against his forehead, a faint gleam of amusement in his eyes. "I was angry. But now, I'm not."

He leaned forward, the heat of his body radiating against mine, his forehead coming to rest against my abdomen. "We now know what this is and isn't. Besides... I know that you're smart enough not to betray me again. " he murmured. "You need me. My people will never bow to the Kamishen who killed their Darius—not without my command. And how else will you reclaim your throne, free your people from Durathar, without me to make them kneel?" he said, his tone unnervingly calm, though it didn't mask the undercurrent of a threat wounding itself through his words.

"I am the only shield you have against the snakes that circle, waiting to strike at your heels."

My hand slipped down, cupping his jaw, guiding his face so his gaze met mine. "And you," I said, my voice low, steady, "don't forget that you need me too. Without my influence over the Kamishen, you would watch this kingdom—and this entire continent—crumble to dust beneath you. The destructive course your kin started cannot end without me."

His smile came soft, almost disarmingly so, but I knew better than to trust it. "I didn't marry you because I couldn't see your purpose," he said, as if his words were meant to soothe rather than bind. "We need each other. We have from the moment our paths first crossed."

Indeed, we did.

My gaze lingered on Azariel's eyes, those celestial betrayers of his bloodline. Whether Kamishen, Tenishen, or Nisshen—moon, stars, or sun—our heritage always revealed itself in the gaze. Azariel, half-breed that he was, bore no exception. His irises were dark as obsidian, like the stone of a mountain, but the pupils, they gleamed like fragments of the heavens themselves, scattering their brilliance in defiance of his mortal frame. Threads of gold wove through the gray, glinting like constellations against the night sky, as though the cosmos had marked him as its own.

I pushed the damp strands of his hair back from his face, my fingertips brushing against the curve of his jaw. His beauty was striking, undeniable—a kind that made you stop, made you look twice. He liked to think those who threw themselves at his feet did so out of fear, for the advantage of mercy through favor or even the chance to bear an heir for the crown. Perhaps some did. But surely not all. How could they ignore the commanding masculinity etched into his features, the strength that spoke of Zurathi blood, a heritage of warriors? Yet the Tenishen in him softened that edge, adding an ethereal allure, a beauty not meant for mortal comprehension. A beauty meant to unmake.

"Hm," I murmured, my voice dipping into something softer, a subtle playfulness threading its way through my tone.

"I wonder why anyone fears you. So soft, so pretty—like the petal of a flower." My thumb traced over the fullness of his lower lip, its velvet texture an echo of the words I spoke.

His lids lowered, his expression tinged with exasperation. "A flower petal?" he repeated, voice heavy with skepticism.

"A shame," I mused, pressing my thumb just slightly further, testing the line between teasing and indulgence. "A shame that such softness is wasted on a tongue so sharp, so venomous. You spit poison, Azariel, where there should be honey." A faint warmth bloomed across his cheeks, a quiet confession that my patronizing words had found their mark.

The wet heat of his lips met my touch, his tongue flicking against the pad of my thumb with an absent defiance. My mind wandered, drawn unbidden to memory—this room, this very closeness. The way his mouth had claimed me, warmth pulling me under like a tide, the strain of his throat wrapping around me as if it, too, had been carved by divine design. A man so beautiful, yet so infuriating. A paradox I could never seem to resist.

My body betrayed me, my cock hardening as it pressed against the hard planes of his chest. Azariel's gaze dropped, the corners of his mouth curving in that infuriatingly knowing way of his. "Shall I remind you just how sharp my tongue can be?" he murmured, his voice smooth and deliberate.

Before I could offer a reply, his hand found its mark, wrapping around the center of my length with a hunger that sent fire streaking through my veins. His movements were unhurried, deliberate, as though savoring the anticipation he knew he was building. I watched, helpless and enthralled, as he lowered his head, the tip of his tongue tracing a slow, maddening line along the underside of my sack, trailing upward until it reached the base of my shaft.

His lips lowered and pressed against me, soft yet insistent, before one testicle disappeared into the heat of his mouth. The sensation was a maddening dance between discomfort and pleasure, the tug of his lips and the lap of his tongue igniting every nerve. A wet sound broke the spell as he released me, and I blinked, startled back into the present, my breaths shallow and uneven.

"Wait," I rasped, the word barely escaping through the haze. "What if Gamal walks in?"

Azariel's stone eyes flicked up to meet mine, glittering with amusement and defiance. "Are you really thinking of other men right now?" His tongue darted out again, dragging along the length of me, teasing a shiver from my body.

"Az," I growled, slipping my fingers into the thick, silken strands of his hair, forcing his gaze upward. "I'm serious."

He tilted his head slightly, the smirk still dancing on his lips even as my grip tightened. "I dismissed him the moment I arrived," he murmured, his voice low. And then he pulled against my hold, his mouth enveloping me with a heat that scattered my thoughts like leaves in the wind.

A groan tore from me, unbidden, as I leaned back against the cool stone beneath me, my free hand bracing against its rough surface. My head tipped back, surrendering to the unbearable bliss of his touch. For all his cruelty, his sharpness, Azariel had a way of turning pleasure into something almost sacred—something I could neither resist nor deny.

The moment I released his hair, my fingers drifted over the sculpted planes of his face, tracing the hollows of his cheeks. The sensation of him taking me so deeply into his mouth was a sin in itself, obscene and depraved, yet it fanned the flames of my desire, leaving me aching for more. Every shift of his lips, every press of his tongue, threatened to unravel me entirely.

He slowed, allowing my length to slip free with a soft, wet sound that felt almost cruel in its loss. His voice, low and teasing, curled around me like smoke. "Would you be open to exploring more?" His tongue flicked out, tracing the sensitive slit at the head of my cock. "I promise I'll be gentle. And I can assure you, it will feel even better than this."

Better than this? I couldn't fathom it. My breath stuttered, but my lips managed to form a single word: "Okay."

His hand slid beneath me, his touch firm but unhurried as he cupped the curve of my hip, fingers slipping beneath to tease the sensitive skin of my ass. Then came the press of his fingertip, light and tentative, against the entrance of my body.

"Wait," I rasped, my voice catching on the edge of uncertainty.

"Trust me," he murmured, his words soft and unhurried, like the first sip of a heady wine. "If it doesn't feel good, I'll stop." And with that, his mouth returned, enveloping me once more in a warmth that dulled the edges of my hesitation.

The teasing circles of his finger grew bolder, each movement coaxing my body to yield. Slowly, gently, he pressed inward, the sensation unfamiliar but not unwelcome. My breath hitched, a gasp breaking free as his finger found something deep within—a spot that sent ripples of pleasure radiating through my core. Heat pooled low in my stomach, heavy and urgent, the ache of my arousal nearly unbearable.

"You're doing so well, Kyo..." he murmured, his voice a silk thread binding me tighter to the moment. His finger curled inside me, pressing in with a rhythm that drew a sound from my throat I hadn't realized I was capable of making. My toes curled in the water, my body taut and trembling as his words washed over me.

A second finger joined the first, stretching, exploring, filling me with an intensity that bordered on too much yet left me craving more. I bit down on my hand, desperate to muffle the moan that spilled from my lips. The tension coiled tighter, a storm building within me, until it reached its crescendo.

My body seized as the release struck, a blinding wave that left me gasping and undone. I barely registered the absence of his mouth, the way he had pulled back to let me shatter under the pressure of his fingers alone. The evidence of my pleasure painted his hand, a few errant streaks marking the expanse of his chest.

He withdrew his fingers slowly, his touch lingering as though savoring the final echoes of my surrender. A low chuckle rumbled from him, dark and satisfied. "Told you it would feel good," he said, his tone rich with amusement and something deeper—something that sent a fresh wave of heat racing through me, even as I struggled to catch my breath.

"You speak too much," I murmured sheepishly, the words slipping past my lips before I could temper them. The heat that bloomed across my cheeks crept unbidden to the tips of my ears, betraying the effect he had on me. I averted my gaze, letting it trail down his body to the water lapping against his waist. There, beneath the rippling surface, was the unmistakable evidence of his lust, hard and thick.

The water shifted as I moved, sinking lower into its embrace, the warmth rising to meet me as he stepped back, granting me space. My hand reached out, tentative yet yearning, the weight of my own boldness heavy in the air between us. "Let me help you with that," I whispered, my fingers hovering just above the hardness of his cock.

Before I could close the distance, his hand caught my wrist, gentle yet firm, the restraint unexpected. His dark eyes softened as they met mine, and he lifted my hand with reverence, pressing a kiss to its palm as if sealing an unspoken promise. "Right now, the only thing I desire is something I have not yet earned," he said, his voice low and steady, each word a tether that kept me anchored to him. He guided my hand to his cheek, holding it there as he leaned into the touch, his warmth seeping into my skin. "So let us focus only on cleaning up."

It was moments like this that unraveled me, that set my heart fluttering with a cadence unfamiliar and terrifying. These fleeting moments when his smile feels genuine and unguarded, unburdened by need to cause fear or pain. When the cracks in his carefully crafted mask reveal something softer beneath. These moments struck me in ways I had never known, leaving me wanting more. *Wanting him.*

·ᛮ·ᛯᛰᛱ

The walk back to Azariel's chambers was silent, the only sound was the soft padding of our boots against the stone floors. Yet, as we turned the final corner, his steps faltered—a brief hesitation, almost imperceptible, but enough for me to nearly collide with his back. My brows knitted as I stepped beside him, following the line of his gaze. Two bazifirs stood stationed outside his door.

This wing of the palace was meant to be empty, the guards dismissed by Azariel's own command. Something was amiss. These men were not outfitted as the palace Bazifir usually were. Gone were the spears and shields, the polished helms that gleamed like sunlight on steel. Instead, they bore swords at their sides, and the absence of their full palace attire spoke of questionable intent.

The air shifted—a taut string pulled too tight—and then Azariel moved. A blur of white consumed my vision as his wings erupted, vast and swift. Feathers scattered in his wake, spiraling through the air as he lunged forward. His hand struck the left Bazifir's throat with unrelenting precision, fingers tightening as he drove the man back against the heavy wooden door. The impact resonated, low and violent, the breath ripped from the man's chest before he could muster a sound.

I turned, my gaze snapping to the second guard. His hand had already dropped to the hilt of his blade, and there was no time to think, only act. My eyes caught the stray feathers as they drifted lazily toward the floor, glinting faintly in the torchlight. My hand lifted instinctively, commanding them to still midair before thrusting forward. They obeyed my will, flying swift and deadly, their quills striking true. The feathers pierced his throat with a wet, sickening sound. He staggered, his hands clawing uselessly at the wounds, blood spilling in dark rivulets between his fingers. His body crumpled slowly against the door, the life draining from him even as he tried to cling to it.

The acrid stench of burning flesh filled the air, sharp and unrelenting. My gaze flicked back to Azariel, just as the head of the first Bazifir hit the ground with a heavy thud, the neck seared clean through, molten and raw. The body slumped shortly after, crumpling at Azariel's feet like a discarded puppet, its strings cut.

The corridor fell silent once more, save for the crackling embers of Azariel's magic as it dissipated into the air. The faint glow still danced along his fingertips, his wings trembling softly as he slowly folded them back. His face was unreadable, but his silence spoke volumes. This was no mere breach of protocol. This was something far darker, and whoever had sent these men would soon learn the cost of crossing their Emperor.

I forced my breath to steady, though the smell of iron and ash lingered in my nose. "Who do you think.." My voice faltered as Azariel's posture shifted, his shoulders rolling back with an air of defiance, his chin lifting as his gaze fixed intently behind me.

I turned, following his line of sight. Two more bazifirs advanced down the corridor, their curved swords already raised for blood.

Azariel strode forward before I could speak again, the grin curling his lips a cruel, feral thing. He wiped the remnants of the first bazifir's essence from his hand onto his trousers, each movement deliberate and taunting. In a flash, twin daggers of searing light materialized in his grasp, their edges shimmering with celestial brilliance. He stalked toward the intruders like a shadow made flesh, a predator toying with his prey.

"Keep one alive for—" My words dissolved into the air, drowned by the swift brutality of his actions. Azariel moved like water in a storm, fluid and merciless. His blade arced, severing the hand of the first Bazifir with a sickening thud before his second dagger tore through the tender flesh of the man's neck, severing it cleanly.

"For questioning.." I finished with a sigh, the futility of my request sinking in. I stretched out my hand, willing the discarded sword of the fallen Bazifir to fly to my palm and moved to Azariel's side, intent on salvaging some sense of control from the chaos he was so clearly reveling in.

The second Bazifir's life cut short as Azariel's blades plunged into his eyes, the hiss of burning flesh sharp against the screams that followed. He drove the blade upward in a swift, brutal arc, its edge piercing the Zurathi's neck with merciless precision. A savage twist followed, and as he wrenched the blade free, a torrent of blood erupted, painting the air in a dark, vivid spray.

"Did you not hear me?" I snapped, my voice sharp with frustration. "How are we supposed to know who sent them if you keep silencing them before we can question them?"

Azariel's laugh was low, mocking, his daggers dissolving into nothingness. "You think this ends with these four?" His gaze swept the corridor, his tone laced with derision. "Trust me, there's more."

"There's another over here," Ilay's calm voice cut through the corridor. His silhouette emerged from the far end of the hall, half-turned toward us, his outstretched hand a silent command to halt to whatever lay down that way.

We followed his gaze, rounding the corner to find another bazifir frozen in place. His body trembled with restrained effort, tension rippling through every taut muscle as though battling unseen chains. His feet remained rooted, bound by unknown forces.

"Tell your Emperor whose orders you are obeying," Ilay demanded, his voice smooth and cold, devoid of emotion.

The Bazifir bared his teeth, venom lacing his words. "I do not answer to half-breeds."

"I cannot hold him for much longer, Your Majesty," Ilay murmured, his voice calm but weighted with strain as he glanced over his shoulder at Azariel. His outstretched hand shifted, an almost imperceptible flick of his wrist before the Bazifir was brought to his knees. It was then I noticed the distortion, contortion of shadow at the Bazifir's feet. Beside his loomed another—a monstrous silhouette, vaguely humanoid yet undeniably other, its clawed grip anchoring his shadow in place—keeping him in place.

This was Ilay's gift from the Veil. A mastery over the darkness that writhed and obeyed his will, twisting reality and binding the unwilling. The Bazifir trembled, his body rigid with defiance, yet unable to break free from the spectral beast that held him captive.

"Who is your master?" Azariel's voice cut through the heavy air, low and sharp, as he stepped forward. His hand closed around the Bazifir's throat with effortless precision, his grip a vice that demanded submission.

The Bazifir's only response was a defiant spit, the wet stain glistening against Azariel's cheek.

Azariel's expression didn't shift, but a dangerous calm settled over him. "Does your small mind keep you from grasping the fear necessary to beg for your life? Fool. I trust defying me was worth it."

To my surprise, he released the Bazifir, his hand falling away as though granting mercy. The mercy was short-lived. A grotesque crack split the air as the Bazifir's body twisted unnaturally, his neck snapped clean, leaving his lifeless form to crumple to the ground. The shadows that had restrained him dissipated, their tendrils uncoiling like a smoke dispersing in the wind.

Ilay's voice broke the silence, measured yet carrying a faint edge of caution. "After the display you made before the councilors, only a fool would act alone in defiance. It is safe to assume this attack was backed by another—or many."

Azariel tilted his head, a faint frown ghosting his lips. "It was Soraya," he murmured, the words spoken so softly it could have been mistaken for a breath. But Ilay and I heard it, our ears attuned to every word he uttered.

Without waiting for a response, Azariel turned on his heel, his pace deliberate as he began to stride down the corridor. Ilay and I exchanged a glance before quickening our steps to fall in line.

"Azariel, wait!" I called out, the urgency in my voice echoing off the walls. "You cannot kill the regent. Not yet, at least."

"She is no longer regent," he replied coldly, without breaking stride. "My union with you stripped her of that title."

"But the court does not yet know this," I countered.

Azariel's jaw tightened, but he didn't argue. Instead, he glanced at Ilay. "Gather the council. Bring them to the throne room."

Ilay came to an abrupt halt, bowing deeply. "As you command, Your Highness."

And with that, the shadows at Ilay's feet coiled and surged upward, consuming him entirely. When they receded, he was gone, leaving no trace but the faint chill of his departure.

Azariel's footsteps slowed and he turned, his golden stoney eyes locking onto mine. "You'll stay with Gamal," he said, his tone measured with authority.

I bristled, my fists fingers tightening around the hilt of the sword. "And if there are more waiting to attack you? What then?"

His gaze sharpened, a flicker of irritation flashing across his features. "Do you think I am incapable of defending myself?"

"And do you think *I am* incapable of the same?" I countered, my voice hardening. "I do not need a personal guard, Azariel."

A faint, almost weary smile tugged at his lips as he stepped closer. His hand rose, his fingers brushing against the stray locks that had fallen across my forehead. "I know that... But your face," he murmured, the words softer now, "needs to remain unseen. This is not about you, Kyo. This is about Lunrae." His voice dipped lower, weighted with frustration and something deeper I couldn't quite place. "I expected backlash. I'd even prepared for it—though I thought it would come sooner. Not on the eve of our departure."

He stepped back then. With a firm rap of his knuckles against the door behind him, Gamal appeared, his expression startled before it shifted into a formal bow. Azariel didn't hesitate. "A coup is being attempted," he said. "Ensure my husband stays here until I return for him."

Without another word, he continued on his path, his figure vanishing down the corridor, his movements precise, unrelenting.

CHAPTER SIXTEEN

AZARIEL

Either my subjects were craftier than I gave them credit for, or they believed themselves clever enough to catch me unaware. The corridors whispered their betrayal in silence, a vast emptiness stretching through the halls where servants and bazifirs once patrolled. Not even the faintest shuffle of sandals on stone. *"There is no true loyalty in this den. Only fear will keep them at bay,"* my father once said. Fear could leash even the wildest hounds, and when fear faltered, gold and power could always replace it.

My steps slowed as I approached Soraya's chamber doors. The air thickened, as if the walls themselves had secrets to keep. Where were her guards?

Surely, she could not think me so feeble. No Duratharian Emperor had ever fallen to the hands of commoners wielding daggers in the dark. And if Soraya thought herself capable of breaking that cycle, she was a greater fool than I imagined

"Soraya," I purred, my voice a silken thread woven with mockery, as I pushed the heavy doors wide. The chamber lay barren, the lingering scent of roses unable to mask her cowardice.

How tedious. A good day soured by these petty machinations. I felt my lips curve into a smile, unbidden, as my thoughts drifted to Kyo. Unpredictable, sharp-tongued Kyo. This union, unorthodox as it was, suited me far better than binding myself to some Duratharian noble whose sole ambition was to use me as a stud for heirs. Kyo was entertaining, fiery—a necessary distraction in a life often dulled by blood and duty.

"Don't squander your time on petty emotions—they are distractions you cannot afford," my father's voice echoed in my mind. *"Killing, conquering, and trampling others to stay atop the throne—that is what brings true elation."*

But surely, distractions couldn't be entirely worthless. What was the point of striving for dominance if there was nothing beyond it—no respite to look forward to? Yet, even as the thought lingered, I knew my father would call such musings weakness. Distractions had their moments, their places. However, this was not one of them.

The throne room loomed ahead, its gilded doors ajar as if inviting me to witness the insult. I pushed them open with ease, the air within brimming with the static of defiance. Rows of bazifirs lined the hall, their shoulders rigid, their eyes fixed forward—not on me, but on her. Soraya, seated upon the single throne. The emperor's throne. My throne. The smaller seat, once hers, was gone, stripped from the dais as if it had never belonged. A calculated move, this removal of her place beside me—a brazen declaration that the seat of power belonged to her alone.

My laughter broke the stillness, dark and low, as I strolled down the center of the hall, the heels of my boots echoing on the marble. The bazifirs did not flinch, not a single gaze shifted in acknowledgment of my presence. Their loyalty was written in the direction of their stares: unwavering, obedient—to her.

"Is this your way of invoking Shahmizan?" I called out, my voice smooth, laced with amusement. "There's no need for such theatrics, Soraya. If you wanted to challenge me, you had only to ask."

I stopped before the dais, tilting my head as I regarded her. Soraya was clad in fitted leathers, her form encased in a bodice reinforced with gleaming metal. Intricate etchings adorned the armor, a testament to both artistry and strength, while the crown upon her head—regal and evocative of her station—lent an air of grace to her otherwise battle-hardened attire. Her expression was calm, maddeningly so, though I caught the faintest flicker of disdain in her eyes—a spark she could never entirely conceal. I should have killed her the moment Darius fell in Yuehama.

Darius.

The name tasted bitter now, like unripe fruit on my tongue. The only tether that had held me back from snuffing out her ambitions had been him. My brother, her shield, and, in many ways, her pawn. He had always kept us apart, as if he knew that one more of her barbs would be the one to break me. Darius was always cordial, though I often wondered why. Was it the bond of brotherhood, a flicker of genuine respect between us? Or was it fear—that deep down, he knew I could surpass him, strip the crown from his head, if I ever willed it?

Not that I ever wanted the throne. To claim otherwise would be a lie, but so too would contentment with being cast into the shadows, relegated to the arena—punisher and executioner like a forgotten afterthought. Darius was molded for the throne, that much was true. But he wasn't molded for himself. He was shaped by Soraya's cunning, Rohan's ambition—a figurehead guided by their hands, too blind to see the cracks in his kingdom, too short-sighted to see the storm brewing just beyond the horizon. Unlike me. I saw it all.

My lips quirked into a grin. "I think I've indulged your defiance long enough. If you want the throne, why don't you take it from me?" My voice dipped lower, almost a growl, the weight of the challenge filling the air between us. "That is our way, isn't it? Or are you too afraid to face me?"

Even as I spoke, a part of me hesitated. Darius' shadow lingered, his memory a nagging echo in the chambers of my mind. And then there was Kyo, his words from the other night softening the edges of my rage. *"Do not descend to their level. You are more cunning than that."* But my bloodlust simmered beneath it all, coiled and waiting, daring her to make the fatal mistake. Let her invoke Shahmizan, let her meet me blade to blade. It would be justice—for my mother, for the years of her venomous manipulations, for the quiet sacrifices I had made to survive in a world that would sooner see me dead.

Soraya's lips curved into a thin smile, and she leaned back against the throne, as if she belonged there. The scarring from the burn on her cheek didn't take from the haughtiness of her demeanor. "Duratharian men and their endless itch for Shahmizan," she said, her tone dripping with a mixture of annoyance and condescension. "There are other ways to dethrone an emperor, Azariel. Not everything has to be resolved with blood."

But blood, I thought as my fists clenched at my sides, *was the only language power truly understood.*

"Your people no longer wish to follow you," she said, her voice venomous and unshaking, a serpent poised to strike. "An emperor without a kingdom. What will you do? Slaughter us all? Replace Durathar's numbers with the Kamishen of Lunrae? Their feeble mage blood would paint an even larger target on our backs. No. We must purge the weak links... starting with *you.*"

A chuckle escaped me, low and sharp, before it spilled into laughter that echoed through the chamber. "You think so little of me," I said, wiping a nonexistent tear from my eye. "Do you truly believe that when I've reduced every Zurathi in this room—including you—to ash, the rest won't kneel? Men are driven by survival, Soraya. Only fools let their pride outweigh their fear."

I stepped closer, my hand resting on the shoulder of one of the bazifirs stationed near her. His jaw tightened, but he did not flinch as I leaned in. I didn't spare him a glance as I whispered, my eyes locked on hers, "If you value your life, do not move." My light stirred beneath my skin, warm and patient at first, before blooming into a blistering heat that flowed into my palm. The pauldrons of his armor began to soften and warp, the metal hissing as it gave way to my will.

The room grew heavy with the scent of scorched leather and flesh, and yet, to his credit, the man remained still, his body trembling but rooted in place. When I released him, the imprint of my hand glowed angrily against his charred skin. I straightened, offering him the faintest curve of my lips. "Good boy."

The other bazifirs shifted uneasily, their gazes darting to me in fleeting, fearful glances before returning to her. Their silence was telling, their fear palpable. I turned back to Soraya, the smile still tugging at the edges of my lips. "You see? Survival is a great motivator."

Her eyes narrowed, her expression a mask of contempt. "You fancy yourself a god among men because of your gifts," she spat, rising from the throne with deliberate grace. "But even gods fall, halfbreed. And so will you." She raised her chin, her voice ringing out with the authority of centuries of tradition. "I invoke the rite of Shahmizan."

My smile widened, slow and deliberate, like a predator baring its fangs. "Excellent," I purred, the word curling off my tongue. This was a game I intended to win.

The bazifirs retreated in tense unison, forming a disciplined ring around the dais where the throne loomed above us—a silent witness to this spectacle.

"Weapons or no weapons?" I asked, my voice calm, but my fingers itching for carnage.

"I need no weapon," she replied, her tone sharp, resolute. "Only the blessing of the Wilds."

Ah, of course. Always the Wilds, with their whispers of untamed power. Power that was seldomly called upon by myself, despite their blood flowing freely within me. My father would have called it stubbornness, a defiance of the very essence that ran through my veins. And he was right. And so, this battle would unfold as Celestial gifts against the raw, untamed force of the Wilds.

She began to chant an old Durathian hymn, her voice low and reverent, invoking the ox spirit, Ghaddar. The ancient cadence curled through the air. Her body began to shift, expanding, the leather of her fitted armor groaning under the strain as her frame grew. Strength rippled through her limbs, her muscles swelling with the unyielding tenacity of the beast she called upon. It was an impressive display, certainly, but power without precision had never frightened me.

She charged, a blur of unrefined force, and I let my wings unfurl. The rush of air as I took to the side was like a whisper of silk, her momentum sending her hurtling past me. Too slow. Too reckless.

"You'll have to do better than that, Soraya," I drawled, landing lightly on my feet. My hands glowed with a soft, golden light as I summoned my own gifts. It coalesced into claws of pure radiance, sharp and burning, wreathing my fists in an elegant ferocity.

She snarled and came at me again, her movements a fraction faster now, but still clumsy compared to my own precision. I darted around her, the claws slashing through the leather at her shoulder, searing into her skin. She let out a growl of pain but swung an arm toward me, and I narrowly dodged the massive blow.

When her fist connected with my ribs moments later, however, I heard the sickening crack before I felt the pain. The force of the impact sent me sprawling, my breath torn from my lungs in a single, humiliating moment. She was strong—brutally so—but her movements still lacked finesse, her strikes telegraphed by her bulk. I wouldn't give her the satisfaction of slowing down.

I was on my feet again in an instant, my ribs screaming but my pride refusing to waver. My light lashed out in sharp bursts, the claws finding her flesh again and again. Burns scored across her arms and thighs, though she seemed to absorb the pain like a stone against a storm. I should cease this game and finish her now.

My gaze fell upon a group gathered just outside the threshold of the throne room. Ilay stood at the forefront, his arm outstretched in command, halting the council I had ordered him to assemble. No one was permitted to interfere, not even the council. Shahmizan was a sacred rite—an ordeal between only two: the emperor and his challenger. Nothing more, nothing less. I felt a flicker of irritation stir within me as I saw the look of concern wash over Ilay's gaze.

Soraya began to chant once more, her voice lower now, more guttural, invoking another spirit. I felt the shift before I saw it: the air thickened with power, and a translucent sheen spread across her form. Crystals sprouted over her body like a second skin, clear as glass but as strong as steel. The spirit of the crystal beetle, Sufra Kankarah.

I rushed her, striking at the armor with my claws, but the light that had burned her moments before now seemed to skitter off its surface, leaving no mark. She laughed, a low, mocking sound, and surged forward again. "What's the point of fire if it cannot scorch? You're nothing Azariel if you cannot turn your flames upon your enemy."

Her fist connected with my side, and it felt like being struck by a boulder. Another blow sent me to my knees, my breath wheezing through gritted teeth. I lashed out again, my claws meeting the crystalline shell, only for pain to erupt in my knuckles as they cracked against the impenetrable surface.

She seized me by the neck, her grip unyielding as she lifted me like a doll. Her strikes came one after another, each one a hammer driving into my ribs, my shoulders, my stomach. Stars exploded in my vision, the air torn from my lungs with every impact.

I summoned my light once more, channeling it into the palms of my hands, directing the searing energy to her wrist and forearm, desperate to burn through the crystal shell and free myself from her grasp. But the light flickered impotently against the armor. She was unyielding, her crystalline fist crashing into me with the weight of a landslide.

For the first time since childhood, I felt the sharp bite of something—fear, a tremor for my own mortality. The tide had shifted, and Soraya's ambition loomed over me, unstoppable, as relentless as the Wilds she had invoked.

Her fist collided with my ribs once more, the sickening crack reverberating pulled me out of my thoughts. Those crystalline fingers tightened around my throat, deliberate and cruel. She was making a spectacle of me, a display of dominance for the court—a stage I understood all too well. If our positions were reversed, I'd have done the same.

"Stop!" A voice cut through the thunder in my ears, sharp and desperate. My gaze shifted, blurred and unsteady, to the threshold of the chamber. Kyo stood there, defiant as ever, with Gamal lingering just behind him. *Fool.* I had told him to stay put, but of course, he hadn't listened. That rebellious streak was both his flaw and his fire.

I summoned my light again, forcing it into my hands, desperate to melt through the crystalline shell that shielded her. But it was too slow. Her grip was unrelenting, her strength monstrous.

"The Shahmizan does not end until one breathes no more," she hissed, her voice curling with venom as her free hand grasped one of my wings. She pulled, and the agonizing tear of flesh filled the air, my own growl escaping before I could cage it. Golden blood sprayed like molten sunlight, staining the ground as she discarded my torn wing with a casual cruelty.

"Watch," she spat, her voice dripping with triumph, "as I clip the little bird's wings and end his pitiful existence—just as his whore of a mother met hers."

Amalthea was my father's undoing. Her death had broken him, leaving him frail enough to wither into an early grave. Was I more like him than I dared to imagine? Caught in the web of my own schemes, I had let myself be drawn to another distraction—my Kyo. My cunning had faltered, my calculations wavered. I too had allowed the seeds of ruin to take root within me—keeping me away from survival.

Her hand reached for my remaining wing, fingers curling like talons. I braced for the inevitable rip, the fresh agony, but the moment never came. Her grip faltered, her hand trembling, as though restrained by invisible chains.

"You dare interfere with your master's rite?" she snarled, her gaze locking onto Kyo. Her body trembled with rage, the crystalline armor creaking as she fought against his unseen hold. The stone-like grip on my throat slackened, but only slightly. My vision swam, darkness curling at the edges.

Was this death? This slow, suffocating unraveling? It was almost quiet, almost serene. I felt no fear, only a strange, cold acceptance. My fingers slipped from her arm, useless now, as the strength left me.

Through the haze, I turned my head, blinking to clear my blurring vision. Kyo sat on the cold marble floor, his hands outstretched, his body trembling under the weight of his magic. Blood trickled from his nose, his eyelids heavy with exhaustion. His defiance burned brighter than his strength.

The word "run" rose to my lips, but no sound followed.

And then, with a sickening wetness at my side, her grip fell away entirely. I collapsed to the ground, air rushing back into my lungs in ragged, desperate gasps. My body convulsed as I coughed, the taste of blood bitter on my tongue. Turning to my side, I finally saw her.

The crystalline shell that had encased her was now crimson, her body within reduced to shattered chunks. Blood coated the inside, as if the armor itself had been reborn into a grotesque, ruby effigy of her form.

Relief came slowly as my body was finally given the chance to heal. My ribs snapped back into place with brutal precision, the raw edges of my torn flesh knitting themselves together. Feathers pushed through tender, reforming wings, their speckled paleness streaked with golden blood.

"Kyo," I whispered, the word heavy with exhaustion and something unspoken. I stumbled toward his collapsed frame, my hands trembling as Gamal knelt at his side.

"He's alive," Gamal said, his voice steady.

"You stubborn shit," I muttered, a quiet reprimand laced with a tenderness. I wiped the blood from his nose with careful fingers before sliding my arms beneath him, one hand under his thighs, the other beneath his shoulders. He was so light, so fragile, in my grasp.

"Take him to my chamber," I ordered, my voice regaining its edge. "Send for Yuka. No one else is to go near him."

Gamal nodded, his obedience wordless. I passed Kyo into his arms and turned, the weight of my council's gaze heavy upon me. "Ilay," I said without looking, "close the doors."

The heavy doors groaned as they shut, sealing just the bazifirs inside with me. Their wide eyes spoke volumes, their fear palpable. My intent had been to preserve our ranks, but they had seen his face. That knowledge made them a danger—a threat to what is mine.

KYO

My body felt heavy, weighted by a warmth that seeped into my bones. When I finally opened my eyes, the familiar opulence of Azariel's chambers greeted me. I stirred, only to feel a surprising weight pressing down on me. Azariel lay sprawled atop me, his arms draped across my sides, his face resting on my stomach. His breath was steady, and for a fleeting moment, I wondered if it had all been a dream.

My fingers moved instinctively, threading through the silken strands of his white hair, soft and unmarred. They drifted down the line of his face, searching for signs of Soraya's brutality, but there was nothing—no blood, no wounds, no remnants of the violence he had endured. My hand slid lower, tracing the curve of his bare back and brushing over his shoulder blades where his wings should have been. The muscles beneath my fingers tensed.

"Why are your hands so cold?" he murmured, his voice thick with sleep.

"Because it gets so damn cold here at night," I muttered, letting my hands fall to my sides. "Now, get off me."

"Why do you think I'm here?" His voice carried that familiar, exasperating laziness as he shifted slightly but didn't move away. "Your body wouldn't stop shivering, no matter how many layers we wrapped you in. It's probably your exhaustion, not Durathar's weather." His words softened, as if sleep still clung to him. "Is it normal for you to pass out like that when you use your magic?"

So it wasn't a dream. The memories came rushing back. "What happened to Soraya?" I asked, my voice steady despite the unease curling in my chest.

"You killed her," he said with a chuckle, his tone light, almost amused. "It was quite the spectacle."

"And her men?"

"I killed them." He propped himself up on his forearms, his stoney eyes glinting faintly as they met mine. "They would've spread tales that the Shahmizan was not won fairly. They'd have called me weak, unfit to rule."

"Oh, we wouldn't want that," I said dryly, the sarcasm slipping from my lips.

His brow furrowed, his expression darkening. "Do you think I'm weak now?"

"Only a fool would deem you weak," I replied, meeting his gaze without hesitation. "And I am no fool." I saw his shoulders relax slightly, the tension easing from his frame. "Though I do think you're stupid."

His eyes narrowed, his mouth curving into a line of unimpressed dismay.

"Don't you ever push me aside again," I said, my voice sharper now, carrying the weight of what had been left unspoken. "Where you go, I go. You are not invincible, Azariel. Your battles are mine. If you fall, I fall. Do you understand?"

For once, there was no glimmer of defiance in his expression, no sharp or witty retort waiting on his tongue. He nodded, his voice quiet when he finally spoke. "I understand." His head lowered slightly, a momentary vulnerability flickering across his face. "Thank you... for saving me."

"I suppose that means you owe me again," I murmured, my fingertips trailing idly along the sinew of his arm. The faint light of dawn crept into the room, soft and hesitant, as though it feared disturbing the sanctity of the morning. Its golden rays kissed the fractures in Azariel's skin, making them shimmer like molten gold against the deep umber of his flesh. He looked otherworldly, a celestial being carved from light and shadow.

"Before we leave for Lunrae today," I continued, "I'd like to add some enhancing sigils to the three of you. They'll stretch the limits of your gifts."

"And what of Gamal?" His voice carried a lazy humor, the faintest smirk playing on his lips. "He's just a human, after all."

"Perhaps, but even a man can stand among giants with the right tools." I met his gaze with a flicker of mirth. "Remember how I tampered with his match? This time, I can give him something more permanent. A proper sigil, one that won't fade."

"You're certain?" His golden eyes narrowed slightly.

I lifted my arm, displaying the intricate dark etchings carved into my forearm. "These have held for years. Sigils don't just fade. Gamal's only failed to stay because my powers were incomplete when I created it. This time, I'll have the proper tools—and the power to match."

"We're a four-man army heading into enemy territory to kill an Emperor. Any advantage we gain could mean the difference between survival and failure. So if you think you can do it, then by all means."

"Where's the confidence you boasted before?" I tilted my head, studying his face with a measured gaze. "I seem to recall you saying we didn't need an army. That our numbers would suffice because we have you."

His jaw tightened—just slightly—but I caught it. A fissure in the veneer of invulnerability he wore so well. "One can never be too cautious," he replied coolly.

It struck me then, the shadow of Soraya's fight still lingering in his posture, his voice. I am sure he would never admit it aloud, but the battle had shaken something in him. I hadn't thought someone so steeped in arrogance and conceit could be shaken at all.

"No, you cannot." My voice softened. "Which is why I'd like to propose something."

He raised a brow, curiosity flickering in his golden-slate gaze. "Go on."

"Eien," I began hesitantly, weighing each word as though they carried the weight of the world. "It's a custom—Kamishen marriage rites. Both partners receive a sigil, binding them together so their emotions resonate through the bond. Not every feeling, just... the overwhelming ones. Pain, fear... and so on." I paused. "If we had been bound, I would have known you were in danger. I could have come sooner." The words lingered in the air, their implications heavier than I cared to admit. Azariel was my key to Yuehama, my weapon to bring Durathar to its knees. But he was also... more. If I had arrived in that throne room moments later—

"Let's do it," he said, the simplicity of his agreement catching me off guard.

"You're certain?" I managed, still trying to gauge his reaction.

"If it strengthens our chances, then yes." He rose from the bed with a languid grace. "I heal fast now, thanks to you breaking my previous sigil. Will this one stay?"

I nodded. "Sigils are celestial magic at their core. They're not mere carvings or tattoos—they embed themselves within you, becoming a part of your essence."

Azariel had already begun dressing, his attention half on me and half on the room as he gathered the layers of his regal attire. "Tell me what you need," he said dismissively, "and I'll ensure it's procured."

He was humoring me far more than I anticipated. I had expected resistance, perhaps even mockery. That he would take offense to the idea of tethering himself to another so intimately, allowing someone access to his vulnerabilities, even in part. But here he was, agreeing without question, without hesitation.

"I just need the same tools—and Gamal and Ilay, of course." I rose from the bed, the weight of last night still clinging to me in the form of rumpled garbs and the faint, glimmering streaks of golden blood staining my side.

Azariel stood near the window, he moved with the casual grace that only he could muster, pulling a linen shirt over his shoulders. The moment felt too ordinary, too calm, and I hated it for that. My feet carried me to him, unbidden, and as he reached to smooth the fabric over his torso, my fingers halted him mid-motion.

"Were your... wings able to heal?" The words came softly, tentatively, as if speaking them too plainly would give life to my fears. The memory of Soraya's grasp rending his wing from his body was burned into my mind. My hand lingered on his back, fingers tracing the smooth expanse of his skin before resting against the ridges of his spine.

Azariel stilled. He didn't answer, didn't turn to look at me. Instead, he pulled the shirt back over his head and let it fall to the floor. I held my breath as he summoned his Tenishen gifts, the pale and marbled expanse of his wings manifesting with a quiet ripple of power.

The air seemed to hum around him as they unfurled—massive, magnificent things. White feathers stretched wide, their mottled brown streaks catching the sunlight that streamed through the window, revealing hidden depths of gold and amber, subtle flashes like the shifting patterns of a falcon's wings in flight.

I reached out tentatively, my fingers brushing against the feathers, skimming the soft edges of them. As I trailed my hand to the base of his wing, where the joint met his back, I felt the faintest tremor ripple beneath my touch.

Azariel turned his head slightly, his expression almost boyish, as though caught off guard by the intimacy of the moment. There was a warmth in his face that I'd never seen before—a shyness, perhaps, though he quickly masked it behind his usual stoicism.

"Back in one piece," he said after clearing his throat, his wings folding neatly against his shoulders. His voice held its usual composure, but there was an edge of gratitude beneath the surface. "Thanks to you."

"You don't have to keep thanking me." My hand fell to my side, my gaze dropping to the floor. "We need each other alive, don't we? It's to be expected."

There was a pause, one that stretched longer than I anticipated. "How were you able to do that to her?" he asked finally, his voice careful, as though treading on fragile ground. "I've seen you manipulate your own blood, but that was... different."

I hesitated, the weight of his question pressing down on me. The memory of what I had done stirred uneasily within me, a churning mix of pride and shame. "I don't know," I admitted. "I've found that I can do things I shouldn't be able to when my emotions are heightened."

Magic is tied to emotion—it is the thread that binds the heart to the divine. Every Kamishen knows this. But what I had done last night went beyond the sacred. It was raw, primal, a violation of the Moon's gifts. I had never witnessed anyone unleash power in the way I had—not to that extent. I had only heard of such things in whispers, fleeting mentions from Renjiro about moments of desperation when boundaries were pushed.

Desperation had wrapped around me like a noose, tightening with every second that he was in Soraya's grasp. Those boundaries we were not to cross broke under the weight of my fear. Azariel was my boundary, just as Yuehama was. The mere thought of losing him was a chasm I could not face. I would defy the spirits themselves, and possibly my own kingdom if it meant keeping him. That realization cut through me, sharp, shameful, and unrelenting. This new dependency, this visceral need for him, was a weakness I could no longer stubbornly ignore.

I could feel the words he had once spoken reverberate through my mind, a cold truth I had outright denied until now. *"Companionship is a liability to survival."*

He was right.

CHAPTER SEVENTEEN

Vizier Sulqadir was left as acting regent. The facade of Azariel traveling to Lunrae alongside Councilor Asahi for Princess Meiyuna was carefully upheld. The death of Soraya and her thirty bazifir served as a chilling reminder to the council, leaving their complaints muted by fear. Though they knew my identity and my role in disrupting the Shahmizan, they kept their dissent buried beneath the weight of caution, too wary of meeting the late Empress's fate. For now, our siege on Yuehama remained a whispered secret.

"How will you two rule two separate kingdoms if you are married?" Gamal's voice cut through the quiet, his fingers idly combing through his brown hair. He turned his attention from the carriage window to Azariel, who lounged across from him with an air of casual detachment.

"Our union is symbolic for our alliance, nothing more," I said, my tone even, eager to fill the long silence of our journey. "Once my uncle is dealt with, I will remain in Yuehama to rebuild, while Azariel returns to his place in Durathar. Peace does not require us to occupy the same court."

Azariel shifted, his elbow resting against the carriage window as his gaze settled on me. There was a teasing lilt to his voice as he replied, "But you'll visit your husband, won't you? What if I grow lonely? It's such a vast distance to endure alone."

I narrowed my eyes at him, my lips pressing into a thin line. "You will simply have to occupy yourself with courtiers or pleasure slaves... My focus will be on restoring trust among my people and rebuilding a court of loyalty after Renjiro's reign."

The carriage began to slow, the rhythm of its wheels faltering until it stopped entirely. Ilay, seated across from me, leaned toward the window, his sharp eyes scanning the horizon. Without a word, he rose and stepped outside, the door creaking faintly as it opened and closed behind him.

It was the third morning since we set out, though the journey was already stretching into the third afternoon. The setting sun bathed the horizon in amber and rose, its light softening the edges of the terrain. We had camped each evening for the horses and guards to rest, but this halt came earlier than usual.

Ilay soon returned, his expression composed as he held the carriage door open. "We are nearing the Tianze River. This is where we part ways with Councilor Asahi."

Stepping out of the carriage, I felt the air change. We had crossed over Yuehama's borders at last. The heat of Durathar had loosened its grip, replaced by a crispness that felt like a balm against my skin and soul. Spring's end lingered in the air, the warmth gentle and familiar. Around us, cherry blossoms fell like soft whispers, their pale pink petals blanketing the lush, green terrain.

I raised my hand, trying to catch a petal as it drifted lazily in the breeze. The sight struck me—how long had it been since I was taken to Durathar? Time had slipped through my fingers, and now the seasons had shifted here in my absence. It had been the cusp of spring when I departed, and now the blossoms were falling, their brief lives already spent.

Azariel approached, his steps quiet, his presence a shadow beside me. "This is my first time stepping beyond Durathar's borders to the northern kingdoms," he said, his voice thoughtful, almost soft. He mirrored my gesture, extending his hand as petals swirled around him. "I've been to Akhsarun, but that land is so similar to Durathar's it hardly felt different. Here, though... it's beautiful."

A single petal landed in my palm, delicate and fleeting. Without a word, I placed it in his open hand. "To think," I said quietly, my gaze fixed on the landscape ahead, "your people wanted to destroy all of this."

Azariel stilled. His fingers curled lightly around the petal, the admiring glint in his expression fading into something quieter, more introspective. As I stepped away, I glanced back to see him standing there, his hand open, his gaze resting on the fragile blossom.

I did not need the tether of Eien to sense how my resentful words lingered between us, cutting deeper than I intended. Though Azariel had looked past our differences, even past the tangled manipulations that had bound us to one another, I could not ignore the fragility of what we were—or what we could never truly be. Ours was a connection destined for ruin, fragile as glass yet carrying the weight of entire kingdoms. The sooner Yuehama was reclaimed, the sooner we could sever this precarious thread between us. Marriages were forged in diplomacy, not emotion, and for good reason. This bond was becoming a weakness.

"Eventually, we will need a change of attire," I said, my voice steadier than my thoughts. I turned to Ilay, who was busy stripping the Lunraean saddles from the horses Asahi had offered us. The beasts were majestic—strong, broad-shouldered creatures bred for nobility, with a commanding presence that betrayed their royal origins. Even without the embossed leather and silver emblems, their sheer size would draw too many wandering eyes.

"Lunraean robes served their purpose when we traveled with the envoy," I continued, smoothing my hands over the horses' flanks, "but they will betray us in these villages. If we are to blend in, we must discard every trace of nobility."

Ilay gave a curt nod. "We'll ride north along the river, find a place to camp, and then stop at the nearest village to gather what we need."

"It is two days' ride to Gahara—the capital—if the roads favor us," I said, fastening a makeshift saddle of layered blankets onto the horse before securing a modest pack to its side. "But we can shorten the journey if we keep pace."

Gamal stepped closer, his brow furrowing as he glanced between the two horses. "Who is riding with whom?"

"I will ride with Kyo," Azariel said, his tone as even and unyielding as stone. His gaze met mine briefly before he crossed the space between us, his movements deliberate. "I am best suited to keep him safe should trouble find us."

Without waiting for a reply, his fingers rose to the loose folds of my collar, lifting the fabric to cover the lower half of my face. The gesture was practical, his expression neutral, but there was something in the intimacy of it that made my breath falter for just a moment. "We cannot risk your people recognizing you, Prince Kyo," he murmured, the title carrying an edge that was neither mocking nor affectionate.

I fought the urge to roll my eyes, biting back a retort as he turned to mount the horse. He swung himself onto its back before extending a hand to me. His palm was warm and steady, and though I resented the necessity of it, I took it, allowing him to pull me up before settling into the saddle before him.

The proximity was inevitable—his presence close and steady behind me. I felt the faint press of his arm and the warmth of his chest against my back as he reached for the reins to adjust them for me. Behind us, Gamal and Ilay mounted the second steed, their quiet murmurs blending with the faint rustle of the river.

We rode to Asahi's carriage, pausing only long enough to offer my thanks once more before we set off. The river stretched out like a rich blue thread before us, its current guiding us northward. The soft glow of twilight painted the horizon in hues of amber and violet, and the cool air carried the faintest hint of cherry blossoms.

Azariel said nothing as we rode, but his silence was weighted, pressing against the space between us. My thoughts drifted as the horse's steady gait lulled me into contemplation. We hadn't made it far along the northern road before the dwindling light of day forced us to halt. There was no use pushing on blindly; we needed what little daylight remained to set up camp.

·孝·翌·芀·米

"What presence does the crown hold in a village such as this?" Ilay asked, his voice low as his horse trotted in rhythm beside mine. His gaze flicked to the trees lining the road, their branches swaying gently in the late morning breeze.

"Chūseki is no more than a fishing hamlet," I replied, brushing a stray strand of hair from my eyes. "Most villages along the Tianze are. The Imperial Guard patrols these roads often, though they rarely venture into the villages themselves. Their presence alone is deterrent enough for bandits."

I hesitated. "At least, that is how it should be." I had rode these roads countless times before, my role as Crown Prince tethering me to the lifeblood of the kingdom's trade. I knew the turns and bends of our trading routes as intimately as the back of my hand, and it was for this reason I had chosen this path to Gahara.

"How likely are you to be recognized here?" Azariel's voice cut through the hum of insects, quiet yet weighted.

"It's possible, but unlikely," I said, the edge of my mask brushing against my cheek as I spoke. "Even if someone noticed a resemblance, they would dismiss it. Once we've changed our attire, I could be any Kamishen of moderate rank. My hair's length is a dead giveaway. It was far longer last time I was here. Past my waist." In the Northern Kingdoms, hair was a banner of one's identity, a marker of social standing and heritage. Nobles wore their hair as both ornament and legacy, the lengths and styles tailored to their stations.

Azariel's fingers drifted through a strand of my hair, slow and deliberate, as if he found something curious in the silken weight of it. "All the same," he murmured, "I'd feel better if you kept the mask on."

I stiffened under his touch, rolling my shoulders slightly. "It's not as though my people would harm me. Unlike yours, my people have no advantage in raising arms against their crown."

Before Azariel could respond, Gamal's voice broke through the rising tension. "Why are there ribbons tied to the trees?" He gestured to the path ahead, where strips of red and orange cloth fluttered from the branches, vivid against the green and blue backdrop. They swayed in time with the breeze, vibrant as firelight.

"Nisduan," I answered, my voice softening. A smile crept to my lips beneath the mask, though it betrayed itself in my tone. "It's one of the three seasonal festivals dedicated to the

— 265 —

Celestial Bodies. Nisduan celebrates the Sun, a herald of the brighter days to come."

As we neared the open gates of Chūseki, we dismounted, leading the horses through narrow, crowded streets. The festive spirit was palpable, woven into the air like the threads of a tapestry. Chatter echoed between wooden stalls, where vendors displayed everything from glossy produce to skilfully painted keepsakes. The scent of steaming buns, grilled fish, and spiced rice mingled with the fresh tang of the river.

Children raced past us, their laughter rising in bursts of joy, each clutching small wooden boats painted in brilliant shades of gold and crimson. One boy skidded to a stop before us, holding up his boat with pride. The image of a sunburst was etched onto its hull in careful detail.

"Cheer for me in the Nisduan boat race!" he exclaimed, a cheeky grin lighting up his face.

I crouched slightly, tugging my mask down just enough to meet his gaze with a warm smile. "Of course. Yours looks like the fastest of them all." The boy's grin widened as he darted off, disappearing into the throng of villagers.

Azariel's hand settled on my shoulder, his fingers light but insistent as he pulled my mask back into place. "It was just a child," I said, my voice laced with exasperation. "Harmless. Besides, no one's paying us any mind. They're too busy preparing for the festivities tonight."

The road ahead shimmered with life, the narrow streets alive with the hum of delighted voices and the sway of golden silk lanterns that bobbed overhead like low-hanging little suns. Gamal's voice broke through the din, curious and low. "What are the festivities?"

"Every two to three years Nisduan falls on the eclipse. The time when the sun and moon intersect, and the stars are brightest—when all the Celestial Bodies can be seen at once. Villages, cities, even Gahara itself light great fires under the eclipse. There's dancing, boat races, feasting." My lips softened into a half-smile beneath my mask, my tone almost reminiscent as I guided my horse through the crowded path. "It is beautiful."

Ilay glanced at me. "Reminds me of Durathar's solstice."

"A little," I conceded, the hint of a laugh in my voice. "But less hedonistic."

Azariel stepped closer, his warmth a quiet gravity that pulled my attention. His voice softened, lower than usual, as if he meant for the question to be mine alone. "Do you like Nisduan?"

"I do."

"Then we should participate."

I faltered, my steps slowing. I turned to him, uncertain. "Participate?"

Azariel's gaze was steady, that rare gentleness in his sharp features that I have grown fond of. "We're not in a rush. Your uncle isn't going anywhere. And," he looked over his shoulder at Gamal and Ilay, the corners of his mouth lifting ever so slightly, "when will you two ever have another chance to experience Yuehama's traditions?" His question lingered, not needing an answer.

For a moment, the thought struck me as indulgent, reckless even. But then I looked around—the warmth of the villagers' smiles, the scent of spiced fish grilling over open flames, the vibrant reds and oranges of ribbons tied to trees. It had been so long since I'd felt Yuehama's heartbeat, its unguarded joy. And perhaps, for the first time in months, we were free. Free from courts full of whispers, free from the vipers coiled in every shadow, waiting to strike. Here, we were just travelers, unnoticed and unbothered.

The realization unfurled within me, fragile but insistent: *why not take this moment? Why not let myself feel the life I had been fighting so hard to reclaim?*

"Okay," I said, my smile blooming like the faint blush of spring blossoms. "Let's do it."

We led the horses toward a small stable on the edge of the village, the stable hand's eyes widening as Azariel handed over a generous amount of coin to ensure the horses remained unnoticed and properly cared for. For the first time in what felt like forever, I felt the faint thrill of anticipation—not for strategy or survival, but for something simpler, something mundane.

It took time—perhaps not as long as I'd anticipated—for a group like ours. We were shadowed in purpose, to blend into the rhythms of Yuehama to assassinate its emperor. Yet Chūseki, with its unassuming charm, wrapped us in a strange kind of anonymity. No one spared us a second glance; their attention was captivated by the joyous hum of Nisduan.

The streets were a kaleidoscope of life, bursting with the aroma of roasted delicacies and the vibrant chatter of merchants hawking trinkets and wares. Lanterns swayed like fireflies in the evening breeze, their warm glow bathing the market in a soft radiance. The echoes of happiness danced alongside the music of flutes and drums. Even the simplest distractions held their allure: the race to scarf down meals against others, the whittling of boats to compete in the village streams, the spirited competitions that drew cheers from onlookers. For some, it was the pull of the night fire, its flames licking at the darkness as dancers moved with fluid grace. For others, it was the awe of the eclipse, a celestial marvel that rendered even the most burdened of hearts humble.

For a fleeting moment, we allowed ourselves to forget—forgot the weight of blades hidden beneath our robes, the silent promises of blood and vengeance. In this sliver of borrowed time, we became nobodies, drifting like leaves on the river's current. Our vigilance softened; the sharp edges of our caution dulled under the beauty of the night. The Spirits seemed to smile upon us, giving us this fragile reprieve, a fleeting reminder of the world beyond duty and violence. A world I needed to protect.

I raised the slender glass bottle of wine to my lips, the heady scent of fermented rice and orange peel laced with a subtle bitterness curling in my nose before the burn settled on my tongue. I took a slow sip, savoring the earthiness, then extended the bottle toward Azariel. He glanced at it but lifted a hand, a polite refusal. I set it down in the grass beside me, the glass catching the faint crimson hue of the eclipse that painted the world in shades of rust and rose.

For a moment, we fell into silence. The air, heavy with the lingering aroma of charred wood from the fire in the distance, and the cool dampness rolling off the river nearby. I let my gaze drift toward the water, where the eclipse's reflection wavered on the surface.

"Why does mine keep sinking?" Gamal's frustrated voice broke through to us from the small distance.

He stood knee-deep in the river, his wooden boat bobbing awkwardly before vanishing beneath the surface again.

"You carved it unevenly," Ilay said flatly, stepping past the water's edge. He retrieved the small boat, shaking water from its fragile hull before inspecting it under the lunar light. A grin split his usually composed face, and then he burst into laughter. "There's a hole in it."

"Let me see."

Ilay laughed harder, holding the poorly whittled craft just out of Gamal's reach. "You didn't just carve it unevenly—you butchered it. I'm certain the children did better than this."

Gamal lunged for the boat, and in doing so, lost his footing. The splash as he hit the water sent Ilay into another fit of amusement, his voice ringing through the quiet night. I couldn't help it—guffaw spilled from me too, warm and unrestrained.

When my gaze flicked to Azariel, I caught him watching me. His lips held the faintest curve of a smile, but it was his eyes that caught me off guard—quiet and steady, like he was memorizing the moment.

The tether of Eien between us thrummed, and I could feel the rhythm of his heartbeat spike, quickening just slightly against mine. A warmth I didn't expect flushed my cheeks. "Why is your heart beating so fast?" The question slipped from my lips before I could think better of it.

"It's not," Azariel replied, his voice cool, composed. But the faint color rising on his face betrayed him, as did the persistent flutter I could feel through our bond.

"Yes, it is," I said with a tilt of my head, raising a brow as a small, knowing smile played on my lips.

The sound of wet footsteps pulled my attention briefly. Gamal and Ilay approached, water clinging to their trousers, their voices still echoing faintly. But when Gamal's gaze flicked between Azariel and me, he stopped abruptly, his knowing expression turning unreadable.

"I think I'll dry off by the fire," he said, his voice composed as he nudged Ilay to follow him. They turned back toward the village, heading through woodland back toward the lively hum of the villagers and the vibrant pulse of the festivities.

I watched them leave, puzzlement furrowing my brow, before I turned back to Azariel. He was still looking at me, but his expression had shifted—contemplative, guarded. And yet, there was something tender in the way his gaze lingered, as if he wasn't sure whether to speak or to hold his tongue. The silence between us was fragile, as if the air itself held its breath, waiting. Then, finally, he spoke, his voice careful, measured. "What did you mean when you said Meiyuna wouldn't truly wish to wed a man such as me?"

I hesitated, my thoughts a tangled web of truths and half-formed feelings. "I... I don't know what I meant by it," I admitted quietly, the words tasting bare and unguarded. "You aren't completely as people described you to be. I see that now. I even saw it then. You are..."

"Like a flower petal?" he interrupted, a faint, almost self-deprecating laugh weaving through his tone. Between his fingers, he held a cherry blossom petal, its delicate edges pale against his skin.

"Yes," I replied, my voice soft as my hand moved instinctively to take it from him. My fingertips brushed the fragile edges of the petal, now curling faintly as it began to dry. He was like a petal—beautiful, fragile in ways unseen, but capable of endurance with the right care.

He watched me closely, his gaze unrelenting. "Would you have still married me if circumstances were different?"

"If there was no political reason to do so?" I asked, my thoughts racing ahead of me. "No," I said at last, the word a quiet surrender. But before he could speak, I continued, my voice softening. "You want me because you see use for me. What happens when you no longer have that use? Will you discard me when someone else serves your purpose? What if—" my breath caught, my words teetering on the edge of confession—"what if I had already fallen in love with you by then? I wouldn't want that worry in a genuine marriage."

His gaze searched mine, raw and open, as though he was stripping me down to my very soul. "Are you in love with me?" he asked, his voice nearly a whisper, vulnerability trembling beneath the words.

I felt the weight of my heart in my chest, its rhythm quickening. "I thought my affections were clear," I whispered back, echoing the very words he once spoke to me. My words were not merely an admission to him but a reckoning within myself—a quiet surrender and acceptance to the feelings I had buried deep, denied, and pushed away for far too long. And before I could second-guess myself, I leaned in, closing the space between us, pressing my lips softly against his.

His lips curved against mine, a subtle smile breaking through the kiss. "In honesty, no," he murmured as he pulled back just slightly, his breath warm against my skin. "They are never clear. You are unpredictable, petty, and conniving."

"Are those supposed to be compliments?"

"They are," he said, his voice low and sincere. He kissed me again, deeper this time, his fingers entwining gently within my hair as if anchoring me to him. "You will always have purpose... All I want is for you to choose me. Accept the way I am and I am yours—wholly, without condition."

A warmth bloomed in my chest, fierce and undeniable. Azariel had lived a life where affection was always bartered, never freely given—where affection was measured by what he could provide or the fear he inspired. His words carried the weight of that truth, the longing of someone who had been loved for everything but himself.

I hadn't realized, until this moment, how deeply I longed to be desired without condition too—to be wanted not for what I could offer or for the roles I played, but for the entirety of who I was. Whether I stood as the epitome of a just and noble prince or merely a man struggling to endure, whether I was tender or unyielding. I craved a love that saw all of me and still chose to stay. It wasn't only the darkness within us that reached out, but the fractured, broken pieces too—seeking solace, seeking wholeness, finding in each other a reflection of wounds that longed to heal.

"Now look whose heart is beating so fast," he whispered, his voice teasing but tender. Azariel's lips found mine again, claiming and certain. His hands slid to my back, pulling me closer, and I moved without thought, straddling his lap. My fingers threaded through his hair as we deepened the kiss, the world around us falling away. In that moment, it was only us, bound by breath, touch, and the quiet promise of something far greater than words could hold.

The heat between us was an undeniable force, raw and unrelenting. I pressed my hand against his chest, urging him back into the soft cradle of the grass. Our lips moved together in a fervent rhythm, mouths devouring, tongues tangling, as though we had been starved for this—starved for each other—for far too long.

My hands, trembling with both urgency and reverence, parted the folds of his tunic and robe, before sliding down his trousers. The linen gave way easily, revealing him to me, hard and aching under my touch. I wrapped my fingers around his cock, stroking slowly at first, savoring the warmth and the way his breath hitched against my lips.

A low moan escaped him, a sound that sent a sharp thrill coursing through me. My hand quickened, betraying the desperation simmering beneath my control. I wanted him, *needed him,* like a flame needs air to burn.

"Why are you rushing?" he murmured, his voice a teasing caress that almost broke through the haze of my desire. His hand found my face, cupping it with a tenderness that made my chest ache. His dark eyes met mine, shimmering with both amusement and something deeper. "Not that I mind you ravaging me," he added, a soft laugh escaping him.

His words made me pause, though only for a moment. *Why was I rushing?* The emotions swirling inside me felt too vast, too all-consuming. Fear. Longing. Desire. If I didn't take this moment, seize it, I might retreat back into the fortress I had built around me, the wall that kept us apart. The thought of pushing him away again was unbearable. I didn't want to think, to hesitate—I wanted him.

"Do you really want me to slow down?" I whispered, my lips brushing against his neck, lingering before my teeth grazed the delicate skin there. A shudder ran through his body as he exhaled sharply. "Because I'm finally going to let you have me," I murmured against his skin, my voice low and daring.

My hand resumed its pace, slower and firmer this time, teasing him as my thumb glided over the slick tip of his length. His hips arched instinctively, meeting my touch, and the quiet rasp of his breath against my ear ignited something primal in me.

I felt my own hardness pressing uncomfortably against my trousers, the ache impossible to ignore. But none of it mattered—none of it—except the way he felt under me, the way he unraveled in my hands, and the way his gaze held mine as though there was no one else in the world but us.

My lips trailed down the expanse of his chest. The golden fractures of his skin glimmered under the soft, red tint of the eclipse, each line kissed with a coppery hue. His chest rose and fell in a slow rhythm, but beneath that calm facade, I felt his heart fluttering, a staccato against my body.

I straightened, undoing the sash around my waist, letting my tunic fall open. The cool night air brushed against my heated skin as I eased my trousers down, my movements deliberate, the anticipation building between us like the stretch of a drawn bow.

Every fiber of me was alive, my pulse racing as I steadied myself above him. One hand rested against the taut muscle of his stomach, the other reaching back to align him with me. The weight of his gaze burned into mine—steady, knowing, and utterly patient.

"Ambitious, are we?" Azariel murmured, his voice carrying a steady, velvet tone as his hands glided up my thighs, lingering just enough to leave heat in their wake.

I had been undone so effortlessly by his fingers before; now I wanted to know how it felt to take him completely, to feel every inch of him as he filled the part of me I had kept guarded.

"No more talking," I commanded. My lips thinned as I focused, my gaze lowering while I pressed my hips down slowly. The slick, heated tip of him pressed against me, my body resisting as I attempted to take him in. This wasn't as easy as I had imagined in the heady rush of emotion. Desire still burned fiercely within me, but my resolve wavered as the reality of the moment grounded me.

I glanced up at him, and his expression nearly undid me entirely. Azariel lay there in quiet worship, his golden eyes heavy with lust but softened by something far more tender. "Do you need help, *Aqaynah*?" he asked, a teasing lilt coloring his voice, though his gaze held no mockery, only a quiet patience.

"No," I breathed, determined to hold onto the reins of this moment. "Just keep your damned cock still."

His lips quirked, the faintest shadow of a smirk. His hands slid higher, cupping the curve of my backside and giving a firm squeeze. One hand released me before his fingers wrapped around the base of his shaft, guiding himself to me. "It's easier if you open yourself up first," he murmured, his tone softer now, coaxing. "Use oil... accept help."

Ambitious and stubborn—that was what I was. If I was going to give him all of me, I needed it to be on my terms. I needed to watch him come undone beneath me, knowing it was my touch, my resolve, that unraveled him.

My hips descended further, taking him in, every inch foreign and overwhelming, the sensation stretching the boundaries of my body and my will. His cock remained steady beneath me, and though discomfort pulsed through me at first, I persisted, my breaths shallow, trembling. The weight of him inside me was immense, a fullness I hadn't known, and as I began to move—lifting myself and sinking back down—I felt the ache begin to ebb, replaced by something deeper, more intoxicating.

Azariel's hands rested firmly on my hips, his fingers pressing into the curve of my flesh, subtle yet certain in their guidance. With every rise and fall, my body grew more accustomed to his girth, the tension loosening, giving way to pleasure. My lips parted, soft pants escaping as heat unfurled low in my stomach.

He began to move beneath me, his hips meeting me, his rhythm syncing effortlessly with my own. His half-lidded gaze smoldered, heavy with lust, and his moans spilled freely into the air. The sound of them wrapped around me, igniting something feral within. I wanted to drown in those sounds, to have them echo only for me, forever.

With a swift motion, he sat up, pulling me close until our chests were flush. His arms tightened around me, firm, possessive, unyielding. "You need to be quieter," he murmured, his voice a low, dangerous growl. "I don't want anyone else hearing those noises coming from you." His hand slid to my throat, firm yet careful, a subtle squeeze that sent a shiver through me. He brought my face to his, his mouth capturing mine in a kiss that devoured, his tongue claiming me, silencing my moans as his movements grew more insistent.

My arms wrapped around his shoulders, nails biting into his back through the fabric of his garbs. Our bodies moved in tandem, the rhythm urgent and unrelenting, every thrust sending waves of sensation rippling through me. Heat coiled deep in my testicles, building with each collision. My own cock, trapped between us, brushed against his stomach with every motion, the friction driving me closer to the precipice.

"I've imagined this," Azariel breathed, his voice rough, his control coming back as he slowed, savoring the moment, drawing it out. "Countless times... But it could never compare to this."

His words pushed me over the edge, the tension within me snapping. Pleasure coursed through me, consuming me whole. I felt his release as well, his body shuddering against mine, the shared rhythm of our breathing and moans melting into a singular harmony.

His lips found mine again, this time softer, tender, lingering as though he wished to pour his soul into me. When the fevered haze began to fade, and our breaths steadied, I pressed my forehead against his, my fingers tracing idle patterns along his shoulder.

"Of course you've fantasized about this," I murmured, my voice light with teasing, though my heart still thundered in my chest.

"Of course," he whispered, a quiet chuckle slipping through his words. His eyes softened as he tilted his head slightly, studying me in a way that left no space for misinterpretation. "Kyo... I think I need to clear something up." Azariel began, his voice low but steady. "Once, I thought your tendency to lead with your emotions was a flaw. Don't misunderstand me—I cherish your genuinity, but I believed it was a burden at times. I couldn't see then what I see now."

His gaze met mine, unwavering, as if every word was a vow. "You've shown me that emotion isn't a weakness. Companionship isn't a liability. It's a force. It drives you, makes you stronger. And because of that, I've stopped hiding what I feel for you. If there's one thing I never want you to suppress, it's this. Us."

He paused, his fingers brushing against my cheek, anchoring me to the moment. "You were right all along. What is survival worth if it's hollow? If it means standing alone?"

"As you said, I am a bad liar," I said. "Even if I tried, I don't think I'd be able to suppress this. It's too much a part of me now."

I glanced over my shoulder, the silver light of the moon shimmering over the lake, its surface glimmering like a field of stars. The eclipse had passed, leaving the world bathed in soft luminescence.

"We missed the ending of the eclipse."

"This was far more breathtaking to watch... I'm sure we'll see another one together," he said softly and I let his words linger, their promise sinking into me like roots taking hold in fertile soil. I closed my eyes and leaned into his touch, allowing myself to accept his vulnerability and my own.

CHAPTER EIGHTEEN

The streets of Gahara stretched before us, alive with the pulse of midday. The sun hung high in the sky, its golden rays illuminating the city like the touch of a divine hand. Every corner brimmed with vitality—a marketplace bustling with traders hawking silk and spices, the air thick with the scent of roasted chestnuts and sweet plum wine. Children darted between the legs of merchants, their laughter a fleeting melody against the rhythm of clanging forges and the low hum of conversation. My boots brushed against the cobblestones, worn smooth by generations, each step a reminder that I was closer than ever to reclaiming what was mine.

The imperial palace loomed in the distance, its golden rooftops glinting like a beacon, daring me to approach. It sat on its elevated perch at the heart of Yuehama, a city within a city. Its walls, an unbroken expanse of ivory stone, rose with an air of invincibility. Beyond them, I could make out the faint silhouettes of pavilions and pagodas, their eaves upturned like the wings of mythical beasts poised for flight. It was more than just a stronghold; it was a testament to power, grandeur, and the heavy burden of rule. My gaze lingered on its majesty, each detail etched into my mind, not as an object of reverence but as a promise yet to be fulfilled. That palace belonged to me, and soon, it would again bear my name.

"Keep moving," I murmured, not glancing back at the men trailing behind me. I led them deeper into the thrumming arteries of the city, past canals where the soft lap of water played against the voices of women washing clothes, past rows of houses where the scent of steamed dumplings and lacquered wood lingered. The air carried a palpable weight here—something ancient, something undeniable. The capital of Yuehama was not just a city; it was a living entity, breathing history into the very stones beneath our feet.

There was no time to linger, no space to let the weight of memory pull me under. The streets of Gahara, alive with midday clamor, offered no comfort, only risk. The hum of the city was a cruel reminder of how close I was to what I had lost, yet perilously far from reclaiming it.

The longer we moved through the open avenues, the more the unease coiled in my chest. Each step felt too loud, each breath a potential betrayal. The Imperial Guards patrolled these streets with purpose, their sharp eyes ever watchful, their movements as precise as the blades they carried.

Ilay and Azariel moved close behind me, their presence both a comfort and a liability. Ilay and Azariel's height and foreign features stood out in stark contrast to the Kamishen and Human populace of Yuehama. Their difference drew eyes, fleeting and curious, but enough to make my pulse quicken.

As we neared a shadowed corner of the street, I slowed my pace and turned to the group, my movements deliberate. I tilted my head toward a dimly lit establishment, a tavern, tucked between two larger buildings. Without a word, I slipped through the doorway, the scent of fermented tea and the low murmur of patrons greeting me like an old companion.

The interior was cloaked in the filtered light of early afternoon, the sunlight streaming through narrow wooden slats and casting golden beams across the polished floorboards. The lanterns that hung low from the beams above were unlit, their silk shades painted with faded scenes of cranes and plum blossoms, swaying gently in the soft breeze that drifted in through an open window. The surfaces of the wooden tables were worn smooth by years of quiet conversations and the weight of shared meals.

Patrons were scattered about, their postures unhurried as they sipped tea or picked at simple meals served in glazed ceramic bowls. A young server wove between them with practiced ease, balancing a tray of cups and chopsticks, her presence a natural part of the tranquil rhythm. It was a sanctuary, hidden in plain sight, where the bustling city just outside felt worlds away.

I chose a corner table tucked deep into the shadows, where the slats of the wooden shutters allowed only the faintest threads of sunlight to seep through. The air was cooler here, distant from the hum of the tavern's heart, the whispers of patrons and the clatter of bowls softened to a murmur. It was a space where thoughts could gather, where watchful eyes couldn't easily follow.

The server brought drinks without ceremony, the clay cups clinking gently as they were set down. For a while, silence reigned, stretching thin as I remained caught in the tangle of my own musings and theirs on their own observations. "The guard will be heavier at night, but the shadows will serve us better then. Fewer servants will linger on the palace grounds." My voice was low, measured, designed to reach no ears but those at the table.

Ilay nodded, his tone mirroring my quiet resolve. "Minds grow wearier under the cover of night. When the darkness deepens, sleep tempts even the most vigilant. Shadows become adversaries in their own right."

"Couldn't you just summon the shadows and take us past the palace walls? Seems there's a lot of ground to cover otherwise." Gamal leaned forward, his curiosity breaking through the tension.

Ilay sighed, the sound more weary than annoyed. "It's not so simple," he began, his voice carefully neutral. "To call upon shadows, I must know the shape of the place they dwell. I cannot pull them from somewhere I have not seen. And transporting others through the Veil demands more of me than you can imagine."

My thoughts drifted to the moment he had summoned the shadows, weaving their darkness around us to transport us from one part of the palace to another. The memory lingered, vivid—the effort etched into his features, the process slower, more deliberate than when he traversed the Veil alone. The sigils I had placed upon him should allow him greater control over the shadows. Enough to command them to transport us all at least once or twice tonight.

I leaned back against the hard wood of the chair, my fingers briefly adjusting the fabric draped across the lower half of my face as I contemplated the fortress ahead. The palace walls were impenetrable, ancient stone reinforced by patrols at their crest and base. Only two gates provided access to the grounds, their iron-bound wood thick enough to resist siege. How had Durathar broken through those defenses mere months ago? Their incursion had been swift, their brute bazifirs slipping past undetected until they surged into the palace itself. We had barely a moment to react.

My gaze shifted to Azariel, who sipped his drink with unhurried poise. "How were your men able to breach the Imperial Palace?" I asked.

"I do not know," he said simply. "Darius commanded the siege. For years, he handled the campaign against Yuehama alone. Toward the end, he grew paranoid, believing our messages were being intercepted. He withheld his plans even from us, leaving much of what happened in shadow."

"Perhaps we should consider a different approach," Ilay murmured, his gaze falling to me with measured caution.

I could see the words forming on his lips before he spoke them, the unspoken suggestion heavy in the air between us. A path paved in bloodshed, the very path I longed to avoid. I would not let this rebellion claim lives unnecessarily. Only Renjiro's. Only the man who stole what was mine.

"Do you truly believe we can do this without collateral damage, *Aqaynah*?" His voice was a low hum, his hand gliding across the table, fingers brushing the fabric of my sleeve before settling lightly against my forearm. The gesture, soft as it was, carried the weight of his question. "There will be those loyal to him, those who will not hesitate to cut you down if it means protecting their new emperor. Will you hesitate?"

His words hung between us, steady and sharp, but his eyes betrayed him. Concern flickered there, a quiet storm beneath the surface. Concern that I would falter, that I would waver at the edge of my resolve. That I might jeopardize not just myself but everyone else if it came to slaughtering my own people.

My gaze met his, unwavering. "I will not hesitate," I said, my voice low and firm. The truth tasted bitter on my tongue, but I swallowed it down. It would be selfish to do otherwise. There is no war without casualties, no reclamation without sacrifice. "I will do what needs to be done for Yuehama."

My eyes drifted to his hand, the umber tones of his fingers resting against my skin, a quiet anchor in the storm of my thoughts. I let the fleeting comfort settle over me before the resolve returned. "The goal is to incapacitate," I continued, voice steadier now, "but if death is necessary... then so be it."

I would carry the weight of those lives. Retribution, I decided, would be made not just in blood but in what I would rebuild. The souls lost in this battle would find their peace in the future I would craft.

The tavern owner's voice cut through our plotting, his warm greeting drawing our attention toward them. Two Imperial Guards had entered, their uniforms stark and pristine even beneath the muted light. They stopped to converse, their mundane conversation carrying faintly across the room.

A smile tugged at my lips beneath the mask, faint but deliberate. My thoughts shifted like the tide, and a new plan began to form in the shadowed corners of my mind. "I have an idea," I said, the weight of my determination steadying my voice. My gaze lingered on the guards for a moment before turning back to the group. "This is how we will get in quietly."

·ꭹ·ꭹꭹꭹ

The quiet of the alley pressed around us, heavy and still, broken only by the sharp clatter of lamellar armor striking the stone. Ilay dropped the Imperial Guard uniforms in a heap, his breath ragged. "Quiet?" he muttered under his breath, his voice laced with incredulity. "Do you have any idea how fast those guys were?"

I let a small chuckle escape, the sound soft in the shadowed alleyway. "You didn't need to have them chase you across half the district. Just enough to make them angry enough to throw you in a cell would have sufficed."

Ilay huffed in response, but the four of us wasted no time. We shed our clothes in hurried silence, swapping them for the armor he had acquired. The metallic scent of steel and faint traces of sweat clung to the uniforms. My fingers worked quickly to secure the chest piece, the ties and plates fitting snugly around my frame.

Azariel appeared before me, holding a helmet in one hand. The dim light of the alley caught the mischief in his eyes as he placed it carefully on my head. He leaned in, his voice low and teasing. "You should wear this again sometime. You know, for fun. I'll play the helpless emperor, and you'll be the guard who saves him."

I tilted my head, my brow lifting in faint amusement. "Is that your idea of foreplay?" I asked, my tone dry but playful. "I've already saved you once. Why don't you save me this time?"

Gamal's light voice cut through the moment, his presence as steady as ever. "Save the coupling for later." He stepped forward, pressing a sword against Azariel's chest with firm resolve, creating a boundary between us.

Azariel chuckled lightly, his hands raised in mock surrender before he strapped the blade to his hip. Gamal's caution hadn't waned in the days since we'd left Durathar. His wariness toward Azariel lingered, a tension born of old scars and the memory of what Durathar had taken from him. I couldn't blame him. There were still moments when Azariel's intentions seemed as murky to me as they likely did to Gamal. But I knew if it came to it, he would choose to defend Azariel. This journey had shaped a comradeship between us all.

"They'll have noticed my absence by now," Ilay said, gathering up the discarded clothes and stowing them behind a stack of crates. "Expect a fight. It's only a matter of time." He turned to me then, his expression cautious but steady. "Are you ready? Once I take us there, there's no turning back."

"There was no turning back the moment we left Durathar," I replied, my voice firm but quiet. "We'll see this through. We have to."

Ilay nodded and stepped further into the shadows of the alley, their darkness deepening unnaturally as we followed. The air grew colder, heavier, and then the blackness became absolute.

"Close your eyes," Ilay said to us.

I obeyed, and the world fell away. No sounds, no scents, no sensation but the creeping chill of the Veil. And then, a warmth—faint but familiar—brushed against the back of my hand. Azariel. His touch, fleeting but deliberate, was a wordless reminder: *I am here.*

Just as suddenly as the cold had come, it vanished. "Open," Ilay said.

I blinked into the dim light of a new space. The air was heavy with damp stone and the faint tang of rust. We had passed through the ivory stone wall that divided the palace grounds from the rest of Gahara, and were in the prison beneath the barracks.

"State your rank and names," barked a voice. A guard stepped forward, his lantern casting jagged shadows on the stone walls. His narrowed eyes flicked over us, suspicion etched into every line of his face.

"I got it," Ilay murmured under his breath. The shadows at the guard's feet stirred unnaturally, creeping up his legs like serpents. His body stiffened, and within moments, he vanished into the encroaching darkness.

"Did you kill him?" I asked, my voice tight as I cast Ilay a sharp look.

But before he could answer, shouts erupted from the cells behind us. "Stop them!" Metal bars clanged, their echo sharp and grating in the confined space.

"Nope, time to go," Gamal cut in with a dry laugh, already moving forward. We followed, the tension coiling tighter with every step. There would be no reprieve now—only the path forward. We neared the top of a stairwell, our pace slowed, the rhythm of our steps deliberate, breathing measured. Each movement was a careful performance, a silent prayer that we might pass unnoticed, just shadows cloaked in the guise of Imperial Guards.

The corridor stretched before us, empty and unyielding, its silence a fragile veil of reassurance. I let out a soft sigh, a relief that tasted almost foreign, as we turned corner after corner, finding no one. The guards were either pacing their patrols in the courtyard or deep in the embrace of sleep within their quarters.

At last my hand pressed against the barrack's exit, and with a soft creak, it opened to reveal the expanse of the palace grounds. It lay before us, a sprawling labyrinth of courtyards and pavilions layered like the tiers of a mountain, the sacred heart of the palace hidden within its innermost sanctum. Nightfall had draped the world in a deep indigo, the air crisp and sharp with the scent of stone, pine and cherry blossoms.

I hesitated on the threshold, my steps faltering as my ears caught the faint murmur of voices in the distance. Low and indistinct, they receded like a tide retreating from the shore—a small mercy, though one that tightened the knot of unease in my chest.

Then, my gaze was caught, transfixed, by a faint glow. It shimmered in the darkness like a phoenix feather, radiant and alive. But it was not the cool celestial light of Azariel's Tenishen lineage or magical reserve. No, this glow was wilder, fiercer—a fire that pulsed with the steady heartbeat of the sun itself. My breath caught in my throat.

"Wait," I whispered, my arm shooting out to halt the others. My eyes traced the retreating figure ahead, my mind grappling with the impossibility of their presence here. *Why would a Nisshen be here in Yuehama?* They were the children of the sun, far from their home on the western continent of Vorynthia.

The soldier's armor glinted faintly in the moonlight, its design an echo of distant lands—a curious blend of ceremonial grandeur and deadly practicality, reminiscent of the formidable Vorynthian warriors. Bronze plates covered his form, sculpted to resemble sinew and muscle, trimmed with gold that shimmered faintly in the dark. But it was not the armor that held me captive; it was the being within it.

Like all Shen, his ears tapered to elegant points, but above his brow curved a pair of obsidian horns, sleek and sharp. Within the black, veins of molten fire coursed like rivers of liquid flame, alive and breathing in time with his steady pulse. His presence was a storm contained, fire and shadow coiled beneath a thin veneer of stillness.

I signaled silently, a brief motion of my hand, urging them to follow me along the opposite path, away from the Kamishen and Nisshen guards. Our steps were soft, muffled against the stone, as we moved like shadows through the courtyards. The air carried the faint perfume of evening-blooming flowers, mingling with the earthy tang of dew settling on ancient stone. Moonlight spilled across the tiled pathways, a silvery stream guiding our path, while lanterns swayed gently in the distance, their glow too faint to reach us.

The courtyards stretched outward in elegant symmetry, their serenity interrupted only by the hushed murmur of distant voices or the faint rustle of fabric in the wind. A koi pond glimmered as we passed, the faint ripple of water stirring its glass-like surface. We clung to the shadows, darting between pillars and alcoves, our breath quiet, our presence undetected.

When at last we reached the palace steps, the imposing structure loomed above us. I paused, my gaze sweeping the expanse of the palace entrance. My pulse quickened—not from exertion, but from the disquiet settling over me like a shroud. *Where are all the guards?* The palace gates should have been teeming with sentries, nearly as fortified as the outer walls. Yet, before us lay only emptiness, a silence that gnawed at the edges of my composure. I glanced back at the courtyards, their sprawling buildings veiled in stillness. We had passed so few guards along the way. Too few.

"Why did we stop?" Azariel's voice was low but edged with mild impatience. His brows furrowed as his gaze flicked between me and the path ahead.

"Something's wrong," I murmured, the weight of the words settling heavily in the air between us.

"What do you mean?" he pressed, his tone shifting from impatience to concern. "Do you think we've been caught?"

I hesitated, my throat dry as I swallowed the unease rising within me. "I don't know," I admitted. "If we had been, we would have been swarmed by now." My eyes lingered on the quiet paths we had traversed, the familiarity of the scene unsettling in its stark unfamiliarity. These routes, these courtyards—I had walked them countless times during my training, patrolled their lengths with my guards. This silence was wrong. It pressed against my senses, a suffocating thing. "Everyone, just... stay cautious."

I turned back to the palace, ascending the stairs with measured steps. My hand pressed against the heavy door, its lacquered surface cool beneath my palm. With a low creak, it opened, revealing the shadowed interior. A vast expanse stretched before me, the hall bathed in moonlight filtering through lattice windows. The polished floors gleamed faintly, their mirrored surface reflecting the pale light. Columns rose like sentinels on either side, their carved motifs seeming to shift in the wavering shadows.

And yet, no guards. Not a single figure stirred within the cavernous space. The stillness was absolute, broken only by the faint whisper of the wind slipping through the cracks. My unease deepened, knotting itself into my chest.

"Where are they?" I whispered, my voice barely audible over the silence.

"What is that smell?" Gamal muttered, his voice low, the back of his hand rising to shield his face as if it might ward off the stench.

I inhaled sharply, the acrid scent biting at the back of my throat. There was something unnervingly familiar about it, something that teased the edges of memory but refused to fully take shape. Ash, metallic—no...

A soft glow unfurled from Azariel's hand, the celestial light blooming like a distant star. Its golden radiance danced along the stone walls of the grand entrance, spilling light into every crevice.

"Spirits," Ilay murmured, his voice a shiver that broke the silence.

My gaze followed his, and the air left my lungs in a sharp, involuntary gasp. *Burned flesh. That's what it was.* The walls were lined with bodies—or what remained of them. Charred flesh hung like grotesque ornaments, the outlines of their forms twisted beyond recognition. The stench became suffocating now that I knew its source.

Azariel's voice broke the silence, light and edged with something akin to admiration. "Looks like something I might've done." His brow lifted, his tone disturbingly casual, as though this horror was art worth appreciating.

A chill rippled through me. "Why.." I swallowed hard, fighting the bile rising in my throat. This is the work of a monster. What kind of being could reduce others to this? And for what purpose? A warning? A message? The questions churned, but no answers surfaced.

The thought unsettled me more than the sight itself. I tore my gaze away from the bodies, my focus narrowing to the path ahead. I couldn't let myself linger here. Not now. "We need to find Renjiro," I said firmly, the words grounding me in a task, in purpose. I stepped forward, each stride deliberate as I moved towards the wing where my uncle should linger at this time. I refused to let my eyes wander back to the grotesque display on the walls. The air felt thicker now, as though the palace itself was breathing, its walls imbued with the malice of what had been done here.

Just as the corridor curved, my steps faltered, drawn by a voice as soft and fleeting as the whisper of wind through willow leaves.

"Kyo."

It was faint, feminine, each syllable brushing against my senses with a kind of gentle urgency. My breath caught as I turned, searching.

"Prince Kyo."

The others halted beside me, our gazes following the sound to a figure cloaked in the muted garb of palace servants. She stood at the end of the corridor, a Kamishen woman whose presence seemed both ordinary and off putting. As we stepped toward her, she receded, slipping farther into the dimly lit hall like smoke dispersing in the breeze.

"She's leading us somewhere," Azariel murmured, his tone unreadable, neither wary nor eager.

"I'm not naive," I bit back, keeping my voice low. "I know this is a trap."

And yet, I followed. We all did.

She guided us deeper, the winding corridors tightening like a noose around my chest. The glow of braziers began to bloom along the path, their flickering light casting long shadows on the lacquered wood. Finally, we arrived before the grand doors of the Imperial Hall—the Throne Room.

The doors loomed tall and somber.

This was where it had all unraveled, where my uncle had orchestrated my downfall. Here was where he betrayed not just me, but the kingdom he swore to protect. This chamber—this throne—was where he surrendered to Durathar's tyranny, binding me in chains of erasure.

The memory clawed at me, the weight of it suffocating. The fury I thought I had controlled now began to stir. It coiled and writhed, my fingers twitching with the need to grasp something, anything, to feel the balance shift in my favor.

Alongside me, the quiet pools recessed into the floor began to ripple, the water trembling as though echoing the storm inside me. A single droplet rose, suspended in the air, then another, and another. They followed me as I stepped forward, a silent procession, fluid and weightless, summoned by the force of my will alone, creating two sentinels of water at my side waiting to strike.

I lowered my mask. If Renjiro stood behind those doors, as I suspected, I wanted him to see me—fully. No disguise. He would meet the gaze of the man he betrayed, and the one who would end him.

The heavy doors creaked open, their sound reverberating like a lament through the chamber. Four Vorynthian Nisshen awaited us, their forms illuminated by the flickering light of the braziers. Their eyes burned with an intensity that defied humanity, the molten glow of their fire a mirror to the sun's merciless blaze.

The one nearest to us held the Kamishen woman in a vice-like grip. Her frail body writhed against his hold, his arm coiled around her neck like a serpent. "It is you," she choked out, her voice trembling, her eyes pleading. The anguish in her gaze struck something deep within me, yet I could not let it soften the steel of my resolve.

A voice rippled from the back of the room, smooth and serpentine. "Unfortunately, she has seen your face," it said, a quiet satisfaction lacing its tone. "And can confirm you still live."

My gaze cut past the Nisshen to him—Renjiro. My uncle. He sat poised upon the throne, *my* throne.

The servant let out a strangled gasp, pulling me back to her. Her delicate hands clawed at the Nisshen's arm as his grip tightened. She was small against him, a fleeting ember struggling against an inferno.

"Let her go," I growled, my voice low and unyielding. The waters beside me surged to life, rising at my command. They coiled and twisted into serpentine whips, their fluid forms cutting through the air toward him. But just as they reached him, they froze, suspended in an unnatural stillness, as though time itself had faltered.

"Always so quick to act." Renjiro rose from the throne, his movements slow, measured, his hand raised as though he alone held dominion over the element. A low chuckle rumbled in his chest, mockery dripping from every syllable. "I admired that about you, Kyo. A true mark of a successor. Such a shame things have come to this."

A sickening crack tore through the chamber, and my breath hitched. The Kamishen woman fell, her body crumpling to the ground like a discarded doll. Her lifeless eyes stared past us, unseeing, her final plea lingering in the air like an unspoken curse.

Fury surged within me, hot and wild, yet I stood frozen, the weight of her sacrifice pressing against my chest. The waters trembled at my sides, waiting, reflecting the storm inside me. I could not look away—not from her, nor from him.

My body moved before I could think, surging forward with the singular aim of reaching Renjiro. But the air before me roared to life, flames unfurling from a Nisshen's outstretched palm. The heat licked at my face, forcing me back as the fire formed an impassable barrier between us.

Azariel was at my side in an instant, his wings unfurling with a sharp crack. The shadows they cast danced with the light of his celestial glow as a blade of pure radiance coalesced in his hand.

"Is this the fruit of your treachery?" I demanded. "The corpses inside the palace walls, the suffering of our people—was it all so you could bow to the Nisshen? You are a traitor to Yuehama, to Tairasa itself!"

Renjiro stepped forward, unhurried, as though savoring each step, each moment of my anguish. His voice was calm, almost detached, yet every word dripped venom. "Our Imperial Guard is weak. Our Shiryū, the Kamishen—all of them are weak. Surely you must see it, Kyo. You've surrounded yourself with children of the stars and veil—" his gaze flickered to Gamal, and his lip curled in disdain, "—and human filth."

Gamal's hands tightened around his twin blades, his eyes sharp as he met Renjiro's insult with a glare that could have cut stone. Beside him, Ilay stood, shadows curling at his feet like living things, their edges dark and jagged as his fury.

"You spoke of the greater good of Tairasa, yet you invited the Nisshen to desecrate our lands!" I spat, my fists trembling. Around me, the waters I commanded writhed like serpents, their forms twisting and pulsing with the rhythm of my anger.

Renjiro's laugh was soft but cold, a dagger of sound. "The Zurathi are the true traitors to Tairasa. Their filth was seeping into every corner of our land. This continent belongs to the Shen. The Nisshen share this vision—they will help me cleanse it."

"You despised Durathar's chains, and yet you traded them for a new master," I retorted, the words searing my throat as they left my lips.

"They are no masters of mine," Renjiro said, his voice hard as steel. "They are kin in purpose. Nothing more."

Kin. The word coiled in my chest, tightening around my breath. "I was your kin!" My voice cracked with the force of it, and I took a step closer, the water around me rising in sharp, jagged arcs. "We had a common goal. To drive back Durathar, to protect Yuehama, to preserve its land and people."

Renjiro's eyes darkened, his gaze colder than I'd ever known it. "You were too weak to ascend with me to this new world I envision," he said, each word cutting like the edge of a blade. He turned to the Nisshen with a gesture that felt like dismissal. "Kill them," he commanded. "Leave my nephew to me."

The Nisshens' horns pulsed with volcanic light, their veins of molten fire glowing deeper, brighter. The flames spread across their forms, licking their skin until it became armor, their hands burning with fiery gauntlets that could rend stone.

This was it—the threshold I had feared yet anticipated. Everything would be decided here, in this cursed hall, under the gaze of the moon and the specter of betrayal. It was all or nothing.

The chamber exploded into chaos as Renjiro's command fell sharply across the silence. The Nisshen surged forward, their forms wreathed in living flame, each step spreading fire's fury across the polished floors. Somewhere in the frenzy, I caught a glimpse of Azariel's wings slicing through the air, Gamal's silhouette blurring into motion. Yet all of it—the sound of clashing, the heat and smoke curling in the air—faded beneath the singular focus that consumed me. Renjiro stood before me, calm as a moonlit lake, and I felt the rage coil tighter in my chest.

"You've always been too reckless, Kyo," he said, his voice a low thrum cutting through the din. "It will always be your undoing. You could have had the advantage had you only learned to temper yourself. You think like a child playing at war." His steps were measured, unhurried, as though I posed no threat, and the contempt in his tone burned sharper than the fire crackling around us.

My fists clenched as the waters at my sides answered my fury. They moved in shimmering arcs. With a twist of my fingers, I hurled them forward, a torrent of jagged streams slicing through the air. Renjiro's hand moved with effortless grace, and the waters within the chamber answered him. They met my attack in mid-air, colliding in an explosion of spray. A symphony of suspended droplets that hung between us like a constellation of opposing wills.

"You overreach," he sneered, stepping closer. The air thickened around me. It pressed against my body like an invisible tide, slowing my movements to a crawl. "Did you think you could cross Yuehama's borders without my notice? I should thank you, truly. Your arrogance has exposed the rot at Lunrae's court."

The Lunrae envoy. Councilor Jiro Asahi. "What did you do?" The words spilled out, unsteady and raw. I faltered once more. My body froze as though seized by unseen chains, and in that instant, I was no longer here but reliving that one night. The waters I once commanded fell from my grasp, cascading to the floor with a hollow, resounding splash—a betrayal of my failure to hold them.

"You still ask the wrong questions. That is your flaw, nephew." His lips curled into something too cruel to be a smile. "Do you not question how Durathar penetrated our borders so easily? How they found your father without stirring the Imperial Guard?"

"Focus, Kyo!" Azariel's voice cut through the haze, sharp and commanding. My gaze flicked to him just in time to see him slam a Nisshen into the ground with unrelenting force. Starlight flaring from his palm as he pinned the fire-born celestial beneath his weight, his body flush to the wooden floor.

"There's one thing I can applaud your kingdom on," Renjiro mused, his focus shifting to him. With a single, deliberate motion, his hand extended toward Azariel. The air trembled as if pulled taut, and Azariel was wrenched from the fallen Vorynthian in an instant. His body arched back, arms outstretched, chest thrust forward in defiance even as Renjiro's magic commanded him closer. This power—the ability to bend the world to your will, to demand it obey as the tides yield to the moon—was as rare as it was terrifying among the Kamishen. For years, I had honed my own strength, my own grasp on this gift, yet I remained acutely aware of my boundaries. Renjiro, however, seemed to have no limitations, his mastery absolute.

"Your people," Renjiro sneered, his words twisting into venom, "see weakness and exploit it."

Azariel struggled against the invisible grip that held him, his body a constant motion of rebellion. Teeth clenched, shoulders straining, his every movement was a silent proclamation that he would not submit. Yet the power of Renjiro's command rippled around him, unwavering.

Even as fury and panic churned within me, I couldn't tear my gaze away from the scene. *Do not take this from me too*, I thought, *not him*, the words a fragile whisper in the storm of my mind. I swallowed the surge of emotions clawing at my throat, forcing them down like bitter medicine. My focus turned inward, seeking my own magic to break the threads of unseen bindings that held us captive.

"That is why I kept you alive, nephew," Renjiro said, his voice smooth, unhurried, as though this chaos was a game in which he had already secured victory. "To exploit those emotions, that lack of impulse control. I thought you would be stubborn enough—foolish enough—to kill the emperor or at least cripple their forces before they crushed you. But it appears I overestimated even that."

With a flick of his wrist, Azariel's body lurched forward once more, yanked closer to Renjiro in a cruel thrust. "I can feel the Eien's energy thrumming between you two," he murmured, his gaze narrowing as it locked onto Azariel. His words were barbed, targeted, yet Azariel met them with a cool and impenetrable gaze.

My fingers twitched as annoyance and helplessness pushed me to act. The waters I once commanded rippled, trickles beginning to rise as I gained more movement.

"You talk a lot," Azariel said suddenly, his voice steady despite the strain I could see in the taut lines of his body. "My husband despises that." His lips curled into a smug smile that seemed almost out of place in the suffocating tension.

And then I saw it—the shadows creeping closer, dark tendrils pooling like ink behind Renjiro's frame. Azariel's shoulders tightened further under the increased strain, his jaw tightening, but that infuriating smirk never wavered.

"It is a mercy that you and Kyo are men," he added, his tone sharp enough to cut. "One shudders to think of the filth your union might have spawned."

Gamal emerged from the shrouded dark, his figure emerging seamlessly out of the creeping shadows. He was a phantom thanks to Ilay, his movements silent yet poised. The bloodstained blade in his hands catching the flicker of the light, a brief crimson gleam like the moon outlined by the sun. In a single fluid motion, he struck. The blades sang through the air. Steel kissed flesh, cutting through the rich fabrics of Renjiro's robes and leaving a thin ribbon of crimson in its wake. Blood bloomed across the cloth, dark and vivid, but Renjiro's body twisted, an instinct honed by years of mastery and battle. The blades, surely aimed for vital strikes, veered just shy of its deadly intent, carving only superficial wounds.

The restraint upon me loosened as Renjiro's gaze snapped toward the source of his pain. The flicker of agony in his eyes was fleeting, quickly replaced by the icy precision of a predator recalibrating its strike. His attention shifted to the immediate threats: Gamal, frozen in the aftermath of his failed blow, and Azariel, still ensnared within my uncle's invisible grip. For the briefest of moments, the room seemed to pause, breaths held and destinies teetering.

We had found his limit.

Without hesitation, I surged forward, pushing my will against his, my resolve like a sharpened blade pressed to a worn tether. The weight that had held me immobile dissipated, and I lifted my hands, summoning the waters that had lain dormant at my feet. They obeyed with eager ferocity. I felt the pull of my connection to the waters as I shaped them into jagged streams, sharp as shattered glass. They hovered, trembling with anticipation, before I hurled them forward with a twist of my fingers. The torrent carved through the air, slicing toward Renjiro with the unrelenting force of my fury. The sound of the waters striking echoed like a thousand arrows meeting their mark.

A cough broke from his lips, a wet, visceral sound that betrayed the crimson pooling in his mouth. Blood stained his teeth like crushed berries, a grim testament to the force that battered him. Renjiro said nothing, but his hands lifted, and with that silent command, so too did the restrained forms of

Gamal and Azariel. Their bodies hung in the air for a breathless moment, as if caught in the hands of an unseen puppeteer, before they were slammed to the ground with a thunderous crash that echoed through the chamber like the toll of a bell.

Azariel—his name burned on my tongue, but I dared not release it, dared not exhale as they were wrenched upward again, only to be dashed against the floor with a force that sent a tremor through my bones.

A sickening crack.

Azariel stirred, his wounds already knitting together, the celestial and the wild converging within him to mend what had been broken. But Gamal—Gamal was only human. His chest rose in shallow, trembling heaves, his lashes fluttering over dazed eyes, blood slicking his lips and pooling at the corner of his mouth.

My fingers pulled, my will reaching—grasping—for the force I had wielded before, the power that had turned Soraya's own body against her. *No more.* The words pulsed through me, insistent, desperate. *Your fight is with me, not them.*

Another slam. The final, lifeless exhale. The moment his struggle ceased.

"Gamal." His name was a whisper, a wound torn open across my soul.

A shadow loomed at his side, monstrous and unearthly, its form a darkened echo of the specter I had seen bind a bazifir before. My gaze flicked toward Ilay, whose trembling frame bore the weight of his effort. His arms were outstretched, his shoulders hunched forward, and his eyes half-lidded with exhaustion. Blood dripped from his nose, a fragile reminder of his limits. Only a quarter Veil, his gifts were a fragile thread stretched far too thin even with my sigils. Yet still, he held Renjiro captive within the shadow's grasp, a tenuous restraint born of desperate resolve.

"Kyo." Ilay's voice was frayed, the edges raw with strain. "End this now. Now."

I stood motionless for a moment, my hands trembling. The water at my feet beckoned, waiting for my command—but I did not reach for it. No, my will sought something deeper, something more primal. I reached instead for the blood that seeped from Renjiro's wounds.

A vision struck me like a blade to the chest—my father's face, lined with quiet strength as his life was stolen. The Kamishen, bound and broken, their dignity stripped as they were led to Durathar like offerings. The arena, where the scent of blood had been my only constant. Gamal, his body crumpled, his breath stolen too soon.

Everything lost. Everything ruined.

The fury surged, dark and unrelenting, sinking its teeth into the hollow spaces of my soul. And so I pulled harder.

The blood answered my call, threads unspooling from Renjiro's body with horrifying speed. His form jerked, spasms racking his limbs as the crimson tendrils snaked through the air, each one glinting in the fractured light. They hovered for a heartbeat, poised and trembling, before I sent them back with deadly precision.

The threads pierced him like spears, driving through his body in a brutal dance of vengeance. For a moment, he hung suspended, an eerie stillness overtaking him as though time itself paused to bear witness. Then, as swiftly as it began, the blood lost its form, collapsing into liquid once more. It fell in a cascade, a crimson waterfall that splattered the floor, soaking into the boards with a sickening finality.

Renjiro's body followed, crumpling to the ground with a hollow thud that seemed to reverberate through the marrow of my bones. It was done.

Instinct guided my steps as I crossed the blood-streaked chamber, my body moving before my mind could catch up. Azariel lay on his side, his breath uneven, a hand clutching his arm. His gaze met mine, sharp and unwavering, as I knelt beside him, the air around us heavy with the lingering echoes of battle.

"Are you hurt?" I asked, my voice low and unsteady, my breaths shallow from exertion. My eyes searched his form, frantic for injuries, though I could already see the faint stitching over his wounds as his body began to mend itself.

"I'm fine." His words were soft yet firm, a tether grounding me amidst the chaos. His hand rose and rested against my cheek, warmth cutting through the nerves that clung to me. I turned slightly, my gaze drawn past him, past the blood-streaked ground, to where Gamal lay.

Ilay knelt beside him, fingers pressed to his throat, waiting. And then, the slow collapse of his shoulders, the way his head bowed, his hands trembling as they fell away.

No words were spoken. None were needed.

I already knew, but something inside me still cracked, splintering like ice beneath too much weight. I should have come alone. The thought was a dagger, sharp and unrelenting. This was my fight. Not theirs.

My hands curled into fists, shaking as I swallowed back the bile rising in my throat. He didn't deserve this. No one did.

"Kyo." Azariel's voice cut through the haze, gentle but insistent. His fingers tilted my chin, pulling my gaze back to his, those stone-gold eyes searching mine. I placed my hand over his, clinging to the warmth.

"He knew—we all knew the risks." His voice was low, meant only for me. "This is not your fault. In his sacrifice, in everyone's, Yuehama is free."

A sob caught in my throat, and before I could stop them, tears slipped down my cheeks, silent as falling petals. Azariel moved, wincing as he pushed himself upright, and then his arms were around me, pulling me against him.

Firm. Steady. Unyielding.

I sank into him, the dam breaking, grief and relief tangling into something too vast to name. The tears kept falling, washing away the terror, the guilt, the weight of all that had been lost.

Yuehama was free. But at what cost?

.‡·☒·ᚥ·⸭

My knees sank into the moss-laden earth, the damp softness cushioning my weight as I bent forward, forearms pressing into the soil. I let my forehead rest against the cool ground, surrendering to the quiet intimacy of this sacred moment. The scent of moss, rich and earthen, filled my lungs, grounding me.

Around me, the night hummed softly—the gentle whisper of crickets, the rustle of wind through the blades of grass. I held still, bowing in silence, as if the world itself was listening.

The measured tread of boots against the stone path grew louder, drawing near, yet I did not lift my head until I felt Azariel's warmth. His arms encircled me as he knelt behind me, a steady, grounding presence against the cold bite of this long exhausting night. My hands instinctively found his, and I leaned into him, his warmth a gift to my weary soul.

My gaze lifted to the dark monolith before me, the great stone carved with names that caught the moonlight, their edges illuminated like silver veins: Seiryu. Emiko. Ayame. My mother and father. My breath caught, and I swallowed the ache that surfaced. For all his treachery, Renjiro had honored my father's wishes for burial. Likely out of fear of angering the Spirits. But, It was one thing for which I could grant him a measure of thanks.

"It's cold. You need rest, *Aqaynah*," Azariel murmured, his lips brushing against my neck before pressing a tender kiss. His voice, like the warmth of his touch, wrapped around me. And though my heart ached, I found gratitude in him. Even in this ruin, Renjiro had unknowingly given me a gift: the man I now called my husband and Emperor. Another thanks I owed him.

Behind us, the clinking of metal heralded another presence. Azariel shifted slightly, his body tensing protectively. The guard's voice broke the stillness.

"We've gathered the remaining Imperial Council," he announced, his tone formal, but I could hear the unease beneath it.

I let my eyes drift to the stone again. Within these palace walls, Renjiro seized power not through honor, but through fear—a weapon sharper than any blade. I could never fully grasp the reasons why. Was it bitterness that my father, older and first in line, had inherited Yuehama's throne? Or was it the lingering resentment that, despite his unmatched strength, Ayame and I still held our rightful claims before him? His fury left no room for mercy. Most of the council and noble families fell under his tyranny, their bodies strung along the halls as grotesque warnings. A grim reminder: compliance was survival, and defiance meant swift annihilation.

The people resisted his demands to align with Vorynthia, but Renjiro crushed their dissent, branding it as weakness, as a lack of resolve. His punishments were brutal, his reforms sweeping. For all his hatred of Durathar and the Zurathi, his methods mirrored their cruelty—a paradox of loathing and reverence that painted him as both tyrant and imitator.

"What do we do about the Nisshen?" the guard pressed.

"Send for them too. They need to know their alliance is no longer wanted."

The guard retreated, his steps fading into the quiet. I turned, resting my shoulder against Azariel's chest. "Will you come with me to Vorynthia?" I said, my words cool and calculated. "I need you to send a message,"

He tilted his head, waiting.

"That Tairasa belongs to the three kingdoms."

His lips curved into a faint smile, one that held neither hesitation nor doubt. "Of course," he replied simply. "I am your sword. I am your shield. Use me however you wish."

I let his words settle in my chest, an anchor amid the storm that loomed. Tairasa would not bend, not to Vorynthia, nor to any force that sought to dominate it. The kingdoms would unite, and together, we would rise and survive.

NOTE FROM THE AUTHOR

Thank you so much for reading my story! I'd be truly grateful if you could take a moment to leave an honest review and rating on Goodreads, Amazon, or any other platform you prefer. Your feedback makes a world of difference for small authors like me. If you'd like to learn more about me, explore my other works, or check out upcoming projects, please visit https://elijahher.com.

Thank you again for your support!

OTHER WORKS BY ELIJAH HER

"Binds of the Forsaken"
An achillean novel about reincarnation, forbidden love. In a modern world, the story follows a fallen angel and his soulmate, a retired mafia prince.

"Her Majesty's Captain"
A sapphic novella about forging your own path, that is inspired by *The Princess Bride*. The story follows a princess and her presumably dead childhood best friend, who isn't actually dead and is now a pirate captain.

and a few web-novels that are only available on Tapas.

CHARACTERS OF AotFP

Kyo Seiryu (He/Him)

Age: 22

Sexual Orientation: ~~Straight~~ Bisexual

Species: Kamishen

Gifts: Water Manipulation, Telekinesis

Personality Type & Sign: ENTP, Aries

Physical Descriptions: Misty Gray Eyes, Dark Onyx Hair, Black Sigils, 5'11" Athletic Build

Favorites: Savory foods, Unagi Don, Mugicha, Gardening, Xiangqi, Painting

Azariel Pahlavan (He/Him)

Age: 24

Sexual Orientation: Pansexual

Species: Zurathi, Tenishen

Gifts: Light Conjuration, Flight, Accelerated Healing

Personality Type & Sign: INTJ, Aquarius

Physical Descriptions: Stoney Gray and Golden Eyes, Snowy White Hair, Golden Fractures, 6'3" Athletic Build

Favorites: Sweet and aromatic cuisines, Baklava, Sharbat, Kyo, Chovgan, Combat Sports

THE CONTINENT OF TAIRASA

Ascendance of the Forgotten Prince takes place on the continent of Tairasa. Tairasa is divided between four kingdoms. Yuehama in the West, Lunrae in the North, Akhsarun in the East and Durathar in the South. The southern and eastern kingdoms are lands of heat, desert and semi-aridity. While the western and northern kingdoms are that of lush mountains and forest. Mountains separate the two landscapes but that did not stop Durathar from crossing borders into the western kingdom of Yuehama.

The inhabitants of Tairasa hold deep reverence for the Spirits, honoring a diverse pantheon that encompasses the celestial bodies—the moon, stars, and sun—as well as the essence of the Wilds and the Land, which includes the spirits of animals, plants, mountains and waters. Many also pay tribute to their ancestors, while others specifically venerate the embodiments of virtues such as strength and love, recognizing their profound influence on daily life and the natural world.

The continents within the world of *Ascendency of the Forgotten Prince* are imbued with their own distinct forms of magic. In Tairasa magic—known as the "gifts of the spirits"—is most prevalent among two groups: the Zurathi, bonded with the untamed Wilds, and the Shen, children of the Celestial Bodies.

The Zurathi draw their power from ancient Wild spirits, forging bonds that grant them fleeting yet formidable blessings. However, these spirits are not easily summoned; they do not heed every call. Such a connection requires a relationship built on trust, whether cultivated directly or inherited through a bloodline.

In contrast, the Shen are born with innate gifts tied to one of the celestial spirits. Their magic flows as naturally as breath but comes at a physical toll over time that varies depending on the individual's capacity. To wield these gifts, precision in hand gestures is essential, as movement becomes the medium through which their magic takes form.

Additionally, the Shen possess access to sigils, intricate creations derived from celestial blessings. Only specific Shen, known as Shiryū, can read and inscribe these sigils, using them to imbue flesh with enhancements or restrictions. The strength of a sigil depends on its creator, and it remains indelible unless undone by the same Shiryū who crafted it.

CHAPTER FOURTEEN
AZARIEL'S POV

Power surged through me, molten and unrelenting, searing through every nerve like a forge stoked too high. My breath came shallow, the corridor stretching into something distant, blurred by the slow, burning thrum beneath my skin.

"Your Highness, I should send for a sage."

Ilay's voice cut through the quiet I hadn't noticed settling around us. His gaze flickered to my wings—one tucked as best as I could manage, though a pulse of pain shot through me at the mere attempt.

"What exactly happened?" he pressed.

Irritation prickled at the edge of my composure. Did he think I was so fragile? That a wound, however inconvenient, required tending as if I were porcelain?

"It is nothing, truly. I am fine. Everything is fine," I said, the words sharper than I intended.

And yet—everything was not fine. I could feel it, this raw, untapped power pressing against the walls of my mind, clawing to be unleashed. A tide rising too fast, too forceful. My anger, my hunger for retribution, coiled tight in my chest. The thought gripped me, intoxicating: I should return. I should carve through them, through every Duratharian who had ever dared cast me a scornful glance, let them melt beneath my touch until only ash remained.

The tension in the corridor thickened, heavy with unspoken thoughts. I caught the glances Ilay and Kaito exchanged—furtive, uncertain. Did they think I was broken? Weakened? My gaze dropped to the trickle of golden blood staining the floor, shimmering as it met the light.

"It's already beginning to heal," I murmured, ignoring the ache as I extended my wing. Pain lanced through me, sharp and precise, but I did not waver. This was my mother's blood at work, the gift of the Celestials mending me, stitching my flesh and bone with quiet inevitability. Feathers pushed through raw skin, new and unyielding.

"I just wish to rest before my meeting with Councilor Asahi," I said, stepping past the threshold of my chambers.

"Then we will leave you to rest," Ilay replied, his voice measured, but I knew him too well. That carefully controlled tone did not fool me.

He turned to leave, nodding for Kaito to follow. "Come along, Kaito. I will bring you back to—"

"No."

The word left me before I had even fully decided upon it.

"Kaito will remain here."

Kaito's gaze lifted at that, though he did not meet my eyes. Ilay, ever composed, dipped his head. "As you wish." The door shut behind him with quiet finality.

Kaito lingered near it, his attention still fixed on the wood, unreadable.

"You have been uncharacteristically silent since we left the council hall," I observed. A pause. Then, softer, almost curious, "Do you fear me now?"

His reaction was swift. "Of course not." The words sounded forced, too quick.

"Then why are your lips silent? What storm brews in your mind?"

A breath of hesitation, then: "Do you truly desire peace between the kingdoms?"

I watched him, weighing my response. "Yes. They may not see it, but survival often demands compromise, not conquest."

Something flickered in his expression, subtle but perceptible. "I agree with your vision," He stepped closer, his fingers reaching—not for my hand, nor my face, but for my wing. Lightly, he traced over the newly formed feathers, a delicate touch against my still-healing wounds. A shiver ran through me, a quiet tremor, chased by something else. Something that was supposed to be unwelcomed at this time. Something I wished, inexplicably, to feel again.

"War has drained the manpower and resources of Yuehama and Durathar. If it continues, it could do the same to Lunrae. With dwindling populations, fewer soldiers, and instability, Tairasa becomes vulnerable to outside threats. Durathar needs allies, not adversaries."

His gaze met mine then, like silvered moonlight against the embers of my own. The fire in me—blazing, consuming—receded, just slightly, tamed beneath the weight of his gaze.

"You understand politics better than I expected," I murmured, watching him with renewed interest. Kaito had worked within the palace walls of Yuehama, studied alongside their Grand Shiryū—but knowledge was not the same as wisdom. And wisdom was not the same as ambition.

Then, as if drawn by impulse, he shattered my thoughts with four words.

"Marry me. Not Meiyuna."

The suggestion was so absurd, so brazen, that I laughed—a sharp, rich sound that curled at the edges. "What? Are you afraid I'll neglect you once I have a wife?" I teased, amusement lingering as I reached for him, my fingers tracing the familiar lines of his cheek. "You've nothing to worry about."

And yet, he pulled away.

That fire in me stirred once more, embers fed to flame, and I let my smile cool into something distant. "Besides..." I mused, my voice slipping into careful indifference, "such a thing is unheard of—two men ascending the same throne as equals."

"You are the Emperor. Decree that it be heard of." His defiance was neither hesitant nor meek, but something bold and unyielding, as if he truly believed the weight of his words could shift the ground.

"Azariel, there is something you must know. I am the—" He turned before he could finish, crossing the room with measured steps. I watched him go, my amusement sharpening to curiosity as he reached for the instruments laid across the table—the ones he had used to carve through my sigils, to sever the chains that bound me.

The fabric of his tunic slipped aside, revealing dark inky sigils woven into the pale stretch of his skin. The needle bit into his flesh first, precise as a calligrapher's brushstroke, and then the blade followed—red welling to the surface in fragile beads.

I moved toward him. "Let me help you," I murmured, my fingers ghosting over the cloth he pressed to his wound. I felt him stiffen beneath my touch as I brushed it aside, the heat of my own light rising between us, seeping from my fingertips.

The scent of charred flesh filled the air. He winced.

My fingers lingered, tracing the edges of skin where my power had sealed the wound. There was something about him. A familiarity I could not place, an echo from a life I had long forgotten.

"You look..." My voice faltered as the thought eluded me, slipping through my grasp like mist beneath the dawn. "It's as if I've found a piece of something I didn't know was missing."

And then he spoke.

"I am Prince Kyo Seiryu. The rightful heir to Yuehama's throne."

The words shattered the fog.

"Kyo," I murmured, my fingers trailing upward, skimming the curve of his collarbone before settling at his throat. His pulse fluttered beneath my touch, the steady rhythm of something far too delicate. "Yes, that's right. Prince Kyo ." My voice dipped lower, richer, as I tightened my grip. "Son of the late Ayame and Emiko. Murderer of Emperor Darius Pahlavan of Durathar."

My fingers pressed in. Not enough to kill. Not yet.

His breath hitched, his hands flying up to grasp at my wrist, desperate, struggling. Weak. A pitiful attempt. A grin curled at my lips as heat coiled in my veins, surging to the surface, seeping out of my palm.

"My people fear me.." I said, my voice dark, contemplative, savoring the way his throat moved against my hand. "But do you know what would make them respect me? Delivering my brother's killer to them on his knees."

I studied him, admiring the beauty of his face—the perfect lines of his jaw, the sharp defiance in those moonlight eyes. I imagined them full of agony, lips parted in a scream as his skin blistered beneath my touch. The thought sent a thrill through me, pleasure curling deep in my loin.

Focus, Azariel. He could still be of use.

I exhaled, forcing the fire in me to settle, for now.

"Give me one reason," I hissed, my grip tightening further, feeling the way his throat strained against my hand, how easily I could crush it, break it—

"Why I shouldn't end you here, *Aqaynah*?"

"Speak to me like a civilized man, not a brute," he rasped, voice hoarse but defiant.

That look—anger, resistance—flickered across his face, a mirror of the first time we met face to face. One hand slipped free from me, curling into a fist, and before I could react, it connected with my face.

A sharp snap rang in my ears, pain blooming briefly across my nose. My head tipped back slightly from the force of it.

I blinked, then exhaled, slow and measured.

"Ow," I muttered flatly, rubbing at the tender bridge of my nose. Strange, how the blow calmed the fire in me rather than stoking it. Probably for the best. He was far more beautiful alive than dead.

"Go on, then. Give me your reason."

"I am your best tool for peace." His voice was steady, but it was the way he touched his throat—the way his fingers ghosted over the mark I had left—that caught my attention. *How pretty.*

"Renjiro and my people will never bow to you," he continued. "Lunrae's submission is no guarantee that Yuehama will follow. The hatred between our kingdoms runs too deep, especially with my uncle at its helm. And even if he did submit, you could never trust him. He is the reason I am here. If he could betray blood, what makes you think he wouldn't betray you?"

"Marrying you could jeopardize my alliance with Lunrae," I said, irritation slipping into my tone like a blade sliding from its sheath.

"Lunrae has already submitted. They'll continue to do so without a marriage tying them to you. And do you think Meiyuna truly wishes to be wed to a man such as you?"

A man such as I.

My wings flexed, responding to the slight before my mind caught up with my body.

"What makes you think your kingdom would serve me—accept me as their Emperor?" My voice sharpened, cutting through the air between us. "My own people scarcely tolerate my rule. What hope do you have that yours will bow to me?"

"Because I know they will." There was no arrogance in his voice, no desperate plea—only certainty. "I will ensure it," he said, conviction hardening in his voice. "I will bend them to your will, Azariel. I will force every kingdom, every throne, to its knees for you. You want unity across the continent—an unshakable alliance. I can give you that."

The words should have pleased me. Should have filled me with that same intoxicating power I craved. Instead, something else surfaced—something raw, something ugly and weak.

"Do you even care for me?"

The words left me before I could stop them, bitter and sharp on my tongue.

"Of course I do, Az."

I laughed, a low, mirthless thing. "Do you?"

I took a step closer, the heat between us shifting, dangerous. "I scorched the flesh from someone's face, Kyo. Reduced their bones to ash. And then I tried to kill the regent. That is not normal. There is something broken within me to have done that. And yet—"

A pain lanced through my chest, unbidden, unwelcome.

Had I let myself be used?

My father's voice echoed in my mind: *Companionship is a liability to survival.*

I had nearly destroyed a vital part of my court for him.

My jaw clenched.

"The first thing you did after all that," I continued, my voice lower now, more dangerous, "was talk about politics."

My wings settled, my fire cooled, but the fury remained—a slow-burning thing, twisting itself around my ribs.

"I have been a fool," I murmured, as if finally seeing the game for what it was. "The reason you don't fear me is because you think you can control me. You've been using me this whole time—using my affection as a leash to drag me in any direction you wish."

"Harden yourself, brother. You will be used." Darius' voice echoed through me. *"I know you are not the monster they say, but they will never see it. They will bow only out of fear, or because they see you as something they can wield—something sharp, something brutal—to instill fear in others."*

The fire in me swelled, coiling and twisting, surging toward an agony I could not contain. It hurt. Not just the betrayal—no, I had long since learned to stomach the sting of treachery. It was something else. Something deeper, something raw.

I had been careful. Hadn't I?

And yet, here I stood, my heart aching with the weight of my own foolishness.

Kyo said something, but the words barely reached me, drowned beneath the roar of my thoughts.

"You've lied to me." My voice was quieter than I intended, but the rage bled through each syllable. "Manipulated me. You used me to your advantage at every turn. And now you want to use me again." I stepped closer, my gaze boring into him, into that calm, infuriatingly composed expression. "Tell me, Kyo—what is the real game here? Unity of the continent is not what you want out of this marriage. You want your throne back, and you intend to use my army to claim it. And my power to keep it."

"You make it sound as though I am the only one guilty here of playing a game. You saw me as a pawn the moment you witnessed me break that sigil. Don't act as though you've been above manipulation yourself."

"And don't act as though you revealed the truth out of guilt," I shot back. "You did so because you saw an opportunity. Because it was convenient."

"*You are nothing but an opportunity for our enemies to use against us. A weak link in a strong bloodline.*" Soraya's voice slithered through my mind like venom and ice.

"Then let it be mutual." Kyo exhaled, the faintest hint of something unreadable passing over his face. "We both seek survival, nothing more. That way, there will be no need to question each other's motives."

I echoed, voice as cool as his, "Nothing more."

I stepped back, though every fiber of my being protested. Distance. I needed distance. If we were going to use each other, then I needed to sever whatever foolish attachment had begun to root itself in my chest—before I did the only thing I could think of that would dull this wretched ache.

My gaze flickered past him, toward the open balcony. Beyond it, the sky stretched vast and endless, the sands shifting below like molten gold beneath the sun.

A memory surfaced.

Flying with my mother. The weightlessness, the wind cradling my wings, the sheer freedom of it. How had I forgotten? Had that, too, been taken from me—buried by the will of a mother who wanted me to hide myself from this treacherous place?

I stepped toward the door as it beckoned me. My voice, when it came, was quiet.

"I am not the only one who learned your face for war, Prince Kyo. I suggest you remain here where it's safe until I return."

"And where are you going?"

"I need space to think. Before I do something I'll regret."

I closed my eyes for a brief moment, swallowing against the heat burning behind them. Instead, I focused on the warmth of the sun against my skin, the sharp scent of the desert air, the faint whisper of jasmine rising from the garden below.

I flexed my wings. The pain that had once plagued them was gone, the muscles stretching with practiced ease.

With a single, powerful movement, I ascended.

I did not look back.

Because I knew—if I did, if I saw him standing there—I would want to return.

Despite everything, there was a part of me that still yearned for him. For his acceptance. His touch. I wanted him to quiet the storm churning within me, to soothe the ache that had embedded itself into my very being.

But I also knew this: if he rejected me, if he shattered the fragile illusion I had clung to once more, then the thing inside me—the volatile, ruinous thing that I kept caged—would rise. And I would do something that would ensure I never felt the way he made me feel again.

That feeling that haunted my waking hours. That invaded my dreams. That made me crave him, again and again.

I didn't care that it wasn't real.

It was an illusion. A beautifully crafted lie.

But it was mine. And I would keep it—no matter the cost.

www.ingramcontent.com/pod-product-compliance
Lightning Source LLC
Chambersburg PA
CBHW030247120726
47903CB00005B/1654